THE ASHFORD PLACE

What Reviewers Say About
Jean Copeland's Work

The Revelation of Beatrice Darby

"*The Revelation of Beatrice Darby* at its epicentre is a story… of discovering oneself and learning to not only live with it but to also love it. This book is definitely worth a read."—*The Lesbian Review*

"Debut author Jean Copeland has come out with a novel that is abnormally superb. The pace whirls like a hula-hoop; the plot is as textured as the fabric in a touch-and-feel board book. And, with more dimension than a stereoscopic flick, the girls in 3-D incite much pulp friction as they defy the torrid, florid, horrid outcomes to which they were formerly fated."—*Curve*

"This story of Bea and her struggle to accept her homosexuality and find a place in the world is absolutely wonderful. …Bea was such an interesting character and her life was that of many gay people of the time—hiding, shame, rejection. In the end though it was uplifting and an amazing first novel for Jean Copeland."
—*Inked Rainbow Reads*

The Second Wave

"This is a must-read for anyone who enjoys romances and for those who like stories with a bit of a nostalgic or historic theme."
—*The Lesbian Review*

"Copeland shines a light on characters rarely depicted in romance, or in pop culture in general."—*The Lesbrary*

"The characters felt so real and I just couldn't stop reading. This is one of those books that will stay with me a long time."—*2017 Rainbow Awards Honorable Mention*

Summer Fling

"The love story between Kate and Jordan was one they make movies about, it was complex but you knew from the beginning these women had found their soul mates in each other." —*Les Reveur*

Visit us at www.boldstrokesbooks.com

By the Author

The Revelation of Beatrice Darby

The Second Wave

Summer Fling

The Ashford Place

THE ASHFORD PLACE

by

Jean Copeland

2019

THE ASHFORD PLACE

© 2019 By Jean Copeland. All Rights Reserved.

ISBN 13: 978-1-63555-316-1

This Trade Paperback Original Is Published By
Bold Strokes Books, Inc.
P.O. Box 249
Valley Falls, NY 12185

First Edition: January 2019

CREDITS
EDITOR: SHELLEY THRASHER
PRODUCTION DESIGN: SUSAN RAMUNDO
COVER DESIGN BY TAMMY SEIDICK

Acknowledgments

First, I must thank my readers who continue to spend their money and their time on my novels. I couldn't keep living the dream of being a published author without you, so thank you. I also want to express my gratitude to the amazing team of women at Bold Strokes Books for their continued support in all the aspects of publishing from brainstorming my proposals to promotion of the finished product and everything in between—Rad, Sandy, Carsen, Ruth, Tammy, Cindy, you all rock! So does my editor, Shelley Thrasher, for her tireless patience correcting my POV and dialogue tag faux pas. You make the editing process feel easy. Lastly, thank you to my friends and family who get excited about every new novel like it's my first. Thank you to Anne Santello for her editing skills, Denise Spallone for her PR work, and to my girlfriend, Jen, and my octogenarian, avid-reader father, James, for their love and support. And finally, a special thanks to my favorite detective for all her technical advice.

CHAPTER ONE

Belle Ashford removed her card from the chip reader at Danville Hardware and grunted as she lifted the box containing two gallons of interior paint, brushes, and other home-improvement miscellany. After declining an offer of assistance from the skinny kid working at a Slim Jim wrapper with his teeth behind the counter, she realized her miscalculation as she shuffled toward the door, her biceps aching in protest.

"Sure you don't need any help, ma'am?" The kid grinned as he tore into the stick of meat with his molars.

Of course, she needed help. Any dolt could see that, but out of principle and his stupid smirk, she replied, "Nope. Got it," in a strangled voice.

She hauled the box with both hands, leaving her defenseless to the tickle of sweat trickling down her cheek. Between contorting her face against the itch and using her shoulder to push open the door, she backed out and into someone walking in.

"Excuse me. Sorry," she said before noticing the sheriff's uniform and gleaming badge on the elderly man.

"Need a hand, young lady?" he said.

"Oh, no thanks." Belle smiled at the frail, lanky man as he held the door for her.

Doesn't anyone have a slow metabolism around here, she wondered after deciding she hadn't wanted to be responsible for killing the old sheriff with a heart attack on her official move-in day.

"You buy the Ashford place?"

"In a manner of speaking." She smiled, slightly creeped out that he knew that fact. "I must have *new girl* written all over my face."

"Small towns," he said with an easy shrug. "Got a lot of fixin' up to do over there."

"I have my work cut out for me."

"Well, you look ready for the job. Sheriff Robert T. Morgan, by the way." He extended an arm sprouting bony fingers.

"Isabelle Ashford." She freed one hand enough for a fingertip handshake. "People call me Belle."

"You don't say?" He leaned against the open door like she was about to offer him tea and scones out of her box of painting supplies. "I didn't know any Ashfords were left around here after Marion passed."

"Just my immediate family. My dad was her nephew through marriage. We all live down around the New Haven area." She repositioned the box, growing impatient with the casual interrogation.

"Jeez. We thought for sure the place would be sold to the town for demolition after the property-tax trust ran dry," he said.

Belle's impatience with the nosy old fella veered to irritation. "Did I ruin your chance for your first strip mall or something?"

He seemed to remember his obligation to be charming and chuckled.

"No, no," he said. "Strip malls aren't our style here. Did you know in 2010, *Connecticut Magazine* voted us most traditional New England town?"

"Most traditional, huh?" She rubbed a flip-flop foot over her rainbow ankle bracelet. "I would've guessed the 'Land that Time Forgot,'" she mumbled.

He cupped a hand to his ear. "What's that now?"

"Nothing," she said, losing her grip on the box. "Well, I should be running along."

"Sure thing. Gonna be a hot one today. Anyways, welcome to Danville, Miss Belle. We look forward to having another generation of Ashfords here."

He tipped his hat and strode into the hardware store.

"Thanks."

Miss Belle? She loaded the box into the back of her Highlander, contemplating what she'd gotten herself into this summer. Thankfully, the inherited house wasn't her permanent residence, just a no-brainer real-estate investment. But upon closer inspection, the DIY flipper appeared to need a lot more Y than she'd originally estimated.

Remember the endgame had become her new mantra. Finally, she'd be able to wake up to a glorious ocean view each morning. Had she dreamed of buying the house and living happily-ever-after there alone? No. But a handful of years as a player and another handful tied up in relationships destined to fail, one of which remained in a bizarre state of limbo, had altered her plan.

"The house is yours," her father had told her months earlier. "Your sister doesn't want any part of it."

"Well, Carolyn's always been the one known for sound judgment."

"She has first-born syndrome to the hilt," he said with a smile. "You, on the other hand…" He slapped his forehead playfully. "But sometimes being a risk-taker works out better in the long run."

"I look forward to the day when that quality starts paying its dividends."

"It will."

Belle relaxed at the confidence in his voice.

"Besides, you love little hands-on jobs on your summers off from teaching," he said.

"Uh, yeah, little ones—like refinishing dressers and end tables people leave on the side of the road."

"All you have to do is pay for the renovations and taxes until you sell it," he said. "Or if you want, keep it."

Belle recoiled. "Keep it? What makes you think I'd ever want to move up to that God-forsaken part of the state?"

"You're gonna have to put a lot of cash and work into it either way, but in the end, it'll be more than worth one summer of your life."

One summer. She had to admit he was right. What did she have to lose? How much could it possibly cost her to renovate a property in worse condition than the House of Usher? Depending on what award *Connecticut Magazine* would give Danville's first open lesbian, maybe she'd keep it after all.

The thought amused her as she pulled out of her parking space.

Lost in the bliss of the breeze blowing her hair around as she drove the winding country road, she hadn't noticed the squad car behind her until its siren squawked twice.

"Oh, shit." Belle tried to assess the officer through her rearview mirror as she pulled over. "Here's where the sheriff's inbred deputy son kidnaps me and locks me in a cage in the basement."

She threw the SUV into park and got her license and registration ready before he approached her window.

"'Morning."

Belle looked up. The inbred mutant was actually a woman—a striking, soft butch with the fiercest tan and tastiest-looking lips she'd ever seen.

"Good morning, Sheriff," Belle said with an obsequious smile. She held out the paperwork, but the officer didn't take it.

"Know why I pulled you over?"

Belle pretended to think. "Driving while not from these parts?"

"Cute." She lifted her sunglasses and studied Belle with creamy coffee eyes nestled in lashes so naturally thick, Max Factor would've rolled in his grave with envy. "No. Your vehicle's emissions has expired."

"Oh. Oh, crap. The notice must've got lost in the mail. It's happened to me before."

"Happens all the time." The officer seemed mildly amused.

"You really pull people over for expired emissions around here?"

She nodded almost apologetically. "Shows you what the crime rate's like."

"That's comforting. So, what now? You throw me in a cell with Otis the drunk for the afternoon?"

"You got jokes," she said with a smirk. "No. Go see Freddie at Auto Plus when you get a chance. He'll take care of you."

"Thanks, Sheriff. I sure do appreciate that."

"It's Deputy. Alexandra Yates."

"Well, nice to meet you, Deputy Yates. I'm Isabelle Ashford." She stuck her hand out the car window. "But something tells me you already know that."

She flashed a mischievous grin. "I even know you go by 'Belle.'"

"This is getting really weird."

"Don't get nervous. I was in the hardware store earlier and heard you talking to Sheriff Bob."

"That hardware store's the place to be."

"It's the only thing open this early besides Ethel's Quiet Corner Café, and I've already had breakfast."

Belle glanced around the road lined with trees and thickets of brush. "So when do the dueling banjo players jump out of the bushes?"

Yates fought off a smile. "Right around the time the city slicker tells her third corny small-town joke."

"Touché," Belle said, raising her eyebrows. "I've taken up enough of your time, Officer. I have to get to tendin' the homestead now, but I'll be sure to go and see Ricky-Bobby about that expired emissions business."

"Thank you kindly, ma'am," Yates said, mocking a country drawl.

"You could do this all day, couldn't you?" Belle said.

"Pretty much."

"That's what I figured. Take care," Belle said with a wink and drove away, beaming over her second run-in with the law in the last half hour. However, that was one lawwoman she wouldn't mind seeing again.

"Keep your pants on, girlie," she reminded herself out loud. "That is not why you're here."

❖

Belle pulled into the gravel driveway that was more overgrown grass and weeds than gravel. But then everything about that place was more what it wasn't supposed to be than what it was. Kind of like her life. A summer away from her ex, Mary, and the played-out drama of her younger friends in and around the lesbian dating scene was precisely the diversion she needed. The idea of refurbishing this enormous disaster filled her with hope. Once she got this wreck all dressed up and habitable again, she could do the same with her personal life.

Now that she'd procured the supplies required for the various jobs she'd tackle in the next few weeks, both indoors and out, she had to decide where to begin.

Peeling her T-shirt from her chest, she groaned when she remembered the house had no central air. In all of her meticulous planning and list-making, she hadn't remembered to buy a window air-conditioning unit. No way would she be able to sleep in a stuffy old house in that heat.

"First-world problems," she muttered, then unloaded the items onto the steps of the veranda that wrapped around the front of the house.

As she headed back to her SUV, she noticed an older golden retriever wagging his tail, patiently waiting—no, expecting to be petted.

"Hey, you." She rubbed his head as he panted. "Who do you belong to?" She checked but no collar. When she gave him a drink from the bottle of water sitting in her car's console, the dog lapped at the flow.

"There, how's that?"

Once his thirst was quenched, the dog sat there staring at her like he was waiting for an invitation.

"What do you want," she asked. "You want to come for a ride to the hardware store?"

He barked and jumped in without further persuasion, parking himself in the passenger seat.

She turned the ignition, blasted the air conditioner, and started backing down the long driveway. "Okay, doggy. Off we go. I'm sure old Sheriff Busybody knows exactly who you belong to."

Parked outside Danville Hardware, again, this time with the car running and a/c blasting, Belle loitered at the rear hatch watching the skinny kid beaded with sweat hoist the new unit into the back of her SUV. She'd made her point about feminist independence earlier. No need to refuse his services again, especially as the day was only getting hotter.

She glanced up and down the storefronts, hoping to steal another glimpse of that deputy, and then sighed. Never a cop around when you need one.

"Thanks, Jimmy." She handed him a five for his trouble.

"Thank you," he said. "Anything else I can do for you?"

"Yeah, there is. Do you know who this dog belongs to?"

He looked into the passenger window. "That's Red the Retriever. He doesn't really belong to anyone."

"A stray? Can't be. He's obviously well cared for."

"He is. Everyone takes care of him. He belongs to the town."

Belle smirked. "How did I not know that?"

"Ethel feeds him omelets in the morning, and he sleeps over at whoever's house he feels like."

"Sounds like a few women I've dated," she muttered.

"Huh?" He used his T-shirt to wipe above his lip.

"Nothing. So, if I let him hang out with me for a while, I won't be branded a dog thief?"

He laughed. "Nope. Not unless you keep him against his will."

"I've tried that a few times, too," she muttered again, getting a kick out of her own private quips.

"Huh?"

"Never mind," she said. "Thanks again, Jimmy. If anyone's looking for the dog, tell them he's up at the Ashford place."

"Will do," he said with a wave and headed back into the store.

"Okay, Red," she said as she drove away. "Since this is my first official night here, my fridge has only the basics, nothing fancy. It'll have to be takeout, so if you have a better dinner offer somewhere else, I won't be offended."

He didn't answer, just plopped down on the seat and closed his eyes for the rest of the ride back.

After dinner and a short nap on a couch that didn't appear to have anything crawling on it, Belle decided to prep the master bedroom for painting tomorrow. She got up slowly so she didn't wake Red, who was asleep on the floor in front of the couch.

She turned on her new iPhone playlist, some kind of jazz fusion, music she'd never listened to before. She wanted something different, a genre that didn't have a collection of age-old memories hanging off it like cobwebs. Glancing around the room, she bopped her head to the funky beat. Had she been delirious when she'd presumed, after a few Home Depot workshops, she could flip this joint on her own in one summer?

She stopped twirling the roll of painter's tape on her index finger and began running strips of it along the faded wood trim.

Sliding along the floor on her knees, she stopped at a small arched door to a crawl space locked with a rusted miniature padlock.

"This is weird." She tugged on the lock.

What the hell was in there that it had to be padlocked from the outside? She stopped yanking on it when her head began to fill with images of the Bates Motel and episodes of *Cold Case Files*. Perhaps alone and in the dark of night wasn't the best scenario in which to start opening up crawl spaces that someone didn't want to be opened. She shuddered as her imagination taunted her with dreadful possibilities.

She let out a shriek when she heard what sounded like a light tapping of nails on the crawl-space door. Red skidded to a halt, apparently considering whether he should make a run for it to another house for the evening.

"Red!" She patted the floor. "You scared the shit out of me."

He licked her chin as if to apologize.

"Well, I've had a bitch of a day and clearly need to get some sleep, so you better skedaddle now." She led him downstairs to the foyer and opened the front door.

He sat down and looked up at her.

"What are you waiting for? Go ahead."

She glanced up the staircase. The bed she'd be sleeping on was in the same room as the ghoul hiding out in the crawl space—with nothing between her and it but a warped wooden door and a tiny, rusted lock.

"Okay, if you insist. But no snoring."

After taking a quick, cool shower and brushing her teeth, she fitted the mattress with sheets from home and cranked up the air conditioner. Even with the list of tomorrow's tasks cluttering her mind, it still found space to entertain thoughts of that attractive deputy from this morning—the light sheen of sweat on her face, those kissable lips, her handcuffs…

Red suddenly jumped on the bed, scaring away her pleasant visions.

"Jeez, Red. How about giving a girl some kind of warning first?"

He circled a few times at the foot of the bed and plopped by her feet. Belle laughed quietly at the sound of him licking his chops in the dark as he settled down. Relieved that he'd chosen to spend the night with her, what with that monster sound asleep behind a locked door, Belle finally fell into a deep slumber.

Chapter Two

After finishing breakfast, Belle indulged in a second cup of coffee on the front veranda with Red, savoring the quiet ambiance of a true country morning. The sun was shining its reassurance, so she felt better about revisiting the master-bedroom situation. It was only eight thirty a.m. Nobody in horror movies ever gets murdered that early in the morning.

Armed with a pair of pliers—plundered from her father's toolbox—which could've extricated someone from an auto wreck, she knelt in front of the crawl-space door and assessed both the risks and rewards of the task. With one eye closed and the other merely a slit, she slowly, gently closed the pliers around the lock.

"Dear God, please don't let anything jump out at me." She glanced down at the dog. "You ready for this, Red?"

He yawned and rested his head on his paws.

After one good squeeze, the lock dropped to the floor in a pile of rusty crumbs.

"On a positive note, if something horrible happens, I'll have a great excuse to call the authorities."

She bobbed her eyebrows at Red, but he offered only a few sweeps of his tail across the dusty floor as encouragement.

After applying some elbow grease to open the swollen door, she shone a flashlight inside the crawl space, blinking rapidly in case a bat or some multi-legged creature shot out and latched onto her eyeballs.

Nothing but a bunch of spider webs, dust bunnies, a screw, a ball-and-paddle set, and a crunched-in shoebox that looked purposefully shoved back against a support beam.

"Okay. Here's where I find the body parts."

She pulled out the box and, after a breath of mental preparation, flicked the top off. No physical remains of any once-living species, but the headless, naked baby doll did give her a bit of a start. How intriguing—and thoroughly macabre.

She placed the flashlight on the floor and sat Indian-style as she picked up the doll. Glancing down the neck hole, she noticed rolled up papers. "What the hell?" she whispered. Scrolls of paper stuffed inside a doll stuffed inside a shoebox stuffed inside a locked crawl space like one of those Russian dolls. The government should be so careful concealing classified documents.

Maybe they were love notes sent to her old aunt by a secret lover, some yokel who said "shucks, ma'am" a lot and operated a tractor. Or maybe a map to a fat bag of cash and jewels buried in the backyard. That would certainly come in handy right now.

Whoever the papers belonged to, they obviously contained someone's darkest secrets. Shame on her for salivating at the chance to invade that privacy.

Then she remembered her father telling her about his cousin, Judy, whom he had barely known, who'd died when she was a teenager. She carefully pulled the scrolls that appeared to have been torn from some type of composition notebook, crisp and yellowed with age, from the torso cavity.

After thumbing through pages of animal sketches, Beatles doodling, and references to a kid named Frankie surrounded by hearts, she concluded they weren't the musings of a lovelorn widow but of an innocent girl. She smiled when she saw the name Annette Funicello written in cursive.

She flipped through a few more pages.

He hurt me again.
I hate when he hurts me.
I hate his guts. I wish he would die.

Belle swallowed hard as she reread the lines that sounded like a sick poetry stanza. Her stomach churned her breakfast at the implication of *"he hurts me."*

Her breath slid out in a hiss. "Were young girls ever safe?"

She tossed the papers aside in disgust but grabbed them again, as curiosity had her in its grip.

He is mean. I don't want to go there anymore.

Underneath the phrases was a sketch of a large head, a man's clean-shaven face with big scary eyes, angry lines over them pointing down, a squiggly line for the mouth, and a large shock of angrily scribbled hair on top. The pressure from the girl's pencil stabs had nearly perforated the paper.

The messages sent Belle's mind into a whirl.

I hate when he touches me. I want to be good.

Beneath the phrases was another sketch of a round head with pigtails and tears under the eyes. At the bottom of the paper, Judy's name written several times in neat cursive, and doodled hearts and sunflowers contrasted the sinister suggestions.

Belle sat quietly in a sea of painting supplies scattered about the floor. Who was this bastard that did this to her? Was he ever caught? Hopefully, he was rotting in hell or at least still rotting in a jail cell. After another moment of reflection, she placed the papers and the doll into the box and pushed it back into the crawl space.

After about an hour spackling various dents and holes throughout the second floor, unable to shut down the haunting reverberations from what she'd read, she returned to the master bedroom and FaceTimed her father.

"How's it going, princess," he asked. "I knew you couldn't get along without my expertise."

Belle laughed. "I do need you, but not for what you're thinking."

"What's up?"

"What do you know about your cousin, Judy?"

"Only what I've already told you," he said. "My uncle, Wes, was killed at work in an accident at the old mill when we were kids. I was only about four or five at the time. Our families never were close, even when he was alive. Why do you ask?"

"Well, I found what I think is Judy's diary, so I wanted to learn more about her."

"Wish I could help, honey," he said. "She was an only child and died when she was a teenager. I'm the youngest of all the cousins, so I don't remember much."

"You know anything about your aunt Marion?"

"Only that she was never the outgoing type, but she really became like a recluse after Uncle Wes died. And this is only what I remember from your grandmother's stories."

"And Judy died how?"

"Aunt Marion said some kind of infection or something, but nobody knew for sure. I remember them saying she was a troubled kid, but if your father drops dead when you're that young, it can happen."

Belle was quiet as she absorbed the details about Judy.

"Too bad your grandmother wasn't still around. She could've told you more."

"Yeah. I wish she was here, too," Belle said.

"What's in that diary," he asked in a playful tone. "Some kind of juicy mystery?"

"Kind of. I think she was abused."

"Oh boy." He was silent for a moment. "Does she name anyone?"

"No, and it's driving me to distraction wanting to know if the guy who did it was ever punished."

"Jeez, Belle. You're talking over fifty years ago. You better let it go, or you'll never get anything done. You sure you don't want me to come help you?"

"Dad, you just had your knee replaced."

"Two months ago. I'm almost one hundred percent."

"*Almost.*" She took on a motherly tone. "Let's wait another month until you're fully recovered, or Mom will break both of my knees."

Her father laughed heartily. "Okay, kid. Don't make yourself crazy over this diary thing."

"I know, but I feel so bad. How could someone hurt a child like that?"

"I can't imagine it, honey. But I know what I'd do if someone ever hurt you or your sister like that."

"I want to find out what happened to him. What if he's still out there molesting kids?"

"If he's even alive after all these years."

"Good point," she said, her thoughts racing several steps ahead. "Maybe I can ask some locals if they knew Judy and Marion."

"Or you can run it by the police. Just don't go around pissing everyone off up there questioning them like you're Angela Lansbury."

"Grandma loved *Murder, She Wrote*," Belle recalled in amusement.

"I know. I can't tell you how many times she watched those reruns while she lived with us."

"I loved watching them with her when I came over." She paused to visit with some fond memories. "Okay. Let me get back to work in here."

"Okay, kid. Stay out of trouble."

"Always. You, too," she said and stuck her tongue out at him.

After they ended the call, she thought about a trip into town later on. She wanted to stop by the farmer's market anyway. Maybe she'd run into some chatty folks who looked like they knew everyone's business.

Better yet, maybe a certain local law enforcer could offer some insight.

❖

Later that afternoon, Belle ventured into civilization on her bicycle instead of by car since the oppressive humidity had yielded to fresh, New England summer air. As she pedaled along the quiet road shaded by a canopy of trees, Judy reappeared in her mind. She'd texted her father asking if he could locate a picture of Judy from his old family album. In the meantime, she'd already created her own image. Probably blond hair, flowered sundress, red sneakers, scraped knees, cherry-Popsicle stains trimming her lips—and a crushed soul hidden beneath all that sweetness and innocence.

"Good afternoon," Belle said as she pulled up to a produce stand and left her bicycle against a nearby tree.

"'Afternoon." The old woman seated under an umbrella attached to her chair smiled as she glanced up from her copy of *Country Home*. "We have a nice variety of greens and the sweetest strawberries around."

"You have any kale?" Belle asked, rummaging through the varietals of lettuce.

"Sure do. First year for it." She dropped her magazine and moved perilously close to invading Belle's personal space. "Last year I decided I'd plant some after you city kids passing through on your way to the new winery kept asking for it."

"Shrewd business move," Belle said. "Except I'm not passing through. I'm here for at least the summer."

"Are you the gal who bought the Ashford place?"

Belle smiled good-naturedly. "Do you guys send out a newsletter or something?"

"Better than that," the woman said. "We got a town crier who never misses a scoop. Happens to be my husband, the sheriff."

"Yes. I've already met him. I'm Belle Ashford. Pleasure to meet you." She wiped a hand wet from veggie-caressing on her shorts before extending it.

"Shirley Morgan. How're you liking it here?"

"I love it," Belle said. "Very quaint."

She grabbed a basket for her bundles of kale and lettuce and proceeded to gently pick through the mountain of ripe strawberries.

When it came to gossips, she got the feeling she'd hit the jackpot with Shirley Morgan.

"Tell me something," she said casually. "Why is the Ashford place such a big deal around here?"

Shirley was silent for a moment. "In case you haven't noticed, we aren't exactly a hotbed of scandal and intrigue. Something has to keep people talking."

"For a minute I thought my photo would end up on the wall in the post office's rogue's gallery for preventing the sale of it."

"Oh, for heaven's sake," Shirley said, spraying rows of greens with a hose. "Why would we be upset by you coming in and fixing up the place?"

"It's almost two acres of buildable land. You guys would've made a killing selling it off to a developer."

"Now that's the problem with this country, ain't it? People selling off beautiful things to make a fast buck."

"I'm sure you could find a few Native Americans who'd give you an 'amen' to that," Belle said.

"You said you were here for the summer? You gonna use the place for a vacation home?"

Belle's smile quickly collapsed at the reminder of her treasonous motive for being there to begin with. "Yeah, uh-huh," she lied.

"Good for you," Shirley said. "You have a husband and kids joining you?"

Belle shook her head and wondered if she shouldn't get the coming-out thing over and done with now. One word to Shirley and by tomorrow the whole community would either throw her a Pride parade or burn an effigy of her on her front lawn. It would be nice to eliminate the suspense.

"Well, I'll keep an ear to the ground for you," Shirley said. "I know a few ladies with single sons if you'd like a hand getting the ball rolling."

"Oh, no, that's okay. I have my hands full with the house." She moved away from Shirley and her matchmaking offer as though they were a contagious disease. After a few minutes faking interest in a rack of handmade wind chimes, she felt safe resuming her mission. "So did you know the Ashfords at all?"

"They were quiet folks, kept mostly to themselves, but sure I knew them. Wes died young in that accident at the mill. But I got to know his widow and the daughter fairly well. My mother-in-law used to teach catechism when I started dating Bob, so I got to know some of the kids."

"You're not harassing the sheriff's wife, are you?"

The low, sultry voice so close to her ear startled Belle—as well as sending a ripple of chills up her neck. She whipped around to find Deputy Alexandra Yates smiling at her, but the real show was the tan, muscled arms straining against her rolled-up short-sleeve uniform.

She regarded Shirley with mock authority. "She's not giving you a hard time with bad country-bumpkin wisecracks, is she?"

"Not at all, Ally," Shirley said. "We're having a lovely time shootin' the breeze and getting to know one another."

Belle flashed Ally a cool, 'so there' smirk, but Ally's return smile was so smoldering Belle nearly squished her handful of ripe strawberries.

"The Ashfords were her people," Shirley said to Ally. "Did you know that?"

"Of course she did," Belle said.

"I liked Mrs. Ashford," Ally said. "She was a little batty in her old age, but I never minded going to her house on wellness checks. She'd always have a snack waiting for me."

"You knew her well?" Belle said.

"As well as anyone could. She wasn't really big on socializing. She ended up with dementia for a while before she passed, but you could still have a conversation with her...sort of."

"Interesting," Belle said. "I didn't know either of them, but since I've taken over the house and learned more of their story, I wish I'd had the chance to get to know Marion before she died."

"She's been gone for five years now," Ally said, "but I'd be happy to answer any questions about her if I can."

Talk about an offer Belle couldn't refuse.

"That would be great," Belle said. "Let me give you my cell. You can text me when you're free."

Ally and Shirley looked at each other like Belle was a traveler from another dimension.

"Or we could go to dinner tomorrow and talk," Ally said.

Belle's knees weakened at the invitation, producing an avalanche of beets from the compartment she'd been leaning against. All three of them remained still until the beets stopped thumping to the ground.

"Whelp, I guess I won't bother asking my friends about their single sons," Shirley said in a deadpan and walked away.

"I'm so graceful," Belle said as she scooped up the beets.

"Could happen to anyone." Ally crouched to help her. "Shirley stacks these bins too high."

"I'd have you over for dinner, but the kitchen is still barely habitable."

"I'm sure you have better things to do around there than cook for someone. Let's meet in town. Do you like Italian? Franco's is fantastic."

Ally had this unnerving habit of pausing for a moment and staring before and after she'd made an important statement. Belle couldn't figure out if it was a cop thing or she was an expert at seduction. Whatever the explanation, Belle reminded herself that, of all the things she needed to accomplish in Danville that summer, falling in love was not high on the list. It wasn't even on the list.

"Franco's sounds perfect."

"Great," Ally said. "I'll make a six o'clock reservation."

"Looking forward to it."

Belle forced the smile off her face so she wouldn't seem too eager. After all, she agreed to dinner plans to gain information about her father's cousin, and to see if justice was ever served or ever could be, not to hook up with a country deputy—devastating good looks notwithstanding.

Talk about a cliché.

After she'd sufficiently reproached herself for getting all riled up over Ally, she paid for her fruits and veggies and headed home.

As Belle waited at a cozy corner table at Franco's Ristorante for Ally to show, she felt the vibration of a text on her phone in her back pocket. Thinking Ally was canceling their date, she was relieved when she remembered they'd never exchanged numbers. The bad news was the text was from her ex, Mary, a robust, grape-cigarillo-smoking cosmetologist with no "inside voice," who likely texted her because things hadn't worked out with the woman she'd met on a free dating site the day after Belle broke up with her.

If you're getting lonely up at that big ole house, I'll come up n keep you company.

Belle wasted no time in replying.

Gee, as tempting as that sounds…Hell no!!!

She shook her head in despair. How had an intelligent woman with all other aspects of her life seemingly in check always managed to attract shallow, over-zealous women with zero self-awareness? She had to draw the line somewhere.

Since turning forty months earlier, Belle was determined to be her best self by becoming the empowered, self-reliant woman she'd so often read about on *HuffPost.* But first she had to renounce her inner serial monogamist and vow to engage only with women truly worthy of her time.

"Sorry to keep you waiting," Ally said before reaching the table.

Belle's phone slipped through her fingers and onto the floor as she approached. Ally in civilian clothes was an even more spectacular sight than Ally in her khaki brown deputy uniform. The off-the-shoulder black top showcased her sculpted upper body, and tight white Capri pants showed off everything else.

"Five minutes doesn't count as keeping someone waiting," Belle said as she rose to give her a light kiss on the cheek. "Thank you for taking time out of your schedule to meet me."

"No problem. You're pretty busy yourself, but we have to eat, right?"

"Right." Belle smiled warmly. "And women cannot live on carbs alone." She pulled out the bottle of sauvignon blanc chilling in a bucket. After Ally nodded, she poured her a glass.

"Thank you." Ally eyed her all the way through her drawn-out first sip. "How's it going up there?"

"It's coming along. Definitely a much bigger undertaking than I'd anticipated. To be honest, I'm not sure what I anticipated. They make it look so easy on those DIY shows. I'm going to have to hire a few people, especially for the outside."

"I can recommend some reputable locals if you want."

"That would be great, thanks. I have to do something radical in that backyard. I'm thinking a stone patio and koi pond."

"Awesome. I happen to love flower gardening," Ally said, absently caressing the tablecloth with her butter knife. "I'd be happy to offer my design services for a very nominal fee."

Oh, God. Was she flirting? Was the "nominal fee" remark a clever attempt at sexual innuendo?

Belle paused for a breath and a sip of wine. She should've let it go, and in the spirit of her new, more discerning dating criteria she would've, but Ally wasn't some second-rate woman rallying what was left of her charm at last call.

She lowered her voice an octave for effect. "What's your idea of nominal?"

"Dinner."

"Dinner?" Belle's disappointment escaped before she could apprehend Ally's meaning. "As in *dinner*?"

"Sure," Ally said. "You can grill me something on your new stone patio when it's all done. I'm a patient woman. I can wait."

"All right. I'll accept your offer, even though I should be ashamed of myself for taking such flagrant advantage of you."

"Just being neighborly." Ally shrugged. "It's what we do for each other around here."

Belle smiled. Ally wasn't flirting. She was a good soul—generous and humble, and not the kind of woman she could lure into bed first and find out if they were compatible enough for a relationship later.

After they'd finished dinner and were on to cappuccinos, Belle contemplated ordering dessert to stay in the presence of such a captivating woman. For once, not only the stunning sex appeal of her companion was keeping her enthralled. Maybe it was the laid-back, bucolic atmosphere, but conversation with Ally was easy and familiar, with no need for affectation and no pressure to impress.

Ally checked her watch. "Wasn't I supposed to answer questions about the Ashfords?"

Belle laughed at how Ally almost seemed able to read her mind. "Yes, you were. See what happens when you add good food and good wine into the mix?"

"And good company," Ally said.

Okay. Now she was flirting, but Belle refused to take the bait so easily. "I'm so curious about them because I found a sort of journal at the house tucked away in a crawl space."

"Oh? Is that why you asked me about Marion?"

"Yeah, but the journal isn't Marion's. It was a girl's."

"How do you know? What's in it?"

"Some typical kid stuff, but unfortunately, I think Judy was the victim of sexual abuse. I mean, she didn't use those terms, but she wrote about a man hurting her. I felt safe assuming the worst."

"If a child's writing about an adult hurting her, it most likely was sexual," Ally said gravely. "Did she write down any names?"

"Just her own, Frankie, and Annette Funicello."

"Given that 'Frankie' is probably Frankie Avalon, I can rule him out as a suspect right off the hop. Where's the journal?"

"At the house, right back where I found it. I can bring it by the station tomorrow if you'd like."

"Would you mind if I swing by after we leave here and pick it up? I won't get any sleep tonight unless I take a look at it."

Belle bit her lip trying to conceal her delight at the thought of Ally coming back to her place in a semi-official capacity. "Sure, that's fine." She came off just cool enough to be convincing.

Ally smiled as she sipped the last of her cappuccino. As long as they were sharing pertinent information, Belle figured she could also ask about Ally herself and, in the process, ascertain her relationship status.

Just as she was about to inquire, her phone vibrated again with another text. No way was she checking it. It had to be Mary. The universe was sending her a clear, awkward reminder that she was to use only her head and not her hormones when it came to interactions with Ally.

Ally seemed distracted anyway as she brushed leftover crumbs on the tablecloth into a minute pile. "Now that I know this, so many other things about the Ashfords make sense."

"Like what?"

"Marion's reclusiveness, the general, strange mystique surrounding them…" Suddenly her eyes flashed with revelation. "Wait a minute. Now I'm wondering that if Judy was abused, did that have anything to do with her untimely death."

"Untimely? She was sick, wasn't she?"

"That was the story, but whoever saw a death certificate?"

Belle was drawn in. "What if she had the clap and got it from the perv who molested her? Then it's murder, isn't it?"

"The clap? And I thought I was careening into far-fetched speculation."

Belle shrugged innocently.

"We don't even have a suspect," Ally said. "An adult male in the home is usually the first person of interest in these cases."

"Eww, you mean my great-uncle could've been a molester?"

"I hope not, but he's dead, too," Ally said. "So that would make all this a moot point."

"No. It couldn't have been him," Belle said. "She was only like five when he died. A five-year-old definitely didn't write this journal, and it was in present tense, like it was ongoing."

"You're certain an older girl wrote it and not a child?"

"You can tell by the tone. You'll see."

The waitress appeared at their table with the check. After a brief squabble over who would pay, they settled on going Dutch. This time, anyway.

Belle was already anticipating their next dinner date.

CHAPTER THREE

B elle carried the scroll of papers into the kitchen and offered Ally a glass of Riesling from a bottle she'd left chilling in the fridge. One should always be prepared for spontaneous entertaining, even in the sticks.

"No, thanks," Ally said. She looked up from her phone, her eyes dazzling with excitement. "That journal entry was written after her father died. The first Frankie and Annette movie came out in 1963. Your uncle died in '59."

Belle sat across from Ally at the table. "You found all that out in the time it took me to run upstairs?"

"I'm a cop. I live for this shit," she said with a grin. "The last mystery I had to solve was five months ago—the case of the demolished mailboxes on Granger Road."

"Ooh, a serial vandal," Belle said with pretend titillation. "Did you nail him?"

"Turns out the scofflaw was old Mr. Borden, who'd accidentally stepped on the gas instead of the brake and took out his neighbor's and his own before turning into his driveway."

"Phew. I wish I'd known what a crime-infested mecca this was before I moved in."

"We're working on cleaning it up." Ally smirked and started reading through the pages.

Belle got up and retrieved two waters from the fridge, then sat back down as Ally read. She watched her eyes float back and forth, her mouth puckering with concern. She was outrageously sexy when she assumed her air of authoritative public servant. And while dressed in that sleek black-and-white evening ensemble? Belle struggled to keep it professional.

"So what do you think?" she said.

Ally exhaled as though needing a moment to expunge the visual of what she'd read from her mind. "Like I said before, everyone's dead. The victim is dead, and so's her mother."

"But what if that pedophile is still alive? He could've been preying on little girls all this time. Maybe he still is."

"Slow down, Belle. I've been a deputy here for almost twelve years. If he was still around doing that, I would've known about it by now."

"Not if his victims are too afraid to come forward. Judy must've been petrified. That's why she journaled about it and then tucked it away."

"We don't know that she didn't tell anyone. When I go back to work on Monday I'll check the records—if the records go back that far. They digitized everything back in the nineties."

Belle huffed. "You mean I have to languish in suspense all weekend?"

Ally disarmed her with a smile. "You're kinda cute when you whine like a spoiled child."

"Don't try to steer me off topic with flattery."

Ally laughed. "What would you like me to do at nine thirty on a Friday night? Besides, I'll have to go into storage and dig through boxes of files to get records from the sixties."

"Let's go now," Belle said, and sprang up from her chair. "I'll help you look. You have a key, don't you?"

Ally held up her hands to temper Belle's enthusiasm. "Look, here's what I'll do. Monday I'll run a computer check for reports of sex assaults as far back as the data goes. If we had a true pedophile in our midst, he would've struck again."

"Yeah. That's true," Belle said. "And for all we know he could've been some shadowy drifter with a sinister past, probably worked as a farmhand. He could've abused Judy during crop season and then wandered off to the next unsuspecting small town."

"You must watch a lot of old movies," Ally said.

"I do. How did you know?"

"Just a hunch," she said with a smile.

"I'm sorry. I didn't mean to get all up in your business. I feel so bad for the girl, and I hate the idea that some creep may never have paid for his crimes."

"I get it," Ally said. "She was an innocent kid and your family. We'd all like to see justice prevail but trust me. It doesn't always work out that way. I was a patrol officer in Hartford for ten years before I came here."

"Really? You left the adrenaline rush of a big city for a gig in Snoresville?"

"I needed to for my sanity. I got tired of seeing thugs cop pleas and serve a quarter of the sentence they deserved. And then I'd have to face their victims afterward. I like what I do in Danville. I help people every day, in all kinds of little ways, and never have to explain to anyone what it means when an ADA nolles charges."

After observing a moment of respect for Ally's commitment to humanity, Belle thumped her water bottle against Ally's. "Here's to small-town living."

"And to justice."

"To justice," Belle added. "May she not be so blind here in Danville."

"Just don't get your hopes up too high, Belle. I'll do what I can on Monday, but the man she's referring to is probably either dead or not living around here anymore. It's been over fifty years."

Belle took a swig of her water. "Well, if anyone can do something about this, you can."

"I appreciate the vote of confidence."

She and Ally held each other in a gaze, jolted out of it a moment later by a bark at the back screen door.

"Red," Ally said. "So this is where you've been keeping yourself."

Belle let him in, and he trotted right over to Ally, who engulfed him in a zealous hug.

"He started hanging around here this week. If someone's looking for him, I can send him home."

"He was Marion's," Ally said. "She rescued him when he was a puppy, but when she started failing, folks pitched in to help her."

"Nobody adopted him when she died?"

"Well, he stays with me most of the time, so technically you can say I did. Chloe loves him, but if he feels more at home here, that's his prerogative."

Chloe? Belle's stomach sank. She should have known a woman as fine as Ally being single was too much to hope for. What a kick in the crotch.

"Isn't Chloe wondering where Red and you are this late on a Friday night?" Belle's tone turned ice-crystal cold.

"I doubt it," Ally said. "I'm sure she's having a great time with her friends."

This duplicitous fucker. Her girlfriend goes out with her friends for the evening, and she wastes no time calling in backup.

"So why didn't you mention Chloe sooner," Belle asked coolly, desperate to control her attitude.

Ally seemed confused. "We were talking about other things. My family hadn't come up."

Family? So Chloe was more than just her girlfriend. "Well, if you go out to dinner with a woman while your wife is out with her friends, I'd hope that's something that would come up right away, like before you even go."

"My wife?" Ally said, chuckling.

Belle stood at the counter and folded her arms in front of her chest. "Partner, spouse, whatever you want to call her."

"Why?" Ally said, scratching at her chin. "Is this a date?"

"Well...I don't know," she said, trying not to stammer. "Is it?"

Ally stood and slowly approached, her eyes smoldering with questionable intentions. "Maybe a kiss will help us decide."

Belle's mouth watered with desire as her inner voice implored her to stop Ally before it was too late to stop herself.

"Not today, cheater," she said, shoving her away.

"Belle, Chloe's my niece," Ally said, laughing. "She lives with me, but she's away at equestrian camp for a few weeks."

Gulp.

"Did I say wife?" Belle said in an exaggerated laugh. "Why would I say wife when I totally meant niece?"

"Your face was priceless," Ally said, still laughing.

"You're quite the prankster, aren't you?" She wasn't even remotely amused.

"I'm sorry. That was a tacky thing to do on what may or may not be our first date." She extended her hand. "Truce?"

Belle reluctantly shook it. "I guess I can let it slide in light of the ambiguity of tonight's theme."

"You're a sport." Ally leveled a playful punch against her arm. "By the way, before I go, do you have any *nieces* you forgot to mention?"

Belle smiled coyly. "Only one. My sister's eighteen-year-old daughter."

"Good to know. Well, thanks for an interesting evening," Ally said as they walked across the creaky wood in the hall heading to the foyer. "Planning to check out the strawberry festival tomorrow?"

"I didn't know about it, although I certainly should have."

Ally stopped at the door and turned toward Belle. "It starts at noon. There'll be music, games, vendors, and all the strawberry products you can possibly consume." She suddenly seemed shy, with her hands in her pocket and her head tilted downward.

Belle liked that side of her. "Someone's coming first thing in the morning to work in the kitchen," she said, "but I suppose I could run out for a bit."

"Good. Hope to see you there."

They stood for an awkward moment at the door. As badly as Belle wanted a good-night kiss for real, she restrained herself. The date issue remained unresolved, and the signs from Ally weren't clear enough through their banter.

Besides, the last thing she needed was an emotional entanglement to derail her from her original purpose. And ultimately leaving without any unnecessary drama.

"What do you say, Red?" Belle asked the dog, who was watching them from the kitchen. "I think Deputy Yates misses you and tried to hide it by putting it on her niece."

"That's not true, Red," Ally said in a sober tone. "It's entirely your choice. If you want to stay here and keep this out-of-towner company, I won't mind. It's mighty hospitable of you."

Belle laughed. "Red, if you want to go home with Ally, I'm okay with that. I'd rather be alone here than have your pity."

"He's a loyal son of a gun," Ally said. "He must still miss Marion."

"Aww, I bet he does."

"Although she's been gone for years, he must find familiarity here."

Belle absently scratched his head. "If that's how it is, I better add dog food to the grocery list. Right, Red?"

He lay down on a tattered throw rug near them.

"Thanks again," Ally said. "Maybe I'll see you tomorrow."

Belle smiled. "I think you will."

She watched Ally's car roll down the driveway and finally exhaled as it drove off.

Not a moment too soon.

After spending the morning watching a pair of burly contractors install a culinary island in the center of the kitchen and remove cabinet doors for sanding, Belle was ready for a bike ride to stimulate her endorphins. She needed the distraction to stop obsessing about how much money she was sinking into the house. She reminded herself that the finished product would look so fierce once she'd christened it with her creative vision, buyers would scramble to meet or exceed her asking price. By next summer, she'd be in her new home in Old Saybrook or some other picturesque coastline locale, hosting friends and family for cookouts on her own private slice of beach heaven.

With the addition of a basket to the front of her bicycle that made her feel like Elmira Gulch, she arrived in town at the height of the strawberry-festival revelry. She propped her bike against a tree and crossed the street to Mrs. Morgan's fruit and veggie stand.

"What's good today, Shirley?"

"'Afternoon, Belle. All things strawberry and or rhubarb," she said. "Pies, jams and preserves, and my special strawberry-rhubarb salsa. I make it with my own secret blend of spices, so don't try to finagle the recipe of out me."

"I wouldn't dream of it."

"Here, try some." Shirley offered a basket of tortilla chips and a bowl of salsa.

"Wow, this is fantastic," Belle said, trying to prevent a piece of tortilla from escaping her lips. "I'll take two jars. And a pie."

"Coming right up." Shirley filled the cloth sack Belle handed her.

Munching on another salsa-heaped chip, Belle glanced around at the crowd. Like a hologram postcard from the tourism department, people played cornhole, sampled festival fare, and lounged in lawn chairs as an acoustic duo harmonized their rendition of Patsy Cline's "I've Got Your Picture."

After completing the transaction, Belle capitalized on the lull in customer traffic at Shirley's stand.

"So, Shirley, remember we talked the other day about Judy and Marion Ashford?"

"Yep."

"What can you tell me about Judy?"

Shirley slowly wiped her hands on a checkered hand towel.

"I remember her being a sweet little girl. Smart and respectful. When I was dating Bob, sometimes Judy and the other girls would hang around after catechism class if I was over at the house." She smiled as she seemed to drift back. "I was about twenty years old, so they liked talking with me about boys and how to do their hair and how to dress. You know how little girls always look up to fashionable older ones."

The word fashionable prompted Belle to take note of Shirley's frumpy denim culottes, plaid blouse, and frizzy gray hair.

"I think Judy stayed because she didn't want to go home, you know? With her father dead, she was alone a lot of the time until her mother came home from her part-time job."

Shirley was repeating some of the info Belle had gleaned from her previously. Her well of knowledge didn't appear to be as deep as Belle had hoped.

"Are any of Judy's childhood friends still here?"

"'Suppose it's possible, but I don't think I could help you out there. I could ask Bob if he remembers any names, or you can ask him yourself. He's over there playing cornhole."

"I don't want to bother him today. But if it wouldn't be too much trouble for you to ask him, I'd sure appreciate it." Belle smiled and wondered why she was starting to talk like a character on *The Andy Griffith Show*.

"Oh sure, honey. I do remember a boy she dated for a while. Carl, no, Craig. He was bad news, always getting into trouble for something. The Wheelers were a bad family."

"Bad how?"

"You know, trashy. Bob was always going over there and breaking up some kind of row either between the father and the wife or the father and the son. He was a mean drunk, Mr. Wheeler was."

"Do any of them still live here?"

"I don't think so. When the husband went to jail, the wife finally got up the nerve to divorce him. I think I heard she took the kids out of state."

"Craig Wheeler." Belle was already reviewing the plethora of online people-search options available. Hopefully, this one wasn't dead, too. "Okay, thanks, Shirley. If your husband can remember anything about Judy's friends, would you let me know?"

"Sure thing. Enjoy the jams."

Belle strolled through the festival grounds, keeping her eye out for Ally. Although she'd had a vivid, blush-worthy dream about her the night before, Belle would vehemently argue with anyone that her motive for wanting to see Ally was purely professional.

She happened along the cornhole tournament and noticed that light-brown uniform and a flash of sunlight reflecting off her highway-patrol sunglasses. Strolling closer, Belle shivered at the sweat glistening on Ally's forearms. She lurked behind some spectators so she could enjoy another moment of clandestine leering.

"Belle," Ally shouted as she waved wildly from across the cornhole lane.

Her cover blown, she waved back and walked toward Ally, who'd already started coming to her.

"Don't you ever get a day off?" she asked.

"Someone has to keep law and order at the strawberry fest." Ally gave her a wink. "Things have been known to get out of hand when Ethel breaks out the sassy strawberry wine from last year's crop."

"Looks like I got here just in time."

"Right," Ally said. "Besides, I like to give Bob a break whenever I can. He's slowed down quite a bit over the last year, but he does love the cornhole."

Belle watched him toss the bean bag into the air as the group of young players cheered him on.

"So, soon there's gonna be a new sheriff in town?"

"By next summer," Ally said. "He said seventy-five is a good age to hang up his hat."

Belle let out a whistle of surprise. "If I'm still teaching freshman comp at that age, please have me put in a home."

"You may be a successful real estate developer by that time and not want to retire."

"Only if I can do business by phone from a beach chair with my feet in the water."

"It's important to have goals."

Belle smiled at Ally's easy way despite her commanding presence. Then she remembered…chocolate sauce. They were doing something naughty with chocolate sauce in her dream.

"Uhhh," she said, stalling to regain focus. "So I was told by my contractor this morning that I should see a guy named Angelo about getting a new stone patio."

"Oh, yeah. He does great work. Loves to bet on the ponies, but the only time that matters is during Triple Crown season. He and the wife vacation in New York for the Belmont Stakes."

Belle smiled.

"What?" Ally asked innocently.

"You're gonna make a great sheriff."

"God, it's true." Ally covered her face in embarrassment. "I officially know everything about everyone in town."

"That's not a bad thing," Belle said. "I got the name of Judy's high school boyfriend out of Shirley."

"Impressive." Ally pushed her sunglasses up into her hair. "Coincidentally, I'm gonna need a deputy next year."

"I'll make you a deal. If we nail the dirtbag who molested Judy, I'll consider sticking around."

"Oh?" Ally's smile shriveled in the sun. "You weren't planning to live here?"

Belle suddenly felt like every bit of the infiltrator Ally's tone suggested. "Um, no, not really, but you never know how things will work out."

"You might finish the house and fall in love with it."

"I just might," Belle said. However, if she were to fall in love that summer, something told her it wouldn't only be with the house.

"Would you have a long commute to the university from here?"

"About an hour—without traffic."

"Eww, that's ugly," Ally said. "Well, I guess I can't blame you."

Was Belle wishful thinking, or did Ally seem disappointed that she wasn't planning to be a permanent transplant?

"Anyway," Ally said with a more professional demeanor. "What was the name Shirley gave you?"

"Wheeler. The boy's name was Craig."

Ally pursed her lips. "Doesn't sound familiar."

"Shirley said the father was a drunk, and when he went to prison, the family moved away. I wonder if he could be our first person of interest. We have motive and opportunity."

Ally laughed almost condescendingly. "*We* have opportunity only if Judy knew the family when she was ten."

"She might have."

"And at this moment, we don't have a motive because being an alcoholic doesn't automatically mean someone's a sex offender."

Belle rolled her eyes. "You might want to ask some of the young women around my campus about that one."

"Point taken, but this situation is entirely different. I know how ramped up you are about this, but you really should prepare yourself for the likely event that we'll never find the perp or, worse, that we will find him but not have enough evidence for a conviction."

Belle had grown impatient with Ally's dismissiveness. "Do you not care about what happened to Judy because she's dead?"

"What kind of question is that?" Ally's eyes were volcanos on the verge of eruption.

"I don't know," Belle said, suddenly feeling like a fool. "If you won't have enough evidence even if you find the guy, why bother at all?"

"Belle, of course I care about her. But I know how these cold cases work. I absolutely will dig around the records dungeon on Monday and also look into the Wheeler family, but I can't make any promises about the outcome."

"Whatever," Belle said dryly. "Just doing my job as a concerned citizen."

"I certainly appreciate that."

"I mean if you folks don't mind a sociopath joining you at your ice cream socials, that's fine with me."

"Don't worry, Ms. Ashford. We'll manage fine. Besides, it's not like you'll be here for long." Ally slipped her sunglasses down over her eyes and added, "You enjoy your day now," before heading back to the cornhole game.

"You, too, Deputy Yates," she yelled back.

She trudged off, muttering to herself, "I'll try not to get murdered so you won't have to tear yourself away from the corndog-eating contest later."

After locating Angelo, the mason, and setting up an appointment for next week, she headed back to the house to check the status of the kitchen.

She pedaled harder along the winding road, still annoyed. Ally was supposed to be a public servant, but as soon as Belle asked her to do something more involved than giving directions to the bank of Porto-lets at the festival, she couldn't have appeared less willing to serve.

Making matters worse was Belle's attraction to her, which only seemed to grow stronger each time they met. That defiant attitude that infuriated her was also extremely appealing.

Hadn't she learned anything from the series of bad decisions she affectionately referred to as "ex-girlfriends?"

CHAPTER FOUR

When Belle arrived home and walked her bike up the patchy driveway, the contractors were packing their tools and depositing construction scraps into her rented refuse container.

"All done?" she said.

"Yes, ma'am," said Ralph Jr. of Ralph Jr.'s General Contracting. "Go have a look."

Red followed them in, presumably to see if Ralph Jr. had returned his new dog-treat jar to the new counter before leaving.

She walked into the kitchen and gasped when she saw the new culinary island and shimmering granite counters. That stylish, modern kitchen couldn't possibly be part of the rest of the house.

"Oh, Ralph, it's gorgeous. And you got it done so fast without having to come back a million times."

"When I start a project, I make sure and see it through." He threw his shoulders back with a smile. "So you're pleased?"

"Very," she said, taking it all in.

"Your cabinet doors are ready for you to paint. They're still in good condition. Sturdy craftsmanship of the early nineteen-hundreds."

Suddenly, a spark of innovation began dancing around her mind. "Ralph, how do you feel about coming back and knocking out this wall for an open kitchen-dining-room floor plan?"

"How's Thursday?"

"You're on," she said as she wrote him a check.

After he left and Red received his dog cookie, Belle took her iPad out to the back porch and began her search for Craig Wheeler. The first hit was for Wheeler and Son Automotive in West Haven. He was still in the state after all.

Without a clue as to what she'd say if he answered, she dialed the phone number and asked for Craig.

"He's not here on Saturdays," the guy said. "Can I help you?"

"Uh, no, thanks. When will he be in?"

"Monday."

This is too easy, Belle thought. This dude was probably referring to the son. "Are you talking about Craig Junior or Senior?"

"There is no junior. You want the old man or his son, Rick?"

"The old man," Belle said, as though he were the confused one.

"Call back Monday then."

Her heart pounding, Belle ended the call and sighed with satisfaction. Finally, someone with a direct tie to Judy who wasn't dead.

She thought about calling Ally, if for no other reason than to gloat over her kick-ass detective skills. Then she remembered they still hadn't exchanged cell numbers. Oh well. She'd rather see the look on Ally's face when she threw the information in it like a pie at a carnival midway.

Around eight o'clock Belle showered, blew dry her hair, and pulled it up in a messy bun. Although she was tired from running around all day, she was restless. As endearing as Red and his sympathetic brown eyes were, conversations with him were rather one-sided unless they involved the topic of treats. Curious to see what nighttime happenings could possibly top the orgiastic excitement of the strawberry festival, she dabbed on some lip gloss and drove into town.

She parked her SUV and strolled along Main Street. Not surprisingly, nearly everything was closed except for the Italian restaurant and an ice cream-coffeehouse type deal.

Maybe she'd underestimated the charm of staying at the house and drinking a bottle of cab with Red's chin in her lap. Except she'd have to drive about a half hour to somewhere with a liquor store that kept normal business hours.

Just as she was about to write off Saturday nights in Danville, the neon glow from an antique Bar and Grille sign and the illuminated pool cue and eight ball under it lured her like a grifter to a con.

After ordering one of the local tap beers, she perched on a bar stool and scanned the crowd. To her surprise and delight, Ally was bent over a pool table lining up her shot. Belle hung back for a while and admired the view, using a group of young guys near her doing shooters for cover.

For her next shot, Ally was positioned directly across from Belle, who'd strategically lowered her V-neck shirt with a tug as she attempted to strike an alluring pose. Ally cracked the cue ball against one of hers, and her eyes followed the trajectory of the cue right up to Belle.

When Belle saw her smirk before pretending not to see her, she headed toward the pool table.

"I guess I was wrong about this place," Belle said.

"Yeah? How so?" Ally's mood seemed tempered, likely by their encounter earlier that afternoon.

"Danville does offer other recreational activities besides swatting flies."

"Congrats. You found the one other thing on your own," Ally said as she made her way around the table.

"Looks like Sully's Snacks and Billiards isn't Danville's best-kept secret after all."

"Not to an amateur super-sleuth like yourself."

This new side of Ally—mildly bitchy with a dash of indifference—was incredibly sexy, as were her khaki short shorts and vintage black Ramones T-shirt.

Belle had better watch herself.

"Would you recommend the buffalo wings?"

"I couldn't call myself a true 'Danvillin'" if I didn't," Ally said, then looked directly at Belle. "You can't either unless you take Sully's super-spicy wing challenge."

"That's a pair of the weirdest sentences I've ever heard," Belle said, rolling her eyes at the lame challenge. "And as much as I'd love to call myself a 'Danvillin'" I'm not willing to risk anaphylactic shock choking down a platter full of lava-coated chicken parts."

"I'm sorry to hear that, Ms. Ashford. I really thought you were gonna fit right in here." Ally sat on a high stool and rested the cue between her legs. "But then you're not planning to stick around anyway, are you?"

"I'm detecting a note of hostility, Deputy. I suppose I owe you an apology for the attitude this afternoon." Without waiting for an invitation, Belle sat on the stool across from her.

Ally's shoulders appeared to slacken at Belle's olive branch. "Apology accepted. I could've been more patient, too. I know what the *CSI* effect does to people."

"What's the *CSI* effect?"

"It's what happens to people who watch too many crime-investigation shows. They think that's how it is in real life. Everyone sees Mariska Hargitay solve all her cases without ever being late for a dinner reservation. In reality, the case of Judy Ashford is more like it—a crime is reported, and we don't have one shred of helpful evidence to go on."

Belle brandished the smile of a precocious child. "Until you rummage through stacks of old, asbestos-covered files Monday."

"Yeah, that and some divine intervention."

Belle rested her elbows on the table. "How about some Isabelle intervention?"

"I have a feeling I'm gonna regret asking, but what's that?"

"I think I located Judy's old high school boyfriend."

"You did? Where is he?"

"He owns a garage down in West Haven. While you're plugging through the archives, I'm going to pay him a visit Monday afternoon."

Ally gave her a skeptical glare. "You're not gonna strut into his shop and ambush him with that journal."

"Um, number one, I don't strut. And number two, I can be a little more tactful than that. I'll bring it up casually. He won't even know what hit him."

"How can you possibly stroll into an auto shop and bring up the owner's dead girlfriend from fifty years ago with tact?"

"I have to get my emissions' test done, remember?" Belle gave her a saucy wink.

Ally chuckled. "Ah, yes. I suppose I deserve some of the blame for this. But I have to admit that's one of the best pretenses I've ever heard."

"I know, right?" Belle said excitedly.

"Except I would not mention the journal to him."

"Why not?"

"Belle, depending on what I can find out tomorrow, this may actually turn into an investigation. You can't go around informing potential suspects about the evidence."

"You think you may be able to open an investigation?"

"I don't know," Ally said as she chalked the tip of her cue stick. "I have to see what's on record with the Wheeler family and determine if there's anything on the Ashfords, too. But I highly recommend you don't take those papers and definitely don't mention anything about a possible sex assault."

Belle sulked. "That doesn't leave me much to talk with him about if I can't mention what she wrote."

"Say you've inherited the Ashford place and that somebody said they knew him and Judy when they were kids."

Belle didn't like how Ally was commandeering the recon mission with Craig she'd planned on her own.

"Better yet," Ally said, "you can hold off on talking to Mr. Wheeler until we see what I can find out Monday. Then I can go with you when you talk with him."

Belle narrowed her eyes. "You're trying to make a coup over my operation."

Ally laughed. "What operation? Look, if there really is a chance of finding out who abused Judy, you won't be doing anyone any favors by mucking it up interrogating a potential suspect. You need to leave that to the professionals."

"What, the mucking-it-up part?"

Ally sighed. "You know what I mean."

"That's what I was trying to do earlier today, but the professional," she said with air quotes, "suggested I forget about it since everyone's dead. Well, guess what, Deputy Professional? Everyone isn't dead."

Ally smirked. "You're a mountain of determination."

"I should say so," Belle said in a huff, smoothing out her wrinkled cocktail napkin.

"Can I buy you another beer?" Ally's eyes dazzled her with insinuation.

Belle sucked in a deep breath, exhaled, and smiled. "I can go for another."

Ally signaled the waitress and pointed to Belle's beer glass. "What do you say we join forces instead of being adversaries? We'll get more accomplished that way."

Ally was showing her subtle talent for wearing down subjects of interrogation. "What do you have in mind?"

"Before you drive all the way down to West Haven to get your emissions tested when you can get it done right here at Freddie's, let me see what I find out Monday morning. If I come up empty, you can unleash your bad-cop wrath on Mr. Wheeler till he throws you off his property."

"That seems fair," Belle said and licked her lips, dry from the beer. "Okay. You got a deal." She held out her hand, and Ally slid her warm palm into it.

"How about a decaf, skinny soy latte to solidify our accord?" Ally said.

Belle looked at her watch. "It's nine fifteen. Isn't it past everyone's bedtime?"

Ally cocked an eyebrow. "Not mine. I have a latte machine at my house."

"So that's your M.O." Belle bit into the orange slice at the bottom of her beer glass. "You lure innocent, unsuspecting newcomers to your love shack with the promise of home-brewed lattes."

"Love shack?" Ally threw her hands onto her hips. "I wanted you to meet my wife."

Belle felt her face deflate.

"Kidding," Ally said as she counted out cash on top of the check. "It's a latte. And I don't have a wife, or girlfriend—not that it would matter to someone just passing through."

Belle's phone vibrated on the table. She grabbed it but was certain Ally caught a glimpse of "Crazy Mary" on the text bar. "A decaf latte sounds like a perfect nightcap," she said.

In the small backyard of Ally's condo, Belle stretched her legs out to the rim of the stone fire pit and stared into the flames as they snapped and hissed. Sitting under a starry sky in the country waiting for a beautiful woman to bring her a latte wasn't part of the blueprint for her summer of restoration—not that she was complaining.

Could the universe have more in store for her than flipping an old house?

"Maybe I should've made these iced," Ally said as she descended the steps. She handed Belle her latte and joined her around the fire.

"It's fine," Belle said. "It's a nice night. Thank you."

"It did cool off, didn't it?"

Belle agreed. "I'm having Angelo build one of these in my yard. I've lived in a condo for so long, I forgot what a luxury it is to have a backyard."

"Yeah. I'm lucky this unit has this one. Where's your condo?"

"North Guilford. If things go according to plan, I'll be putting it on the market soon."

"Are you renting it out now?"

Belle paused a moment, considering how much she should reveal. "Uh, no. I'm currently waiting for the other, uh, occupant to move her stuff out."

"And by other occupant, do you mean your ex?"

Belle clenched her teeth in dread of Ally's reaction.

"That wouldn't happen to be Crazy Mary, would it?" Ally asked.

"It would, in fact." Belle glanced at her and thought she noticed an eye roll in the glow from the fire.

"Fascinating," Ally said casually. "So when you say crazy, are you using it in the colloquial sense?"

Belle giggled. "She's harmless, albeit annoying. But she was the wake-up call I needed."

Ally grimaced. "You were a relationship Rip Van Winkle?"

"A what?"

"You know, asleep for twenty years before realizing anything was wrong."

"You might say that. But I saw forty looming well before it arrived, like ten years before. Most of my friends were marrying and starting families by then, so I got paranoid thinking I'd be alone for the rest of my life if I didn't stop screwing around."

"That's so early two-thousand," Ally said. "I have a couple of friends who didn't meet their life partners until their forties. Some things don't fit into a timetable."

"What can I say? I was the kid who hated to be left out of anything. And when Connecticut passed civil unions, I was getting invited to ceremonies as often as birthday parties. The pressure resulted in a lot of hasty decision-making—culminating with Mary."

"The classic U-Haul lesbian. I've known one or two in my time. So what brought you out of the dark?"

"I think realizing how much energy I'd wasted dreading turning forty as this phantasmagoric plunge into the abyss. Then I woke up one day three months ago on my fortieth birthday, and the sun was shining, and I went to work, got my car washed, and then went out with Mary for a birthday dinner.

"As I watched her hobble over to the bar in wedge heels fluffing up her over-processed hair, it dawned on me that I was living with a woman I probably wouldn't want to engage with at the DMV, let alone build a life with."

Ally was silent for a moment, looking slightly aghast. "Did you at least stay for the free birthday cake?"

"Naturally. There was no reason to make the cake suffer."

Ally laughed. "So, now she won't leave?"

"I'd told her I'd give her a month to find her own place, but that turned to two, then three. Finally, the deed transfer came through for my aunt's house, and I said I'm going to stay up here, and that every last trace of her better be out of there by the end of June."

"How's that working out for you?"

"I'm having my attorney file an eviction notice this week."

"No good deed, huh?"

"Exactly," Belle said.

"So does this mean you've sworn off relationships as part of your recovery?"

"And completed my transformation into a walking cliché? No. But I realized I need to take some time to focus on me, my goals, and what I'd like out of the back half of my life."

"That's very sensible," Ally said. "I arrived at a similar conclusion myself a while ago. It's part of what brought me here."

"How'd it work out?"

"Rather well. Highly recommend it."

"Awesome," Belle said. "Then it's fate that we became friends. You can be my mentor of sensible life choices."

Ally smiled. "I'm glad we've become friends, too, but I don't know if I'm up to the task of being your guardian of good choices. Seems like a full-time job."

"Cute." Belle returned her gaze to the fire with a frown. Did Ally really have to agree so readily to the idea of being just friends?

"I'm gonna grab some waters," Ally said, rising from her chair. "I also have Pellegrino if you'd prefer. Or wine. I have a selection inside that I usually drink by myself."

"I don't think I should start on wine. You might end up with an uninvited overnight guest."

"That wouldn't be such a bad thing," Ally said and headed inside to the kitchen.

That returned the smile to Belle's face. It placed other parts of her on notice as well. If she was sincere about making better life choices, now was the right time to start. It would be so easy to pin Ally against the wall, plant a wet one on her, and blame it on the wine.

She followed Ally inside. "How about a rain check? Maybe we can visit that nearby winery, so I can start my own collection."

"We have two within a relatively close proximity," Ally said. "We can make an afternoon of it and hit them both if you'd like."

"That's a fantastic idea." Belle sucked at the last drop of foam in her cup.

"Can you sneak off for an afternoon some weekend?"

As she was about to answer, Belle placed her cup in the sink at the same time as Ally. They bumped shoulders and faced each other, Ally's glistening lips almost daring her to act.

What was one kiss between friends?

Belle stared at them, momentarily paralyzed with indecision. Kissing her was absolutely out of the question. No way. A move she'd regret seconds after doing it. But those lips—so soft, so luscious, so...

"Would you prefer during the week instead?" Ally asked.

"Huh? Uh, no, a weekend is perfect. Whatever suits your work schedule." Belle extricated herself from the dicey situation by heading to the front door. "I'm sure I'll need an afternoon away from that house soon," she said over her shoulder. "Thanks for the latte."

"Any time."

Belle stood in the open doorway staring at Ally's mouth.

"Either kiss me good night or shake my hand," Ally said in a drawl. "You're letting moths in standing there like you're trying to introduce me to Jesus."

"I know what I want to do, and I know what I should do. Unfortunately, they aren't the same thing."

"In that case, let's split the difference." Ally wrapped Belle in a light hug. "Thanks for a nice night. I'll call you Monday if I come up with anything."

"Don't forget." Belle smiled to diffuse the awkwardness. "I have to get my expired emissions done before I get pulled over again."

"You got it," Ally said with a salute.

The short walk down Ally's driveway felt like a road to nowhere. When she shut her car door, she drew in a deep breath before starting the engine.

So how was a platonic friendship with someone you're physically attracted to supposed to work anyway? She'd never pulled it off when she was in college. But then she wasn't a college girl anymore. She was forty—the age when a woman finally had the strength to conquer her urges and use logic and reason regarding matters of the heart.

Or not.

CHAPTER FIVE

Belle spent most of Monday morning chewing her way through the backyard weed farm with her father's lawn mower until it finally ran out of gas. By the time she'd finished clearing out the overgrown grass, rocks, and sticks nearest the house, she would undoubtedly owe him a new mower.

She checked the time on her phone—11:35 a.m. and still no word from Ally. She'd kicked around the idea of shooting her a friendly "how's it going" text as a gentle reminder that she was dying from curiosity but decided to give her till high noon. As soon as she shoved her phone back into her pocket, it vibrated.

"Hey," Ally said, all business. "A computer check came up empty, and I couldn't find any reports of sexual assaults on minors in the paper files from 1960 to 1964."

"Damn," Belle said, disappointed. For some reason she was under the impression that, after a few keystrokes, Ally would be able to solve the entire case. Maybe she was right about the *CSI* effect after all.

"I hear ya, but I'm not surprised. In those days, it was an even easier crime to get away with."

"So it's possible the pedophile that did this hasn't or never will be caught."

"As much as I hate to say it, yes. It's very possible."

Belle moaned in frustration as she paced the yard. "How about the Wheeler family? Did you get a chance to check into that?"

"Yes, and it was interesting," Ally said. "I found a bunch of charges for old man Wheeler—public drunkenness, disorderly conduct, several domestics involving the wife and son, Craig—but no sex assault or misconduct with minors."

Belle lost her train of thought for a moment as she listened to Ally sounding like a professional investigator. She wished she had asked her to stop by the station to explain all that in person. She must've looked so intense and sexy.

"Uh, forgive my lack of enthusiasm," Belle said, "but what's so interesting about that? It's exactly what I would've expected from an angry alcoholic."

"It is? The other day you were ready to castrate old man Wheeler without even giving him his day in court. Now he's off your list of suspects?"

Belle giggled flirtatiously. "Well, I've had a seasoned sheriff's deputy educating me about persons of interest and motive and all that."

"I'm glad you've been paying attention," Ally said, returning the flirtation. "The interesting part wasn't what I found on Mr. Wheeler. It's what I found on Craig. The kid was a menace."

"What do you mean?"

"He was constantly in trouble and definitely in the running for most inept petty criminal in history. I'm surprised he made it out of his teens alive."

"What kind of trouble?"

"You name it—criminal mischief, assault, breaking and entering, and several possession charges. He was a walking, one-man crime spree."

"Well, look at his father. With that upbringing he wasn't gonna be in line for the National Honor Society."

Ally offered a sympathetic grumble. "Are you still planning to go see him?"

"Yeah. I'll take a ride tomorrow," Belle said, slapping at various itches on her legs. "Hopefully he'll be at the repair shop."

"You might want to hire an armed bodyguard to go with you."

"Are you offering your services?"

Ally laughed. "No. I'm working my day job, which I need to get back to now. Tomorrow I'll see if I can sneak off to search more of the paper files for sex assaults."

"Thanks for doing this, Ally," Belle said in a warm voice. "I owe you big time."

"Ally, huh? I guess we're back to a first-name basis."

"I hope you weren't offended that I didn't choose door number one Saturday night. It wasn't you, believe me."

"Not that I would've minded terribly if you had," Ally said, her voice low and velvety, "but I think you made the right choice. Well done. You passed your first post-breakup challenge."

"You mean your lingering glance at the sink was just a test?"

"Lingering glance?" Ally's tone was a clear plea of pretend ignorance to Belle's charge. "I gave you nothing of the kind."

Belle smiled into the phone. "But you wouldn't have minded if I kissed you?"

"I'm an understanding person. I realize change doesn't come easy, so if you'd slipped back into your old, flirty ways, I couldn't hold it against you."

"That's mighty magnanimous of you, Deputy."

Ally giggled. "Hey, listen. On a serious note, be careful if you talk to Wheeler. Stay in a public space."

"I got this. Some geriatric delinquent is no match for me. I work out."

"And remember what I told you about saying too much."

"Ten-four," Belle said.

"Okay. Call me immediately if you gather anything new."

Belle agreed and ended the conversation.

She gripped the lawn-mower handle, smiling like a gremlin. "She likes me."

In theory, walking up to a stranger and informing him that she'd unearthed some buried piece of his past seemed like an intriguing proposition. But as she pulled into Wheeler and Son Automotive, her palms were sweating from her death grip on the steering wheel. She could get her vehicle tested, pay the forty bucks in testing and late fees, and drive away, but then how would she live with herself after such a cowardly abdication of her moral duty? An innocent child had been hurt, a child who shared her bloodline, and this Craig person was essentially the only living human being who might have some insight into the perpetrator's identity.

She sat in the waiting room thumbing through a wrinkled copy of *Automotive Digest* from two years earlier, scrutinizing every sweaty, greasy guy in a Wheeler T-shirt who walked in and out. Not one of them looked a day over thirty. She finally approached the counter to inquire about Craig, fearing her car would be ready with her ulterior motive still unrealized.

Out of the back office came a man with a slight build, eyeglasses, and white, thinning hair.

"I'm Craig," he said. "How can I help you?"

The contrast in how she'd pictured him left her momentarily speechless. Since learning of him from Shirley Morgan, she imagined him as either a grass-smoking hippie with straggly hair, a peace sign dangling from a rawhide neck choker, and bushy sideburns, or loaded with prison tattoos. Maybe he'd looked like that forty years ago, but today he kind of resembled her dad.

"Hi, uh, I'm Isabelle Ashford," she said, trembling inside. "I recently moved up to Danville, and I heard you used to date my father's cousin, Judy Ashford."

"Wow. That's sure a blast from the past." Although he'd offered a cordial smile and handshake, his eyes reflected the unsettled feeling clearly evoked by the name.

"It's nice that you still remember her."

"Oh, sure," he said with a bittersweet smile. "She was my first girl. Sweet kid."

"Did you know her long?"

"Oh, yeah. We met in grammar school. She was my little sister's friend. We started dating when I was a junior and she was in ninth grade."

"Really?" Belle's look of reproach must've made him self-conscious.

"You know, kid stuff—going to the show, getting burgers and stuff."

"Did you guys ever play together when you were little?"

"She and my sister did, but I didn't really notice her until she got older," he said with a grin.

Belle tried to contain her fervor at the news that it was possible for Craig's creep father to have had access to Judy. She couldn't wait to report back to Ally.

"So did they play together a lot at your house?" Belle rested her hip against the counter with the confidence of a veteran investigator.

He shook his head. "I think they spent most days at her house. I went there sometimes, when I was bored. Her father died when she was young, and her mother was real overprotective. Always tried to get Judy to stay home. My sister and I didn't mind 'cause she'd make us lunch and sometimes supper, too."

"Were you still dating Judy when she passed away?"

His smile crashed as though she'd teleported him back to that moment. He shook his head. "The year before it happened, I got shipped off to juvie for six months, then got sent over to 'Nam. I found out about Judy in a letter from my sister. Couldn't make her funeral or nothing."

When Belle saw the fresh pain under his heavy eyelids, she almost choked up. In her zeal to solve an ancient mystery, she'd never considered the possibility of encountering someone for whom she might be opening ancient wounds.

"I'm so sorry you went through that, Mr. Wheeler."

He pulled himself together as only a vet could. "Eh, it was a lifetime ago. But boy, I had a hell of a time getting over not being there. Maybe if I wasn't off fighting in that damn jungle, I could've found her in time."

"What do you mean? In time for what?"

He regarded Belle like she was dense. "So they coulda pumped her stomach."

Belle was floored. "I'm sorry. I'm a little confused. I thought she died from some sickness."

"Swallowing a bottle of downers'll make you sick, all right."

"Wait. She died of a drug overdose?"

He gave a solemn nod.

"Was it suicide?"

He shrugged. "She didn't leave a note."

"Was she acting depressed or suicidal before it happened?"

Craig narrowed his eyes. "Are you a cop or something?"

"No, no. Just too empathetic for my own good. She was my dad's cousin, so I kinda feel like I owe it to him to find out. Anyway, if she was suicidal, I assume you would've known it before anyone."

He seemed to disagree. "The only contact we had for a year was through letters. But she was always a moody one, dark, you know? Even before I got sent away, she'd sometimes go days without speaking to me. Even when I went to her house after school, we'd sit there watching TV for hours without her saying a word."

"Ms. Ashford, you're all set." A young man emerged from the garage and pointed to her car waiting outside.

Damn him! The one time in the history of the universe anyone had ever rooted for the service to take longer than promised…

Craig looked at his watch. "Well, I have to get going. Hope I helped you out."

"You did, Mr. Wheeler. And I'm sorry if I brought back painful memories."

"No problem," he said with a twitch of his shoulder. "You brought back a few good ones, too."

On the long ride back to Danville, Belle attempted to expunge from her mind the haunting images of old Craig Wheeler's face as she prompted him to relive seemingly the worst period of his life. She also tried to reconcile why Judy's death was passed off as some mysterious illness when the real cause was obvious. Given the era, it probably had to do with the stigma of addiction and suicide. Those things didn't happen in "good" families, and they certainly weren't talked about openly if they did.

As she approached the exit, she called Ally via Bluetooth to find out where she was working. Could she have texted her the info? Well, yeah. But miss a chance to see her in her snug-fitting, khaki-brown deputy uniform? Never.

She parked down the street from a utility truck and workers doing repairs on a power line.

"Hey," she said, sucking wind as she jogged toward Ally, who was waving a car through the work zone. "You're not going to believe this."

"What's up?"

"Judy didn't die from some illness. She died from a frickin' drug overdose."

"Really? That's what Craig Wheeler told you?"

Belle nodded slowly.

"Hmm. I'll see if I can find her death certificate and find out what the coroner ruled it. What else did he say?"

"Just that he and his sister spent more time at Judy's house than theirs, so I'm guessing their old man probably wasn't the guy who assaulted her."

"I wouldn't rule him out entirely."

"Now you're calling him a suspect?" Belle said. "The other day you were defending him, saying 'a wicked alcoholic does not a child molester make.'"

"That was before your brilliant detective work established a connection between him and Judy."

Belle beamed with pride. "Oh yeah? I did that?"

"You did," Ally said, holding up her hand for a high-five. "Now I'd like to question Craig to see if it was always their pattern to play over at Judy's house. Maybe Judy stopped playing at the Wheelers once the father started molesting her."

Belle stomped her foot in the dirt on the side of the road. "Why didn't I think of that?"

"Hey, you did a great job on your first suspect interview."

"Thanks." Belle gave a wistful smile. "He must've really loved her for him to get choked up after all these years. They were like a modern Romeo and Juliet, except he gets sent to juvie, and she ODs."

"Modern, indeed." Ally's stern cop exterior finally seemed to give a little.

"So tragic."

Ally flicked away a droplet of sweat from under her mirrored sunglasses. "Yeah, it is," she said peevishly. "Thanks for swooping in and annihilating my image of Danville being the kind of wholesome community you'd love to raise your kids in."

Belle laughed. "I'm sorry. That was never my intention."

"You know what they say about good intentions."

"I wish I'd never found that stupid headless doll. I'm spending way more of my mental energy on this abstract notion of avenging Judy than I am on renovations. Time is money, you know."

"Yes. I'm well aware that our little hamlet is nothing more to you than one big cash cow."

Belle couldn't determine whether or not that was dark humor, but she was slightly insulted nonetheless. "That's not true. I've only been here a few weeks, but the place and the people are really growing on me. It may turn out that my purpose here is much bigger than flipping an old house. It's almost like Judy left that cryptic message there so I would find it."

"Oh boy," Ally said. "Now you're hearing voices from the grave?"

"You don't believe in fate?"

Ally scoffed. "After twenty-two years in uniform, I believe in facts that can be supported with evidence. Messages from the other side don't hold up in court." She broke into a half smile. "No matter how cute and persistent the receiver of the message is."

Belle crossed her arms and squinted from the sun as she challenged Ally. "Don't think your schmooziness will distract me from my mission. I'm on to something, and you know it."

Ally humored her with a nod as she waved through another car.

"If Judy's death certificate says it was a drug overdose, can you do anything with that?"

"No, but I'd like to take a look at those pages again, if you don't mind. I'll also talk to Bob and see if he can remember anything. He was the deputy sheriff when she died."

"His wife remembers them. Maybe I should question her again. Should I mention what Craig said about the drugs?"

"I wouldn't. She has a mouth bigger than the Connecticut River. Don't give her any details. Let her give them to you. I'll talk to Bob about Craig's OD claim."

"Sounds like a plan," Belle said.

Ally smiled.

"You really think I'm cute?"

"Adorable. But something tells me you already know that."

"Don't be ridiculous," Belle said as she flapped her eyelashes flirtatiously.

"Can I get back to work now?"

"Oh, yeah, by all means," she said, slowly walking backwards toward her car. "I have a ton of things to do myself."

"See you around."

"Yes, you will, I mean if you want," Belle said, stopping for a moment. "Do you want?"

Ally nodded and seemed to laugh in spite of herself. "Happy trails." She waved as she meandered backward toward the utility truck.

Belle jumped in her SUV and drove off, forgetting where she was headed as Ally's smirking, too-cool act drove her to distraction.

After a long day of painting the upstairs bathroom, resurrecting ghosts of the past, and trying to keep it professional with Deputy Yates, Belle seized the chance to have her first soak in the newly cleaned and reglazed original claw-foot bathtub. With a glass of Riesling in one hand and her iPad in the other, she watched in the soft glow of candlelight a YouTube video on toilet installation.

"Ugh. This is where I've met my match. I better leave that to the professionals."

She placed the iPad on the floor and reclined against the back of the tub. Sipping her wine, she savored the first brief respite she'd afforded herself in weeks. She closed her eyes, let out a deep sigh, and listened to the faint night sounds of nocturnal critters drifting in through the open window.

Then, after what seemed like only seconds of bliss, Red's deep, roaring bark jolted half of the wine out of her glass and into her bath water.

"What the hell," she said, then shouted, "Red, what the hell are you barking at?"

He answered her with more barking.

She wrapped herself in a towel, suds and all, and crept down the staircase to make sure Red wasn't trying to inform her that the house was going up in flames. He stood in the foyer wagging his tail.

"What's the matter, boy?" she said, heading to the front window. "Did Timmy fall down the well again, that clumsy fuck?"

A hard knock on the door nearly startled her out of her towel. She opened the door only enough to poke her head out.

"Hi," Ally said. "Hope I'm not interrupting anything."

Belle opened the door wide enough for Ally to get the full picture. "You're either interrupting or right on time."

Ally laughed in obvious embarrassment. "And this would be why you didn't answer my text. I'm sorry. I just wanted to pick up the journal."

"Well, since you're already here, you might as well help me finish the bottle of Riesling I opened for my first bubble bath in forever."

"I could not have set this scene any better in my imagination, but I'm sure you'd like to get back to your bubbles. I'll pick it up tomorrow."

"No, no. You made the trip. Come in. I'll throw on some sweats and grab the diary."

"Are you sure?" Ally walked in slowly, seeming tentative.

"Positive." Belle grabbed her arm and pulled her inside. "Have a seat." She indicated the sofa before flying up the stairs.

Her heart pounded as she picked through a pile of clean, unfolded laundry on her bed. A pair of Nike shorts, a Reebok T-shirt, and a pair of granny panties were the best she could do on no notice. She snatched the bottle of wine from the bathroom and flew downstairs to find Red on the couch, too, half in Ally's lap.

"Well, well. Isn't this cozy?" she said.

"We have a history." Ally gave Red a big smooch on his whiskers.

Belle sat on the other side of the dog and handed Ally a glass of wine. "So, Red, this puts you in a rather awkward position."

"Oh, don't make him choose. I'm comfortable with a threesome."

"I am, too. But isn't there a consent issue where Red's concerned?"

"He's well aware that he can come and go as he pleases," Ally said. "Speaking of that, has he been here every day?"

"Since I started sleeping here a few weeks ago."

"I don't know how I'm going to break it to Chloe when she comes home from equestrian camp."

"Aww, I can't take a kid's dog. You can have him when she comes home."

Ally pretended to talk to Red. "I don't know, Red. How do you feel about this? Want to stay here with Belle?"

He let out a groan and stretched across them. Belle and Ally laughed and gave him one-handed head and belly rubs.

"I'll bring him to your house next week," Belle said in a whisper.

"No, that's fine. Chloe's been nagging me for a rescue greyhound for months, so now I'll have to get her one."

"You're a good aunt. Is she staying with you for the summer?"

Ally shook her head and sipped her wine. "I've been her legal guardian for the last six years. My sister's an addict, and who knows where Chloe's father is. They were never married."

"Oh. I'm sorry to hear that."

"She had a tough start, but she's an amazing kid—smart, artistic, sensitive."

"I'm sure most of the credit for that goes to your caring, stable influence."

"I'd love to take credit, but she's a unique girl, a survivor from the minute she was conceived. It's funny how I never wanted or planned to have children, especially at forty, but raising her has added so much to my life."

"That's awesome," Belle said. "You two are lucky to have each other."

Ally nodded. "How about you? Did you ever want kids?"

Belle sipped her wine to prevent a reflexive *hell, no* from launching out of her mouth like a ballistic missile. "I never gave it much thought, but I did have a cat I had to put to sleep a few months ago."

"Oh." Ally's mind was clearly working to make the connection. "I'm sorry."

"So Chloe sounds like a great kid. I'd love to meet her."

"We can arrange that," Ally said. "Have you heard from your ex anymore?"

"Uh, no, and that's how I prefer it."

"Then it's totally over and not just on lesbian hiatus?"

Belle laughed. "You have some interesting relationship terminology. What's a lesbian hiatus?"

"You know how lesbians have to break up a minimum of three times before it's officially over?"

"Yeah…" Belle said through more laughter.

"Well, the time in between is the hiatus. That's usually when some poor, unsuspecting wretch gets lured in, only to be cast off when the hiatus is over and the original couple decides to try it again."

"You seem disturbingly knowledgeable about this phenomenon. Were you the caster-offer or the wretch?"

Ally laughed. "When my ex and I were together we saw enough of our friends traipse through that minefield, but after we split, I was the wretch."

"Eww, I'm sorry," Belle said, hoping to avoid having to confess that she'd been both in her time. "No. Mary is absolutely a done deal. My lawyer said in thirty days it'll be signed and sealed."

"Were you together long?"

"Eleven months. Lived together for seven."

"Eleven months? And you were already living together and broken up?"

"I told you I was a tad hasty with Mary," Belle said. "But in all fairness, it was kind of a whirlwind when we met. The physical attraction was instant, we shared some interests, and I'd just turned thirty-nine. The bell was about to toll. So one night after four months and way too much tequila, I asked her to move in."

"Phew," Ally said. "If you'd said too much Riesling, I would've been outta here."

"Look, I'm not proud to admit to that misguided act of desperation, but I think anyone would be lying if they said they'd never made some type of desperate relationship choice. Okay, I may have made more than the average person, but that's why I don't drink tequila anymore."

Ally laughed and absently slapped Belle on the thigh. "Why do you think I'm keeping my mouth shut?"

"You should start talking now. I've said enough."

"None of my decisions involved tequila or shacking up after four months, but I think I can take some of the heat off you."

"I'd appreciate that."

"Okay. Here it goes. The ex I mentioned, my partner of thirteen-plus years and a fellow member of the Hartford PD... God, I can't believe I'm telling you this." Ally covered her eyes with the hand that was resting on Red's head.

"Come on," Belle said. "You can't stop now."

"Okay, okay. She cheated on me at least once that I know of, and I forgave her, but when I said I wanted us to take custody of Chloe, she said it was time to pursue different paths in life."

Belle recoiled with contempt. "Really? After thirteen years? Good riddance."

"Here's the desperate-choice part—at first I didn't take custody of Chloe so Jericca wouldn't leave me."

"Jericca? What kind of douchebag name is *Jericca*?"

"Her parents supposedly couldn't agree on naming her Jessica or Erica," Ally said, "but that's not the point."

"I get it. You chose a woman over someone important in your life. It's not a crime. Lots of people have had to make that choice."

"But I chose a woman with no integrity over an innocent child, a member of my own family."

Belle was surprised to learn that Ally had not always been the model of moral decency she'd pegged her as. But then who was?

She gave Ally's hand a squeeze. "It sounds to me like you've more than made amends for it."

"I have, but sometimes when Chloe is having a bad day or upset about whatever upsets twelve-year-old girls, I remember how I was almost another adult in her life who let her down."

Belle's heart ached at the regret Ally wore on her face. "Absolution is always hardest to get from ourselves. I'll bet she doesn't even think about that time in her life," she said as she refilled their glasses. "I mean equestrian camp and a new rescue greyhound when she comes home? That's winning at life if you ask me."

"Thanks, Belle."

"No need to thank me. I didn't want to drink this whole bottle myself, which I would've had you not popped in."

"I don't mean for the wine," Ally said with a warm smile.

Belle smiled back, her insides all jittery. "Besides, if anything, you've probably learned to be healthfully discerning in your subsequent relationships."

"I haven't had a relationship since Jericca. I've dated, but nothing serious."

"How can that be? You're a lesbian who wears a uniform."

"I'm a discerning lesbian in a uniform."

"That day you pulled me over and started flirting with me, I assumed you had a wife or girlfriend and were a typical player cop."

"I beg your pardon. I'm not a player. And if you recall, I was the victim of the typical cheating cop."

"Sorry," Belle said, holding up her hands in surrender. "Painting with broad strokes again."

"I should say so. And secondly, I was not flirting with you. I was doing my job in a friendly manner. That's all."

"That's actually disappointing. I've always had a secret cop fantasy."

Ally scowled. "Of course you have."

"I'm kidding. Honestly, I've never had one of those. I have a nurse fantasy."

"What a relief. I thought you were unoriginal."

"I'm teasing, Deputy." Belle gave her a gentle kick in the side of her leg. "But if I did have a cop fantasy, you'd be the perfect specimen to…never mind. This second glass is going to my head."

"No, no, I'd like to hear this."

"No, it's nothing. I mean nothing you haven't heard before, I'm sure."

Ally's mocha eyes were like lasers boring through her. "Try me."

Usually as smooth as soft-serve when it came to the ladies, Belle suddenly felt tongue-tied. "Well, you're incredibly attractive. And you have this way about you, I don't know. I haven't been able to name it, but for some reason, I already feel comfortable around you. Maybe it's because you're in law enforcement. I came all the way up to this part of the state by myself, not knowing a single soul, but I feel like I found a friend in you. Corny, isn't it?"

"Not at all." Ally's smile affirmed her agreement.

Red jumped off the couch, stretched his limbs, and plopped down on the cool wood floor in the foyer.

"Obviously Red thinks you're corny," Ally said, and they both laughed.

"Dammit. I left the diary upstairs," Belle said after she sipped her wine. "I'll get it."

"Mind if I come with?" Ally said. "I'd like to see what you've done so far up there."

"Sure," Belle said after a slight hesitation. The line between innocent flirtation and full-on seduction seemed to be vanishing. "I still have a lot to do, but it's coming along."

As they arrived at the top of the stairs, Belle felt the heat of Ally's presence against her back. They walked into the master bedroom, and Belle went to the scroll of papers sitting on the dresser.

"This looks great," Ally said. "I love the gray."

"Thanks. It's called Storm Cloud. I'm going to get some lavender and yellow accents when I'm ready for staging. Luckily, the flooring up here is in better condition than I thought."

"It's going to look amazing." Ally glanced around the room as though imagining her own decor innovations.

Belle glanced at Ally's tan, shapely calves and slender torso. She loved tall girls, especially tall, intelligent girls with a warm personality. Now she had a single one standing in her bedroom, and all the old instincts were stampeding back. They could crawl into her bed only inches away and cap off the night sharing that sweet sensuality that only women, skin on skin, could share.

But would Ally go for it? She had a past and seemed like she'd been through it all during her days in the Hartford scene, but how far in her past was it?

Belle took the papers from the dresser and walked toward Ally, who still seemed lost in her imagination. "Here you go," she said softly.

Ally turned to her, and their eyes locked. She reached for the papers, but Belle held on. It was a standoff. When Ally smiled, Belle released them to her and moved in for the kill.

Standing on her tiptoes, she kissed Ally tenderly, savoring the silky texture of her lips sweetened with wine. To Belle's surprise,

Ally hadn't backed away. She threw her free hand around Belle's waist and pulled her closer.

As their delicate kisses grew harder, more passionate, Belle wrapped both arms around Ally's neck.

They undulated together in the rush of intensity between them. Belle had already made peace with swerving off the moral highroad and was about to steer Ally toward her bed, when Ally suddenly, gently pushed her away.

"We shouldn't do this, Belle. I'm sorry."

"Why not?" she said, all steamy like car windows at a drive-in.

"I don't want to move so fast," Ally said.

"You're right, you're right. Sorry about that." She tried to save face by touching up her messy bun in the mirror above her dresser.

"Well, you don't have to be sorry. I mean, it was nice."

"It was," she said to Ally's reflection in the mirror. She turned and braced herself against the dresser. "Too nice."

"Right. I think we're both wise enough to realize how complicated we'll make things if we go any further."

"Yeah, yeah. Right now isn't the right time," she said, not because she believed it, but because it seemed like the appropriate thing to say.

Ally arched an eyebrow. "Especially for you."

"What do you mean 'especially for me'?"

"You're barely out of your last relationship, and you won't even be here in another month or two." Ally began pacing. "And my life, well, it's structured and stable, the way one's life should be when one is raising a kid."

"And someone like me would make you unstable?" Belle tried not to show how much the suggestion offended her.

"Not you. The situation."

"Well, gee, I guess my plan to destroy your life has been foiled." Belle rushed past Ally, her bare feet slapping the hardwood steps as she clopped down the stairs.

"Belle." Ally chased her down to the foyer. "That's not what I meant. C'mon. You know that."

She sighed. "I know. I'm sorry for overreacting. I just thought we had something between us, and I acted without thinking."

"Hey." Ally nudged her and smiled. "If things were different, who knows what would've happened up there. It's not just you feeling some type of way."

"Thanks, but you don't have to patronize me." She opened the door for Ally.

"I'm not, Belle. I just…I hope you're not mad at me." Ally stood in the doorway.

She offered a sincere smile. "How could I be mad at you for speaking the truth? It's cool. Don't worry. Happy rereading," she added, indicating the journal pages.

Ally saluted with the scroll to her forehead as she stepped out onto the porch. She stopped before heading down the steps. "For the record, I wasn't trying to sugarcoat anything."

Belle offered a stoic smile to ease the tension.

She closed the door after Ally made it to her truck, then went upstairs. Her light, airy mood was mashed down by a mixture of disappointment at Ally's rejection and her own impetuosity that never failed to dig her into a spacious hole in which she could bury herself.

When would she ever learn?

CHAPTER SIX

With the stone patio finished, Belle enjoyed her first alfresco breakfast at the new umbrella/table set she'd recently purchased. She'd broken her own house-flipping cardinal rule of not spending big money to add personal accents or items for staging. But then she argued that if a house had a new stone patio and fire pit, wasn't some elegant outdoor furniture needed to complete the picture?

She tore off a piece of her croissant for Red, who was waiting patiently for her to drop something on its way to her mouth, as was often the occurrence. As they both chewed, she glanced out across the yard to the lush woods framing the property. Almost two acres. Decent chunk of real estate. Plenty of space to host summer shindigs. Even if the future owners were inclined to install an in-ground pool, they'd still have plenty of room for cornhole or badminton tournaments. And when the koi pond was installed off to the side of the yard? With all those amenities, this place would be the ideal summer destination.

Someone might even want to open it up as a cozy little LGBT-pet-friendly bed and breakfast, dripping in rustic Connecticut charm.

"What do you think, Red?" she said, patting him on the head. "Would you like to be an assistant innkeeper?"

He started panting as she massaged him behind his ears.

To Belle's delight, Ally came around the corner of the house, her face shaded with a Danville Sheriff's Department baseball cap. She had to stop looking so good at any given time of the day. It wasn't fair.

"'Morning," she said as she approached. "Hope it's not a bad time."

"Nope. Red and I were having a little breakfast before I tackle the first-floor spackling. Would you like some coffee?"

"No, thanks. I just came from Ethel's." Ally stood across from her as she glanced around. "This patio is gorgeous. I love the flagstone."

"Angelo does great work. Thanks for the recommendation," Belle said, cooler than wet grass at sunrise. "He's going to make a fire pit over there at the edge and a koi pond under that oak tree."

"Wow. That's going to look fantastic." Ally took a sip of her bottled water as she glanced around.

"Thanks. I have to say, this place is growing on me."

"That could be dangerous when it comes time to sell."

Belle shrugged as she sipped her coffee. "My heart is still set on that beach house."

It was a proud moment for Belle, acting so cool in the presence of the woman who set her briquettes aflame.

"Would you care to sit down?" Belle asked.

"Oh, thanks," Ally said absently, dragging a chair out and sitting. "So I looked up Judy's death certificate. The cause of death is listed as phenobarbital poisoning."

"What kind of drug is that?"

"Sleeping pills. They're in the tranquilizer family. 'Mother's little helper' they used to call them."

"The 'downers' Craig had mentioned. You think Judy got into her mother's sleeping pills to commit suicide?"

"The manner wasn't ruled a suicide. They put 'undetermined.' That type of medication is easy to misuse. If she was just looking for a high and washed them down with booze, it could've killed her accidentally."

"Then we'll never know for sure," Belle said.

"Not unless you can locate another friend who can provide more insight into her mental state back then."

"I'll see if Craig will give me his sister's name so I can track her down."

"I also finally had a chance to talk to Bob about everything. He said he remembers Craig because he and the Wheeler family were so much trouble during his first few years as a deputy."

"Does he remember anything about Judy?"

"He said sort of, because his mother taught catechism, but then he said she taught practically every kid in town for forty years, so his recollection's foggy when it comes to specific ones."

"Did you ask him about sex-assault cases on minors?"

"I did, but again, he said nothing stood out in his memory, which isn't surprising. The guy's in his mid-seventies."

"Well, I refuse to believe there weren't any."

"I'm sure it happened as often as it does now," Ally said. "But keep in mind that back in the day, kids feared authority figures and adults in general more than they do now. If another adult disciplined a kid for bad behavior, he'd go home and get it again from his own parents. Really, it could've been anyone—a teacher, a priest, an uncle. All we know for sure is that the perp was male."

Belle sighed and slumped in her patio chair.

Ally picked at the label on her water. "I'll keep going through the paper files for complaints and arrests when I have time, but you should prepare yourself for the real possibility that we won't ever find out who assaulted Judy or if her death was a suicide."

"I know," Belle said. "It was so long ago. Even if you find out something new, it's not like it'll benefit Judy in any way."

"If she were looking down now, I'm sure she'd appreciate your efforts to get justice for her. I mean, even if we found the guy, do you know how unlikely it would be that we'd get a conviction?"

"Don't even tell me that."

"It's the truth. You can't cross-examine a few pages from a journal. The guy's defense attorney would claim she was emotionally unstable from her father's tragic death and made the whole thing up. And a jury would probably believe it, especially if you parade a feeble old grandfather in front of them."

Belle rolled her eyes with disdain. "Anyway, I'll see if I can contact Craig's sister, and if that doesn't work out, I'll have to drop it."

Ally got up and stretched. "That's a good idea. Bob would give you the same advice."

"It's not like I don't have anything better to do around here." Belle stood up. "Thanks for trying."

"No problem."

They suddenly slipped into an awkward silence. Belle wanted desperately to say something, but over the last several days, she'd realized her attraction to Ally was much more than physical and at that point, the friend route was without question the sensible path to follow.

"Okay then." Ally started to walk away but stopped and gestured between them. "We're okay, right?"

"Pfffft. Oh yeah. We're great."

"Okay, good," Ally said. "Let me know how you make out with the sister."

"You got it."

As Ally walked away, Belle dismissed the tug at her heart that grew more extreme each time Ally left her.

Before she had time to become too maudlin over Ally, Angelo, the mason, drove his mini Bearcat tractor up the lawn toward the towering oak tree, the location Belle had chosen for the koi pond.

"'Morning," he shouted over the puttering engine. "Figured I'd dig out the hole for the pond first, then finish up the rest of the stonework. That okay?"

"Sure, whatever. I'll be inside working, so give a holler if you need anything."

He waved, threw his tractor in gear, and it chugged up the slight incline to the oak tree.

Belle walked inside and began patching two holes in the hallway. As she sanded the jagged plaster edges, she wondered about their origin. One looked as though it could've been from a punch. She made a fist and fit it into the hole. She couldn't imagine a young girl having enough aggression or physical strength to hit a hole in the wall like that. Judy and Aunt Marion were the only ones who'd lived there…unless the holes were made before Uncle Wes was killed.

Or had someone else been there?

A chill ran through her. The house was starting to feel like it had a soul. It was creeping into her head, telling her stories of violence and secrecy, whether she wanted to hear them or not. As awkward as she felt about it, she had to call Craig and get his sister's name for one last stab at a resolution.

After completing the patch jobs, she washed her hands and the spackle knives in the kitchen sink.

"Miss Ashford," Angelo called from the yard.

She walked out onto the patio wiping her hands on paper towel. "What's up, Angelo?"

Red was standing with him, peering down into a large hole.

"The backhoe hit something. Can you come over here?"

She trotted across the yard and looked down at the partially unearthed object. "What is it?"

"It looks like one of those old milk-delivery bins. I think that's rope around it, or what's left of rope. Should I dig it out?"

"I don't know." If she'd thought she felt creeped out before… "It's probably a dead pet or something. Is it gonna release some kind of poltergeist thing if we do?"

He glanced at her like she was nuts. "An old pile of cat bones? I bet those bins are worth something. I'll see if I can get it out in one piece. You can take it to the consignment shop."

Belle grimaced. "After I take it to the fumigator's."

He grabbed his shovel and dug around the bin until he was able to free it. He placed it on the grass and looked at her. "Well? Go ahead. Open it."

"No way. You open it. You're a man."

"What does that have to do with anything?"

"Men are used to gross things. Besides, it's not often I'm on the beneficial side of a sexist stereotype."

"Fine. I'm not scared. It's not like whatever's in there is still alive." But he stood there in the half circle he formed with her and the dog staring at the box, scratching his balding, sunburnt head.

"What are you waiting for?" she asked

"If this is a buried treasure, I want half."

"All right," she shouted, queasy with anticipation.

He used the shovel to flick off the layers of ropes, which gave way with little effort. Then he attempted to lift the lid with his foot, but it wouldn't budge.

"Looks like it's rusted shut. I'm gonna need a screwdriver to open it, but I may ruin it if I do. Should I leave it?"

She willed herself to be patient with him. "No. You shouldn't. Get your screwdriver."

When Angelo went to his truck, Belle bent to look at the bin and shook it with her foot to see if the contents rattled. Nothing but the slight hiss of a small mass moving from one side to the other. It probably was the dust of the entombed remains of a family pet.

"Ick."

Perhaps she'd offer it to Angelo, and he would take it to the consignment shop.

"Okay, here we go," he said as he returned brandishing a large screwdriver. "Watch out, Red." He gently pushed the dog aside as he worked at the lid.

As he was about to pry it open, Belle slipped behind the Bearcat for cover. When he inserted the screwdriver fully under the rim and pressed down, the lid sprang up with a shower of rust flakes.

"It's a garbage bag." He poked it gently with the point of the screwdriver. "Something's in it though."

Belle placed her hand over her heart. "What's left of dear Fluffy or Fido, no doubt," she said solemnly. "Okay, this is ghoulish." She turned to him with a sweet, obsequious smile. "Can you please rebury it in the woods back there? You can keep the container if you think it's worth anything."

"It's in decent condition…considering. I bet I can bang this dent out. All right." He grabbed his shovel. "I'll chuck the bag in a hole and bury it."

"Thank you. There's a bottle of your favorite alcohol in it for this."

She walked back to the house to call Ralph Jr. to see when he was going to finish the wall demolition between the kitchen and dining room. As she waited for him to answer his cell, she glanced out the window into the backyard.

"What the fuck?" Angelo bellowed so loudly, birds scattered from the trees in all directions.

She ran out to see what the commotion was and met Angelo coming out of the woods, his perpetually bronzed face whiter than Sheetrock.

"What's the matter?"

He pointed his thumb over his shoulder. "That's no fucking cat in that bag."

"What do you mean?" she said, trying to remain calm.

He led her into the woods and pointed to the overturned container. The contents in the partially decomposed trash bag had broken through and spilled into the shallow hole Angelo had dug.

She gasped at the tattered newborn blanket and tiny skull beside it.

"Oh my God," she whispered, trying to subdue her gag reflex. "That looks like a baby's head."

His face contorted as he rolled the head with the tip of his work boot.

"Don't do that. Don't touch anything." She turned away from the scene and called Ally's cell.

"You calling the cops?"

She nodded as they hurried out of the woods into the sunlit yard.

"What do you want me to do about the…"

All she heard was the ringing of Ally's phone as she ran toward the house.

Belle sat at the patio table with her knees up to her chin and a glass of red wine to her lips. She was beginning to think her hands would never stop shaking.

Yes, she was breaking her summer rule of no alcohol during the day, but discovering the bones of a dead infant in her own yard was a legitimate-enough excuse.

What was taking Ally so long in there? Whatever the reason, Belle was quite content to wait right where she was.

Finally, Ally emerged from the woods and headed toward her. "How are you doing?"

"I'm day-drinking a bottle of wine all by myself. Does that answer your question?"

Ally gave her shoulders a quick, comforting massage.

"How much longer is that scary guy with the camera gonna be skulking around my yard? He's freaking me out."

"Horace?" Ally said fondly. "He's our evidence guy. He's brilliant. He may look like he just crawled out of an open grave, but he's a real sweetheart and awesome at his job."

"He certainly looks like he enjoys it."

Ally puckered her lips trying not to smile. "He's almost done processing the scene. We're waiting on the ME's office to get here."

"What happens then?"

"She also has to process the scene, take photos, and give Horace the blanket, trash bag, and the container for testing. Then she'll take the bones to the ME's office in Farmington."

"What'll they do with them?"

"First, verify they're human, a technicality because they obviously are. Then hopefully, she'll be able to determine a cause of death. Meanwhile, forensics will try to collect DNA so we can see about IDing the remains."

"It had to belong to either Aunt Marion or Judy, don't you think?"

"No other family ever lived here?" Ally said.

"It's always been in the Ashford family. My great-grandfather built the house in the early 1920s. He had the lot next door, too, for farming. But I can check with my dad. He might know something I don't."

Ally nodded as she wrote notes on a pad.

"I bet it was Judy's, and it was stillborn," Belle said, recovering from her near catatonic state. "That's why she committed suicide, from the grief. It's all coming together now."

"Take it easy, Quincy. One step at a time. We have to see if we can gather viable genetic material first, although it's more than likely it belonged to one of them."

"Yeah, Judy."

"You can't assume that. Marion could've had a stillborn baby at home, and in her despondence, she could've buried it in the yard so she could stay close to it."

"Eww, really?"

"Maybe. Or…" Ally seemed to drift off in speculation. "The pregnancy could've been the result of an affair Marion had. Or it could've belonged to some neighbor girl who wasn't married and didn't want anyone to know she was pregnant. It could've belonged to anyone who crept back there in the cover of night and buried it."

"Are you suggesting the baby could've been murdered?"

"Belle, right now this is a murder scene," Ally said. "The assumption is it was murdered and stuffed into that container, at least until the ME can determine otherwise."

"I can't believe someone in my family would do that."

"It was known to happen back then. Hell, it still happens today. Why do you think we have safe-haven laws—so girls don't have to dump babies in trash cans at high school dances."

"Ugh. I don't know how much more of this topic I can take," she said as she refilled her glass.

Ally frowned. "It's definitely the worst part of a job in law enforcement."

Sheriff Morgan came around the corner, hiking up his pants as he slowly made his way toward them.

"Bob, you didn't have to come out," Ally said. "When I called, Shirley said you still weren't feeling well."

"Ahh, I feel as good as I'm ever gonna feel." He turned his gaunt face to Belle and removed his hat. "I'm sorry about all this, Miss Ashford. You let me know if there's anything we can do for you."

"Thank you, Sheriff Morgan," she said as she guzzled from her wineglass. "All I'd like is to find out who it belonged to and how it got there."

"Well, that's what we're gonna want to find out, too," he said. "But I won't say it's gonna be easy. We don't have DNA going back that far."

"She knows we'll have the best investigators on the case," Ally said. "If we can get a profile, we can run it through the system and see if we get any hits."

"Ahh, 'at's a long shot," he said, "but if the ME wants to expend the resources, you may get lucky." He coughed hard as he glanced out into the yard at Horace gathering soil samples at the burial site. "You can handle this?"

Ally nodded. "Go get some rest, Boss," she said warmly.

"Well, okay then. I'll check in with you later." He turned to leave. "You phone the house if you need me. I'll make sure Shirley wakes me the minute you call."

"Will do," Ally said with a pat to his arm.

He tipped his hat to Belle and ambled back toward the front of the house.

"Jeez, he looks like he's about to drive a Buick through the front of a Dunkin' Donuts," Belle said. "He's not ready to retire?"

Ally chortled, albeit reluctantly. "He's very ready, and he practically has. His wife said he's determined to finish out the year."

"He doesn't sound very optimistic about solving this."

"He's old-school. But he was right when he said it's not gonna be easy."

"Should I give a sample or something? If it's Judy's, would our DNA be similar?"

"Only if Judy's mother was your father's sister. Mitochondrial DNA is found in the mother's bloodline."

"I'm not even gonna ask what all that means." She sighed, her eyelids growing heavy as she dumped down another glass of wine.

"Why don't you get back to your work inside?" Ally said, sounding genuinely concerned. "It's gonna get worse when Horace comes out of the woods with the bones in an evidence bag."

Belle gulped in disgust. "With all due respect, Deputy, do you honestly think I can just slip on my Home Depot apron and get back to wall-spackling after this?"

"I'm sorry. I know you're still shaken up, so I don't think you should be here to watch him saunter out carrying a body bag." Ally paused as Belle drained the last of the bottle's contents into her glass. "Or drink yourself to death."

Belle looked at the empty wine bottle. "You make a solid point." She stood on unsteady legs.

"Let me help you inside." Ally looped her arm under Belle's. "Maybe a catnap wouldn't be such a bad idea."

"I'm not an alcoholic, you know," she said as she stumbled into Ally.

"I know you're not." Ally threw her arm around her for more support as she led her inside. "It's been a morning and a half."

"Right?" Belle shouted as she pitched more of her weight into Ally.

"Let's go into the living room so you can lie down."

"Splendid. Oh, but I need to make some business calls first." She slurred her words as Ally poured her onto the sofa.

"Why don't you hold off on the calls until you've had a chance to rest?"

"There's no time," she said, springing up from her prone position. "I have to call Ralph Jr. I have to make appointments for window estimates. I have to call Angelo and find out when he's gonna finish the koi pond."

"You want to put a koi pond in an exhumed makeshift grave? Yuck!"

"Well, sure. It sounds bad when you say it like that." Her eyes closed as she fell back onto a decorative throw pillow.

"G'night, Sleeping Beauty," Ally said.

Belle thought she felt warm lips on her forehead before the muffled sound of Ally's shoes trailed off across the hardwood floor.

Later in the afternoon, Belle woke with a dull throbbing in her head. She went into the kitchen, grabbed a bottle of cold water and a nectarine, and nibbled at the skin of the fruit as she gathered her wits.

She was almost starting to feel normal until she heard the backup warning beeps from the medical examiner's truck as it rolled backward down the slope of her yard toward the front. The yellow crime-scene tape around the would-be koi pond and at the perimeter of the woods turned the skin on the back of her arms bumpy.

"This is gonna do wonders for the resale value," she muttered.

She again thought about the list of calls she still needed to make concerning the house, but first she had to phone her father. After relaying to him the grisly details of her latest discovery, she went silent for a moment, trying to stave off a deluge of tears threatening to break free.

"Isabelle," he said, sounding worried. "Are you still there?"

"Yeah." She wiped her cheeks and nose on her bare arm.

"I'm sorry, honey. If I'd had any idea about any of these things, I would've suggested we throw the house on the market as-is the minute I got the notice."

"There's no way you could've known, Dad. That side of your family was exceptionally adept at keeping secrets."

"Why don't you come home? Walk away from it, and put it up for sale right now."

"I can't do that. I'd feel like I'm walking away from Judy and that baby."

"That's not true at all. You can't do a thing to help either of them. And it's certainly not worth your sanity."

"I'm okay, Dad. Really. I've become acquainted with a policewoman, and she's been so helpful. I didn't mean to worry you."

"Belle, none of this is your responsibility. You can leave anytime you want, especially if you don't feel safe."

Belle laughed mirthlessly. "What do I have to be afraid of except a few ghosts from the past?"

Her father sighed into the phone. "I wish I could be more help, but I don't know enough about that side of the family."

"It's okay, Dad. You've helped a lot." She wanted to reassure him it was settled, but she was already planning another visit to Craig Wheeler's auto shop.

Belle ended the call with her father feeling a little better. She had been thinking that getting justice for Judy was her responsibility. Add to that the possibility that an infant that might or might not have been murdered might or might not have been family?

It was overwhelming.

She decided to put all the family drama aside until tomorrow and direct her energy toward more work around the house.

Still in her hand, Belle's phone chimed and vibrated with a text from Ally. She smiled at the assortment of emojis Ally used, which included a skull and the bulging-eye face, after asking how she was doing.

I'm king of the world, Belle typed back, along with, *Thanks for asking and for putting me to bed on the sofa. You're sweet.* She punctuated it with a heart emoji.

Happy to oblige, ma'am ☺, Ally replied.

It's comforting to know my property-tax dollars are going to good use.

We take our role as public servants seriously up here.

I'm almost tempted to stay here and be the next Ashford generation to die in this house.

LMAO!!! You're bad. I have to admit I love your sense of humor.

Belle reveled in scoring a point or two with her dark humor. *I'm bad. Don't encourage me. My mom would kill me if she heard me talking like that.*

In my line of work, occasional gallows humor doesn't go unnoticed...or unappreciated.

Ha-ha. Let me know as soon as you hear anything, ok?

You got it. Then a second text came through. *Let me know if you need anything. Or if you just want to talk.*

Did she mean as a friend? A law-enforcement officer? Or something more? Without the use of emojis, how was she supposed to know?

She placed her phone screen down and walked away.

She had to stop reading into things.

CHAPTER SEVEN

After scarfing down a combo order of delivered Szechuan chicken, Belle sat in a warm coconut-oil bath, listening to the rain as she googled various names and phrases relating to Danville, Connecticut.

Nothing new came up that she hadn't already learned her first week there. When she'd previously referred to it as Snoresville, that was no misnomer.

Sheriff Bob had kept a vigil over the town for forty years, the fifteen before that as deputy, and was as decorated as a law-enforcement officer could hope to be. For most of his tenure, Ethel had been running her Quiet Corner café, which by now had become legendary, an official must-see Northeastern Connecticut tourist stop, according to travel brochures. Aside from the storied strawberry festival and the *Connecticut Magazine* award years earlier, Danville was about as eventful as a minister's wife's funeral.

Except for the mysterious dead baby in a backyard tomb and a sex offender that had once prowled their happy little hamlet.

After the bath, she settled in bed to catch up on some articles of interest in her academic journals. Red was asleep, stretched out along the length of her legs as they both relished the cool of the A/C.

Her phone vibrated, and she grinned when she saw the text bar from Ally. She must be checking up on her again. She was certainly thoughtful…unless she considered that part of her job.

I'm fine, Belle typed back. *Surely you must have something more exciting to do tonight than keep tabs on me.*

Not really, Ally replied with a smiley face.

Ha-ha. I'm sorry to hear that. But thank you for the text.

Even if I did have something exciting to do tonight, I still would've texted.

Belle gasped. No cute emoji, no "lol." She was being sincere. And if Belle knew her verbal foreplay, so coming on to her. She scrunched her face as she thought of how to respond. Should she play hard-to-get? Coyly clueless? Or full-on flirt?

I feel so special, she typed, and punctuated it with a kiss emoji—not the plain one, the one with the heart. Yup, full-on flirt. As if there was any doubt.

You are special. Ally added the same kiss emoji.

Belle's actual heart was pounding now. *I am???*

Totally! You've brought more excitement to my job in the last few weeks than I've seen in all my twelve years here.

"Your job? Seriously?" Belle said out loud. She had a good mind to leave her hanging in unanswered-text purgatory for that one, but she wasn't about to let her off the hook so easily.

That's all that's special about me?

Belle smiled expectantly at the blank screen. Nothing. Maybe she'd pushed it too far by sending off a loaded question. She was about to save face with a "just kidding," when Ally's text popped up.

Definitely not, but I can't say what else in a text. You could use it against me if I ever run for public office. Wink emoji.

That brought the smile back to Belle's face. "Oooh, you're good, Deputy," she said out loud again. Red lifted his sleepy head up as if she were talking to him.

Why? Is it dirty??? Top that, smart-ass.

Lmao!! Ally wrote. *First you have to tell me if that kiss emoji you used before was an offer??*

What??? And Belle thought she was pushing it?

You used it too, she replied.

But I asked you first.

Ally was unbearable at this. But Belle was loving it. She got up and began pacing to work off the escalating nervous energy.

Ok, since you keep insisting…yes, if you were here, it would be an offer. She hit the kiss emoji like five times.

So it's a limited-time-offer thing? Ally wrote.

'Fraid so. Matter of fact, it expires in three minutes.

Belle smiled and bit at her cuticles as she awaited Ally's reply. She wandered out into the hall and paced the landing, keeping her eyes fixed to the message for the three wavering dots, but they weren't popping up. Ally must've been responding to a call—somebody's chickens went missing or something.

Her battery almost drained, Belle went down into the kitchen and plugged the phone into a charger she kept in the wall above the counter. She caught herself grinning as she poured a glass of water and squeezed in a lemon wedge.

Why did Ally have to be so much fun and sweet on top of being so damn physically attractive? It was as though the universe was intentionally trying to complicate matters for her. First those haunting scrolls of writings, then the bones, and now a woman who seemed to possess every quality Belle had always desired in one but wasn't nearly delusional enough to believe she'd ever find. All she'd set out for was an easy-breezy, carefree summer fixing up an old house, making a healthy profit, and then being all "Peace out, back-woods bitches!"

Was that so much to ask?

Clearly.

Red began barking, preceding a knock at the front door.

"Oh, crap," Belle said, hoping it wasn't Mary. She'd ignored several texts from her over the last few days and wouldn't have been surprised if she'd elected to take a more proactive approach.

She fastened the chain lock on the door and opened it a crack in the event it was Mary or a machete-wielding psychopath. Six of one…

"Did I make it in time?" Ally stood on the porch grinning as she pretended to consult her wristwatch, her tan shoulders glistening with raindrops.

Belle whipped the chain off the lock and flung open the door. "What took you so long?"

Ally cupped Belle's face in her hands and pulled her in for a long, slow, sensual kiss that scorched her to the bone.

She threw her arms around Ally's neck as her knees came close to buckling under her, but Ally was already leading her toward the couch.

They collapsed together into a heap of arms and legs and dewy kisses.

For a moment Belle secretly debated whether to make this mistake, but as Ally's tongue made its way into her mouth, she stopped caring and surrendered to the pleasure about to apprehend her.

She allowed her hands to roam over Ally's back, down the curves of her narrow sides, stopping to squeeze her firm ass.

Ally groaned. "I may not be able to keep it casual after this."

"That's what I'm hoping," Belle replied in a breathy whisper.

They ground into each other as their skin grew damp with sweat. Belle could hardly contain her desire as she stroked Ally's smooth, muscular arms.

"Let's go upstairs," Belle said. "I need more room to properly devour you."

"If you have second thoughts on the way up, I'll understand." Ally tugged her to her feet, never letting their lips disengage.

"Way past that happening." Belle grabbed Ally's hand and towed her up the staircase.

Once in the room, Belle stopped at the dresser to light a scented candle as Ally caressed her arms from behind and gently kissed the back of her neck. When she turned around, Ally staring back at her in the candlelight was surreal—her bronze skin, strong jawline, heavy eyes full of desire made Belle tremble, left her hungering for Ally's body against hers.

She unbuttoned Ally's jeans as she guided her to the bed. Ally had her out of her comfy loungewear before they'd made it into the missionary position.

The way Ally took her time kissing her chin and throat, exploring her body with her lips left Belle writhing with anticipation. How exquisite to have Ally's strong hands around her breasts, her tongue tantalizing her in a style in which no one else had ever seemed proficient.

As her lips brushed across Belle's lower stomach, Belle gripped the slats in the headboard in an attempt to control herself under Ally's charge.

"Ally, I can't take much more of this torture," she said, breathless.

An evil giggle emanated from Ally's throat as she slid up to Belle's lips to give her one last sensual kiss before endeavoring to find her other treasures.

As they gazed into each other's eyes for a tender, timeless moment, Belle nearly blurted out she was in love with her. In that moment, she was reasonably sure that if she had, Ally would've returned the sentiment.

After bringing each other to ecstasy numerous times, Belle lay sideways against Ally, a human body pillow to Ally's warm, lanky frame. She held onto her so tight, she wondered if Ally already knew what she'd wanted to say. Was Ally feeling it, too, and just as hesitant to speak it?

If she was, she'd kept it to herself as she lay there, her breathing growing slower, shallower, until Belle knew she was asleep.

As badly as she wanted to say the words and hear them whispered back, she decided to let sleeping deputies lie.

The next morning Belle woke early, thanks to a cantankerous squirrel tap-dancing on her air-conditioning window unit. Country living, she thought as she scanned the room for something to pelt the noisy critter with.

She sat up in bed, stretched, and tried to clear the fog of disorientation from her mind. Ally was gone, and she felt as if the last two days had been a bleary-eyed dream—or a Wes Craven movie come alive in her own back yard. If Wes Craven was still alive and tossed in a little lesbian-porn plot twist.

After putting on a cup of coffee, she shuffled across the hardwood floor to let Red in—Ally must've opened the door for him when she'd slipped out like a burglar. As she sipped the hot coffee, she began negotiating with herself as to how she should feel about this business of Ally bolting on her without so much as a good-bye scrawled in lipstick on her mirror.

On the one hand, she had every right to be disappointed—even furious with Ally for treating her like the winner at last call. They'd had an amazing night together. Belle felt a genuine connection with her, and from the dreamy look in her eyes, Ally did, too.

On the other hand, perhaps she'd done the polite thing in ducking out, sparing them a painful morning-after encounter where they would've contrived awkward small talk until they finished breakfast or until Ally had scavenged for her clothes scattered over the bedroom before attempting a graceful exit—at which no one in the history of one-night stands had ever succeeded.

Should she text her? Would a phone call be more appropriate? The fact that she was even contemplating doing either alarmed her. If last night had truly been a no-strings hookup, she wouldn't care. But it wasn't just a hookup, not to Belle anyway.

She wanted what Ally had said in a moment of passion to be true.

Making love with her left an indelible mark on her, a metaphoric one, in addition to the physical one Ally left near her hip bone. She'd been awake for hardly thirty minutes and was already missing her face, longing to hear her voice, craving her touch.

If she'd remembered what falling in love felt like, this was it.

In any event, she'd accomplished little on her to-do list yesterday and was antsy about getting back into her work on the house. Except now she'd also be languishing in excruciating curiosity about what would happen next between them, whether or not they'd find DNA on the bones, and whether a nasty case of second thoughts had precipitated Ally's hasty exit.

Whatever. She had better things to do than worry about what Ally was thinking.

After a quick shower, she made the phone calls she'd neglected the day before, then decided she was hungry for breakfast, an Ethel's Quiet Corner Café breakfast, to be exact.

During the bicycle ride into town, she refused to admit she was hoping Ally would be there. When she sauntered in, she headed straight toward the counter. So focused was she on not appearing like she was looking for someone, it had to have been laughably noticeable to the casual observer that was her entire purpose for being there.

She sat at the counter glancing at the headlines on a used copy of *USA Today* as she choked down an egg-white, spinach, and goat-cheese omelet.

How does Ally eat these? She should've gone with the bacon-and-cheddar omelet—arteries be damned.

"More coffee, honey," Ethel asked while she refilled her cup.

"Thanks," Belle said, sipping it black. "Say, has Ally been in?"

"Not for breakfast, but she should be here any time. She called in a lunch order." Ethel smiled as she wiped down the counter around Belle. "You a friend of hers?"

"Yeah, I guess I am, even though I'm new here," Belle said. "I'm renovating the Ashford place."

"Oh, yeah. I heard about you. Welcome. Breakfast is on me then." She grabbed the check from the counter before Belle could react.

"Ethel, please, that's not necessary." She reached for the slip of paper. "Your charm is a warm-enough welcome."

"I won't hear another word about it." Ethel crumpled up the check and tossed it into the trash.

"That's awfully kind of you." Belle smiled as she lifted the cup of steaming coffee to her lips again.

"There's my favorite lady lawman."

Ethel's announcement startled Belle, causing her to singe her lips on the coffee.

"Hey, Ethel," Ally said and gave Belle a friendly pat on the shoulder. "Good morning, Belle—what's left of it."

"Is it?" She made a face and turned her head only slightly toward Ally.

"How's Bob feeling?" Ethel said, seeming oblivious to the tension between them.

Ally frowned. "You know Bob. He'll never admit he feels like crap."

Ethel grabbed the bag of takeout and handed it to Ally. "I threw in a cup of chicken soup for him. Make sure he eats it."

"I will." Ally smiled as she handed Ethel the money.

Belle fumed as Ally stood next to her. Was she really going to act like they were nothing more than casual acquaintances?

"You have a super day, Deputy," Belle said, looking straight ahead, her tone crisp enough to ice the hot coffee.

Ally glanced at Belle's empty paper placemat. "Walk out with me if you're done."

Walk out with her? Who did she think she was, ordering her around like that?

"Okay, fine." Belle sprang from her stool. "Thank you, Ethel. I'll be back to patronize your lovely establishment again soon."

"I hope so," Ethel said with a wave.

She trailed Ally outside, her omelet agitating in her stomach.

"I get the sense you're not happy about something," Ally said when they cleared the front of the café.

"Nothing gets past a crack investigator like you."

"Belle, I'm sorry I left without saying good-bye. Honestly, I didn't know how I should handle the situation, and by the time I'd figured it out, I would've been late for work. I was going to call you."

"Hey, I get it. You didn't want me thinking it meant anything more than what it was—a good lay."

"That's not true."

"So it wasn't a good lay?"

"No, Belle, it was great, amazing. Probably the best I've ever had. That's the problem."

That remark earned Ally more of Belle's snarky side-eye. "You and I have a very different definition of the word 'problem.'"

Ally wiped the sweat from under the brim of her cap. "Belle, you're not understanding me. I'm feeling more for you than I think I should, given our individual circumstances. Look, I'm picking Chloe up from camp this weekend. I'm not gonna be the spontaneous, passionate woman you seem drawn to. I've had a tough time with her over the last few months."

Belle sighed. "If I wasn't such an empathetic person, I'd be royally pissed at you for assuming I'm so shallow."

"I don't think you're shallow at all. I know you have a lot going on in your life, too. I can't imagine how a woman with a crabby twelve-year-old who's also helping out her dying friend and his wife would fit into your world right now."

"Sheriff Morgan is dying?"

Ally tilted her head for Belle to walk with her back to the station. "He'd kill me if he knew I told anyone, but his lung cancer has metastasized. The tumors aren't responding to the chemo. He told me he'd only agreed to this last round for Shirley's sake."

"I'm so sorry to hear that."

"He and Shirley are like grandparents to Chloe. They watched her a lot for me over the years. And Bob's been a friend and mentor to me since I came on."

Belle's heart sank. Now she felt childish for jumping to conclusions.

"I'm sorry," she said again, taking Ally's hand. "What's going on with Chloe?"

"She's been so moody recently and had some discipline issues at school this year, which is totally unlike her. I think puberty hormones are doing a job on her. She got her period about six months ago, and maybe she's resenting that her mother isn't around for this crucial stage."

"Well, I can only speak from what I've heard, but it sounds like you're the best mother she could ask for."

"We're super close, but she knows I'm not her real mother. Lately, she's been of the mindset that her mother chose drugs over her."

"Ugh. And how do you convince a twelve-year-old otherwise?"

"I've explained to her many times that drug addiction is an illness. Some moms die from a physical sickness, and others go away because of mental sickness. She gets the concept, but I don't know…I just hope I'm protecting her from growing up feeling like she was abandoned."

Belle's eyes grew cloudy as she processed the pain on Ally's face. What a ton of shit she was dealing with.

"Hey, I'm sorry," Ally said. "I didn't mean to dump all this on you. I haven't really talked to anyone about it before." Ally's plaintive smile tugged at Belle's heart. "Now you're probably happy I left without saying good-bye."

"Not at all," Belle said softly. "I'm just not furious with you anymore. And I'm glad you shared this with me."

"Really?" Ally flashed that signature smirk that drove Belle wild. "I would think you've already met your lesbian-drama quota for the year."

Belle shrugged. "You're not drama, Ally. This is what adult life looks like sometimes. As for Mary, she's a non-issue. My lawyer is handling the eviction."

Ally looked around, squinting at the sun's glare bouncing off everything in their surroundings. "Well, I'm not sure where we go from here, but if you ever want to get a drink or a bite to eat, I owe you a venting session after listening to me. However, if you'd prefer to keep it professional through the investigation, I'll understand that, too."

Belle studied her handsome face for a moment, contemplating the deliciously appealing paradox of "woman of steel" law enforcer and vulnerable surrogate mom grappling to do right by her equally vulnerable niece. She realized she no longer had a choice in whether to pursue whatever this complexly irresistible thing was with Ally.

"This time I choose door number one," Belle said, heavy on the flirtation. "I'd love to meet Chloe sometime, too, if you're not worried I'd be a bad influence on her with my sordid past."

"I'm worried you're a bad influence on me."

Belle laughed. "Yeah, right! With your seduction skills, I'm sure it's the other way around."

Ally leaned toward Belle's ear. "Seducing a woman like you doesn't require a skill set. It's raw, natural instinct."

"I'm seriously about to swoon," Belle said, waving a hand in front of her face.

"You're funny." Ally seemed relieved at the lightness into which their conversation had drifted. "Well, I better get in there with lunch before Bob issues a silver alert on me." She was about to walk away but stopped and held Belle's hand. "I'm glad I ran into you this morning."

"Yeah, some coincidence, huh?"

Belle winked and headed back to her bicycle parked outside Ethel's. She wheeled around and walked backward a few steps for a last glance before Ally went into the station.

When Belle arrived home, Ralph Jr.'s van was in the driveway, and the squeal of some type of electric saw peeled out from the kitchen.

"Ralph, you're amazing," she said. "You move faster than a centipede across my bathroom floor."

He smiled. "Happy customers are repeat customers."

She looked through the two-by-four wall frame remaining after Ralph's sledge hammer and electric handsaw had their turns at the Sheetrock. "I can already see how fantastic this will look."

He smiled again and kicked the Sheetrock and decades-old wallpaper scraps aside as he prepared to cut out the remaining wood.

After offering him a bottle of water that he politely declined, she leaned against the counter and sipped hers. "Ralph, did you ever do any work for my aunt, Marion?"

"Did it look like I ever did any work for her when you got here?"

"Fair enough. Did you know her at all?"

He shook his head. "Only as the old recluse people occasionally told stories about. You weren't close?"

"Not at all. In our family, she was the old recluse people occasionally told stories about."

Ralph chuckled. "Whelp, if anyone around here knew her, it'd be Ethel or the Morgans. They've lived here forever and seem to know everybody."

He was right about that. Another meal at Ethel's Quiet Corner Café would soon be in order. She would've loved to pump the Morgans for information, but now that she knew their predicament, she realized they had enough to worry about without some stranger poking around in the embers of their memories.

Given the light breeze and low humidity, it was a day to spend outside scouting locations where Ally should plant her flower garden and where Angelo should re-dig the koi pond in back. That is, if she could convince him he wouldn't disinter any more goblins.

The next morning, Belle was restless. After weeks of inhaling clouds of dust, and paint and cleaning-product fumes, she'd allowed herself a day off. Ralph Jr. was coming to complete the wall removal and install the new hardwood floor from the kitchen into the now-contiguous dining room.

Besides, she needed a change of scenery. Danville and her recently acquired house of horrors had left her stewing in some bad mojo. The bright spot was Ally, but even that had its complications. After their chat yesterday, she realized that even though they were on the same page, they needed to slow the pace.

She'd popped in on her parents for lunch to update them on the strange and fantastical things brewing up there in the quiet corner, eliciting much the reaction she'd anticipated.

"I wasn't comfortable with you alone so far away from the beginning," her mother said as she cleared the lunch dishes. "Now I don't like it at all. You should stay home while the contractors finish their work."

"She can't stay home and let them have the run of the house," her father said. "I'll go with her."

Her mother spun around at the sink. "Like hell you will. You're not going anywhere until your follow-up appointment next week."

Belle made the time-out sign with her hands. "Uh, guys, nobody needs to babysit me. I'm fine. Whatever crime or crimes occurred there happened ages ago. As Deputy Yates explained, it's been so long the person or people involved are probably all dead."

Her mother brought over a pitcher of fresh lemonade and sat down at the table. "I think it's just awful about that baby. I'm sick over it. I hope to God they can catch whoever's responsible."

"I wonder whose it was," her father said.

"That's what I want to know."

"Wouldn't Judy be the obvious choice," her mother asked.

"I highly doubt it belonged to my aunt Marion."

"I don't know why you say it like that," her mother said. "Your aunt was very attractive in her day. After she lost your uncle, maybe she was lonely and met a nice gentleman…"

"And took him home and banged him without protection?" Belle finished her mother's sentence with a giggle. "Mom, are you saying Daddy's uptight aunt got her groove back after her husband croaked?"

"Oh, Isabelle, stop it. Don't be flip about such a sad situation."

"What have the cops said about it?" her father asked.

"It's in the hands of the medical examiner's office now. They're analyzing everything to see if they can extract some DNA and determine a cause of death."

"In the meantime," her mother said, "don't go around getting strangers involved. You're so cut off from everyone up there in that dinky little town. Do they even have 911?"

Belle laughed. "Yes, I'm sure they do. Don't worry, Mom. I've gotten very friendly with the deputy sheriff. She's been a big help during all this."

"How friendly?" Her father grinned.

Belle felt her smile expand to her earlobes.

"Are you seeing someone new?" her mother asked.

"Yes and no," Belle said.

"Is Mary out of your condo?" her father asked.

"Yes and no."

Her parents both glared at her from across the table like attorneys cross-examining her.

"Are you doing your overlapping thing again?"

"Mom!" Belle feigned insult. "I beg your pardon. I'm not that woman anymore. Mary and I are done, kaput, finito. We have been for many months now."

"I'd like to see you settled down with someone like your friends are. I want you to have your gay happily-ever-after."

Her father remained silent, trying not to smile.

"Well, thanks for lunch," Belle said, rising from her chair. "Have to be on my way."

Her mother clutched her forearm. "Belle, we want to know what's going on in your life. You always rush out whenever the topic turns to your personal affairs."

"Sorry. Old habits." She sat down again. "I like Ally. I think she likes me, but we're both not sure it's the right time to pursue anything beyond that."

"Is Mary out of your condo or isn't she?" her father asked.

"She will be as soon as she's served with the eviction notice."

He shook his head. "I don't know where you find these women."

Her mother admonished him with a look. "She's forty years old. She knows what she's doing." Her head jerked toward Belle. "You know what you're doing, right?"

"Yes, Mom." She smiled at her parents' antics and rose from the chair. "This time I really have to get going. Thanks for lunch."

She kissed them both and headed toward the door.

"Let us know how you make out with everything," her mother said.

"And don't move anyone into the new house," her father added.

"Bye, parents," she said, waving without looking back.

She started up her SUV. As long as she was down by the shoreline, she might as well pay Craig Wheeler a visit at his garage.

❖

"Well, if it isn't Nancy Drew again," he said as he came out of his office and met her at the counter.

"Hi, Mr. Wheeler. I hope you don't mind me dropping by."

"No problem. And call me Craig."

"Okay." She paused before launching into her pitch. She'd rehearsed what she was going to say during the car ride down, but when she was standing right in front of him about to spring on him the news of baby remains that might or might not be the fruit of his adolescent loins, all that preparation kinda flew out the window.

She opted for a less incendiary approach.

"I, uh, was wondering if you think your sister would be willing to talk to me about Judy. You'd said they were good friends."

"They were. And I don't think she'd mind. The only glitch for you would be that she's three thousand miles away."

Belle groaned. "California?"

"She's lived in San Diego for the last thirty years. But I can give you her email address and let her know you'll be contacting her."

Email? She wanted to say the year 2000 called and wanted its mode of communication back, but at the moment it took more energy than she had. "That would be a big help," she said instead.

He took out his cell phone and thrust it at her. "I think I have an email app on my phone. You wanna check it? Look for Charlene Highland."

As Belle scanned through the few names in his contacts, she contemplated how furious Ally might be with her when she found out she'd spoken to Craig about the baby. But if she'd discussed it with her beforehand, Ally would've told her to stay out of it, leave it to the professionals, blah, blah, blah. She didn't want to be shut out. The women of the Ashford place were her family, even if she hadn't known them personally. Judy was her dad's first cousin, and her short life seemed so tragic.

So was that pile of little bones. She had a right to be involved.

"Is this it?" She showed him his phone, then snapped a picture of it with her own. "Great. Thank you."

"Say, you're going through a lot of trouble searching for answers you'll probably never find. At this point, after forty-some-odd years, does it really matter whether her overdose was accidental or not?"

"I think someone should know her story. I'm basically all the family she has left who cares. Something made her swallow a mouthful of pills." She lightened her approach a bit. "Besides, who doesn't love a good mystery, especially if it's in her own backyard?"

He seemed distant for a moment, as if unpacking darker memories of Judy he'd stored away decades ago. Belle inched closer in anticipation.

"Well, good luck," he said with a shrug and turned to walk away. His newfound indifference toward his alleged first love irked her.

"Uh, Mr. Wheeler, sorry, uh, Craig. I didn't come here just for your sister's contact info."

"No?" His thin lips pursed in obvious annoyance.

"Can we talk for a minute in private?"

"Sure." He sighed. "Come on." He led her into his cubbyhole of an office and offered her a seat on a dingy orange vinyl chair as he closed the door. "Okay, shoot."

"A contractor was excavating an area in my yard and made a rather gruesome discovery."

"What was it?"

"A container with a baby's skeleton in it."

"You're kidding?" Although surprised, he didn't appear to connect any dots.

"I wish I was. They've been there for many years. Do you think it could've been Judy's?"

The suggestion silenced him for a moment, his face a palette of various grays and greens.

"Any chance it was yours?" she said delicately.

He finally exhaled and ran a hand through his thinning hair. "Jeez, I suppose it's possible. I mean we had a scare once, but it turned out she wasn't—at least that's what she told me. If it was mine, she never said anything to me about it."

Not surprising. If Judy had planned to get rid of it, she wouldn't have. Then again it could've been Craig's, and he knew about it and had helped her dispose of it.

She gulped air. Was she sitting directly in front of the murderer tipping him off that he was about to be the subject of a police probe?

Ahh. So that was why Ally hadn't wanted her talking to Craig and giving him any sensitive information.

Oops.

She struggled to conceal her growing panic and claustrophobia at being locked in a murderer's tiny office after informing him the remains of his victim were finally recovered.

She stood up and reached for the doorknob. "Well, I better be on my way so I can email your sister."

"Wait a minute."

His tone chilled her as she bobbled and then dropped her phone on the floor. "People know I'm here," she blurted.

"Huh?"

"What? Nothing."

"What, uh, what are they gonna do with the baby's body?"

"I don't know," she said, still nervous. "I mean, if they can't identify who it belonged to, I'll make sure it, I mean he or she, gets a proper burial."

"Oh," he said somberly.

"You wanna submit a DNA sample to see if it was yours?" she added, feeling braver now that it seemed as though he didn't intend to make her his next victim right then and there.

"How do I do that?"

"Give me your cell number, and I'll have an investigator call you. You might have to come up to the Danville police department. Would that be okay?"

"Uh, yeah, I can probably do that." He didn't sound particularly on board.

She took his phone number and shook his hand.

As she was about to leave, he asked, "Hey, were you ever able to locate any of the boarders Mrs. Ashford had?"

Record scratch.

"Wait, what?" She whirled around, her hanging jaw taking an extra second to catch up.

"The boarders," he said. "I remember a young, big woman with big, round eyeglasses who rented a room for a while—a school-teacher or something. And a guy. He was an army reject 'cause he was missing two fingers. He smoked a lot of grass, but while he was there, it was the only time the outside of the house was kept up."

"Why didn't you tell me any of this when I was here before?"

"I didn't think of it. You only asked me about my relationship with Judy and her overdose. What did I know that it mattered that they had boarders?"

Belle scratched at her head in frustration. This thing was starting to spiral.

"You don't happen to remember their names, do you?"

"The guy's name was Phil. We called him Three-fingers Phil. That's how I remember. I got no clue about the woman's name. Maybe the baby was hers, not Judy's."

"Did the guy and woman rent there at the same time?"

Craig shook his head. "From what I remember she only had one renter at a time."

"Can you remember anyone else who was there?"

He shook his head again. "I got sent off to juvie when Phil was there. That tight-assed sheriff caught the two of us smoking pot in the Ashfords' yard. I got mouthy with him, and he arrested me. That was the last time I was in Danville. I did ninety days. Then on my eighteenth birthday I joined the marines and went to 'Nam. That straightened my ass out."

"Sheriff Morgan?"

"Yeah, that prick. Excuse my language. I had a lot of issues when I was a kid, got in a lot of trouble, you know. He'd finally had it with me, recommended to the judge that I go away."

She thought about old Bob and how her impressions of him didn't match the prick picture at all. But then when had teenagers ever appreciated a strict authority figure? "Seems like you ended up on the right path though."

"Yeah, I guess I did, but I never saw Judy after that. I used to think if he hadn't sent me away, things would've turned out different for her." His lip quivered ever so perceptibly, and he turned his head.

Belle touched his shoulder. "Craig, you were a kid yourself then. I'm sure you were there for her in every possible way."

"Thanks," he said, then lowered his voice. "Oh, and let me know about that sample. I would like to know if the child was mine."

"I will," she replied. "Thanks for your help."

Once in her car, Belle fired off a polite email to Craig's sister asking if she wouldn't mind talking to her about Judy and what she remembered about their childhood together. Hopefully, she would answer the email right away and include her telephone number.

As she headed up the interstate, confidence fueled her as now it seemed Craig's involvement would help the case rather than hurt it. Belle decided this latest development was significant enough that she should convey it to Ally in person. She was already visualizing them celebrating the new lead over cocktails.

Then maybe they'd continue celebrating in private.

But only if Ally suggested it.

By the time Belle arrived back in Danville, Ally's shift was ending. She drove directly to the station and stormed in, breathless with excitement.

"Boarders," she said, sucking wind. "My aunt had boarders at the house."

"What? How do you know?" Ally closed the file draw she was standing at and met her at her desk.

Belle propped a hand on her hip. "Well, *how* I know isn't as relevant as the news itself. This breaks the case wide open… doesn't it?"

Ally shot her a stern glare. "Please tell me you didn't talk to Craig Wheeler again."

"Okay. Then we'll skip that part. Marion had a guy and a woman living there at separate times. This boarder guy must've been the one who molested Judy. Isn't this great?"

Ally sighed, clearly trying to focus on the positives. "You didn't happen to get the names of either of the boarders, did you?"

"He didn't know the woman's name, but the guy was known as Three-fingers Phil."

Ally laughed dryly as she lifted her eyeglasses and massaged the skin on the bridge of her nose. "I guess we can rule out strangulation as a cause of death."

"May I continue?" Belle said. "Craig—I mean this person I talked to—didn't remember the guy's last name. Don't I get any points for scoring a nickname?"

"A nickname might help." Ally sat in front of her computer. "I can run that in our in-house system right now. But I'll need a first and last name to run in the nationwide law-enforcement databases. Still, it's a long shot he'd be in there now if he was a criminal way back then."

Ally punched at her keyboard as Belle stood behind her, her face practically brushing Ally's ear.

"If you find him, he could be the key to the whole thing," Belle said. "You could have the daddy and the molester in one shot."

"He could've been the father, but there's also the possibility, however slim, that it was your aunt's baby."

"Think so?"

Ally shrugged. "It's all open to conjecture at this point. He could've impregnated her during consensual sex, but she didn't keep it for whatever reason, or like I said before, it could've been a stillbirth. I'll call the ME's office. They should have an official cause of death by now."

"I don't think it was my aunt's. My money's on Three-fingers Phil being some young drifter who messed with Judy and knocked her up."

"Now that you've placed another woman in the house, it also could have been hers. She was pregnant, didn't want anyone to know, so she travels up to the sticks of Connecticut and has it at some out-of-the-way boarding house. We're going to need DNA here."

"That whole scenario is so creepy. Who would let total strangers sleep in their houses with them?"

"That's what they did back then. Hell, some people still don't lock their doors."

"It's all fun and games until the home invasion. Doesn't anyone watch *Forensic Files?*" Belle said with scorn.

"Nothing is coming up in LInX for that nickname. I'm gonna need a first and last name to run him in our records and CONNECT. I'll ask Ethel and the Morgans if they recall a boarder named Phil."

"I can ask Ethel if you want. She said she hopes I come back to the café soon."

"Belle, I'm trying to be as polite as I can about this, but you're gonna have to stand down. You're not an official investigator. If we ever do nail someone for this, his lawyer will no doubt find a way to use your involvement as a loophole and squeeze the old guy through it, thus ending all hope of justice for Judy. Is that what you want?"

Belle frowned. "No. But this is exhilarating, way more fun than trying to teach college freshmen in summer English comp the difference between *there*, *their*, and *they're*."

"Then I suggest you join the police academy like the rest of us had to." Ally picked up her desk phone and pressed the keys.

Belle plopped in the chair beside Ally's desk. "Are you always this cranky when you're working a case?"

Ally glared at her. "Hi. This is Deputy Yates from the Danville sheriff's department. I'm checking on the status of an autopsy." She read off the case numbers, then covered the mouthpiece with her hand and whispered, "I'm only cranky when people jeopardize said case by ignoring my very clear orders."

Belle chewed on a strand of hair from her ponytail and gave Ally a dirty smile. "That's hot, you giving me orders."

"Oh, is it? Then you might try following them this time." She put her hand up. "Yes, I'm here. Go ahead." She nodded and made notes on a pad as she listened.

Belle craned her neck to read what she was writing, but the script was cramped and illegible from where she sat.

"No sign of blunt-force trauma," Ally said before the phone was back in its cradle.

"What does that mean?"

"The ME didn't find any signs of breaks or fractures in the bones. If the baby was murdered, it wasn't violent."

"A non-violent murder? That's a thing?"

"If it was born alive and then killed, the evidence suggests it was probably smothered. But without a body, only undamaged bones, the ME will list the manner of death as undetermined. We'd never get a murder conviction."

Belle scoffed at what she was hearing. "So that poor thing's soul will never rest in peace."

Ally grabbed her keys and travel coffee mug off the desk and headed toward the door. "Don't give up hope yet." She stopped at the door and squeezed Belle's arm. "If we can locate an eye witness or the killer, and get a confession out of him, then it's still possible."

"Oh, that sounds easy enough."

Ally added a bonus caress to Belle's back. "Thanks to you, I have a few more leads to follow up."

Belle went heavy on the pouty eyes, loving how easy the ploy seemed to trigger Ally's tender side.

"Are you hungry?" Ally asked.

Belle shrugged.

"How about we head over to Sully's for some wings and beer? I'll let you beat me in a few games of pool," she added with a grin.

Belle felt her face ease into a smile. "Only if you promise to say good-bye this time."

"I think that's fair."

As they drove away in separate cars, Belle exhaled. What was it about Ally that left her breathless?

Whatever it was, she wanted more.

CHAPTER EIGHT

B elle marveled at Ally's efficiency in stripping the meat off the bones of her buffalo wings. She hadn't allowed even one drop of excess sauce beyond the perimeter of her lips, whereas Belle had surrounded herself with enough crumpled, orangey napkins to torch up a summer bonfire right there at the table.

"You take the last one," Ally said with a dainty lick of her thumb.

"No way. I had more than you."

"You did not." Ally shot her an imperious look. "If I can direct your attention to this pile of bones, you'll notice I have more on my side."

"No, you don't." Belle flicked them around with her finger. "You arranged them to look that way."

Ally grinned. "Are you accusing me of evidence tampering, Ms. Ashford?"

Belle laughed. "You're just defensive now that I've figured out how you can eat wings and beer and still maintain your slender, rockin' bod. You pawn the excess fattening stuff off on your dinner dates."

"Rockin' body, huh?" Ally narrowed her smoky, seductive eyes. "I guess you would know."

"I speak with authority on that subject. The memory of it can be quite forceful at times."

Ally downed the last of her beer. "So can the dream of it."

Belle stared at her for a moment, allowing the thought of Ally having dirty dreams about her soak in.

"Should we get the check and shoot some pool?" Ally asked.

"You're not having a second drink?" Belle was suddenly worried Ally was trying to cut the evening short. "C'mon. You can't fly on one wing."

"You know how many calories are in craft beer?"

"There are ways of working off an extra two hundred calories."

"I'm aware of that. And with every alcoholic beverage I drink, I come that much closer to suggesting one to you."

"I'm always open to suggestions." She took Ally's hand. "From you."

She squeezed Belle's fingers as her brow crinkled in concern. "I'm picking up Chloe Friday."

Belle smiled, still holding her hand. "Good. I'm looking forward to meeting her."

"Have you ever dated a woman with a kid before?"

"A couple, but their kids were in college."

Ally didn't seem convinced. Belle signaled their waitress over and gave her the two-finger point for another round of beer.

"For what it's worth, I like kids," she added. "I teach young adults for a living, and although I've never pursued having my own children, I also never ruled out having them in my life."

"Okay." Ally's smile gleamed with relief. "Thanks for clarifying."

The waitress brought their beers, and Ally took a slow sip of hers, savoring the flavor with an "ahhhhhh."

"Is everything okay?" Belle asked.

Ally paused as if what she'd say next would irrevocably change the course of their relationship. Belle froze in anticipation.

"I like you, Belle. A lot," she said finally, issuing forth a breath she'd seemed to be holding for centuries. "And I'm not quite sure what to do with all the emotion you're stirring in me."

"I like you, too, Ally. My heart hasn't had a minute's peace since we made love. And the fact that our lives are crowded with people and things demanding our attention hasn't deterred my feelings in the least."

Ally sat back in her chair and folded her arms. "I know. I keep trying to reason with myself that I shouldn't get involved with you right now, but like you said, it doesn't matter. I can't stop thinking about you."

"What do you think about?"

Ally looked down as a blush tinted her caramel cheeks crimson. "Um, lots of things—but mainly your inviting smile, your determination, your passion for justice for a troubled teen and an infant you didn't even know. Those are rare, remarkable qualities."

"That's so sweet." Belle's throat lumped at the sincerity in Ally's eyes. "When you think about it, you and I have something major in common."

"Great sex and a love of craft beer?" Ally said.

She giggled. "Besides that. We both have careers that involve looking out for the welfare of kids. I think that's a perfect place to start."

Ally raised her glass to Belle's.

"And the sex was great, wasn't it?" Belle said.

Ally whistled her agreement. "But you know, that could've been beginner's luck. I don't think you can define the state of anything after one experience."

"How about we take a rain check on pool and go back to my place…you know, to verify?"

"Fantastic idea," Ally said.

After they made love, they lay in Belle's bed draped in moonlight shining through the naked window. Ally cuddled close, her head resting on Belle's shoulder. They said nothing for a while, stroking each other's arms with the tips of their fingers, Belle drinking in the scent and texture of Ally's soft skin.

Holding her in peaceful silence erased any doubt Belle might have had as to the authenticity of her feelings. Once again, the words *I love you* wrestled to be free, but she reminded herself that even though they'd met more than six weeks ago, it had been an even shorter time since they'd crossed the threshold and become more than friends.

"I love how the trees are making crazy shapes in the moon-light," Ally whispered.

"When it comes to this house, a full moon and craziness are part of the ambience. I should have the realtor showcase that feature."

Ally pointed to her nose in agreement. "It's funny how many times I came here on wellness checks for Marion and never noticed anything out of the ordinary."

"Not that I'm doubting your intuition as an officer, but I find that so hard to believe, given what I've discovered after being here only two months."

"She seemed like your typical elderly woman who'd outlived her family. After she retired from working as a visiting nurse, it seemed like she spent her remaining days with pets and pictures of Judy all over the house. It was actually rather sad. My official wellness checks became more like visits with an old friend. She'd always have a pot of tea and something baked from scratch waiting for me."

"Really? How often would you check in on her?"

"It got to be a standing date, once a week for at least that year before she died. Then she fell, so we put her in a home to rehab, but she passed a week later."

When Ally suddenly became silent in the semi-darkness, Belle hugged her tighter.

"She wasn't supposed to be there permanently. I told her it was only until she got better." Ally's voice was somber, almost in rhythm with the shadows of tree branches slow-dancing against the wall.

"I didn't realize you had an actual friendship with her."

"She was a kind woman, but aloof," Ally said. "Her personality seemed almost muted, like losing her daughter shut down her ability to connect with anyone after that. I suppose I could've asked her more about herself, but I felt like I was prying. I just listened to whatever she had to say." She laughed softly. "But she did love my arrest stories from my days in patrol."

"I'm glad she had you to talk to in her last days. That must've made her feel good. And safe."

"I enjoyed having tea with her. But I must say, never once did I imagine one day I'd be back in this house in bed with her gorgeous great-niece. Or investigating long-dormant crimes."

Belle laughed. "That must be a bit of a mind-freak."

"Yeah, a little bit." Ally giggled, then added, "But I can't imagine any place I'd rather be right now…as macabre as that may seem."

Belle kissed her head. "I'll take macabre if it's with you."

"You and I should go into business writing wedding vows."

Belle guffawed at the suggestion and locked Ally in a bear hug. They jostled each other under the covers until their silliness ebbed. Belle then pulled Ally up, and they began kissing tenderly, exploring each other as if they were discovering their desires for the first time.

Soon their hands were exploring each other in other places.

Ally's kisses and caresses swept over her like passionate winds, and she swayed and bowed like a palm tree under her masterful touch. No other woman had ever taken her on such a sensual journey.

Nothing could pull her out of it—except for the sound of… thunder?

No, wait. That wasn't thunder pounding on the front door.

"I think someone's at your door," Ally said.

"Who the hell could be here at this hour?" Belle glanced at her phone on the nightstand. Almost eleven p.m.

"Let's go see." Ally jumped up and gathered her pants and shirt.

Belle sat up and bunched the sheet up to her chin. "Um, no. I didn't invite anyone over. Let's ignore it."

The pounding was louder and more persistent this time.

"I don't think your guest cares what time it is."

Belle flung the covers aside and grabbed her clothes, begrudging whoever had the gall to keep knocking at such an inopportune moment.

As they walked downstairs together, a voice emanated from the front porch.

"Open the door, Belle. I know you're in there."

Belle skidded to a stop at the bottom of the stairs, causing Ally to rear-end her. "For the love of Christ," she whispered.

"I'm guessing you know her."

"It's fucking Mary."

Ally jerked Belle toward her by the shoulders. "Your ex, Mary? The one who lives in your condo? And probably believes you're still a couple?"

"Correction. Who *used to* live in my condo. She got the eviction notice. That explains why she kept blowing up my phone with texts and calls."

"Didn't you answer her?"

"She was already served. I didn't think it was necessary."

"Clearly an oversight on your part."

"I didn't think she'd stalk me up here."

"You have her listed as 'Crazy Mary' in your phone contacts. How could you have missed this?"

"I thought I was just being clever. Perhaps I underestimated her."

"Ya think? Please answer the door and see what she wants. Do you want me to go upstairs or stay with you while you answer it?"

"Do you have your gun?"

"No. I don't have my gun," Ally snapped. "Do I need it?"

"No, but it would be the perfect touch if she saw it in a holster on your hip."

"Open the door, Belle. I'd like to know exactly what I've gotten myself into with you."

"With me? I'm not the one banging on someone's door in the middle of the night."

"Belle, stop pretending you're not home," Mary shouted. "I can fucking hear you talking in there."

"I'm leaving out the back," Ally said.

Belle grabbed her arm. "No, don't. Please. Go upstairs. I'll take care of this."

She refused to budge as she skewered Belle with skepticism.

"Ally, please. This isn't as horrendous as it seems."

"There's not a lot of room for interpretation here."

Belle jumped at the next round of battering. "Please."

Reluctantly, Ally retreated up the stairs as requested.

Belle whipped open the door. "What?"

"You fucking twat! You actually went to a lawyer and got me evicted?"

"That's what people do when the tenant ignores their repeated requests to leave."

"Tenant? How could you be so cold?"

"Mary, you seem to have forgotten that I gave you months to find your own place without even charging you rent. You ignored my texts, but did I come pounding on your door? Which, in this case, would also be my door."

"I can't believe you're already on to someone else. Does she know what a bed-hopper you are?"

Belle stepped out onto the porch and closed the door behind her.

"I am not a bed-hopper, and you know it," she whispered. "You and I both know that when you moved in, we realized right away it was a mistake, so don't give me this wounded-heart shit because you're angry I threw you out."

"I was planning to be out by the end of summer when you were done up here. I'm still trying to get my jewelry-design website up and running. Money's been tight lately, really tight."

"So you're not up here to try to win me back?"

Mary's cigarette laugh rumbled like an idling muscle car. "I am still pissed at you and do think we could've made it work if you'd given it more effort, but no. I'm not trying to get you back. What I would like to win, however, is a check from you so I can afford to move my stuff into storage for a month until I can find my own place. I've been crashing on Lyla's couch for the past three days."

As hard as Belle tried to figure out how that was her problem, she agreed anyway to expedite the unpleasant matter. "Hang on. I'll be right back."

"I can't even come in and see what you've done to the place so far?"

"Look at the pics on my Instagram," she said, slowly pushing Mary off the entry step with the door as she closed it.

Ally was halfway down the staircase. "I'm gonna head out now. If it takes you that long to tell an ex to get lost, it's obviously not over."

"No, no, no." Belle ran up the stairs and grabbed her hands. "That's not even close to being accurate. Please trust me. Let me give her a check, and then I'll explain everything."

She ran into the kitchen for her checkbook and tried sorting out the mental cluster-fuck that had sucked her in like a vortex just when things couldn't have been going any better. Ally would have to be a saint to overlook this.

"I can only spare two hundred dollars." She handed Mary the check. "And this is a loan. Got it?" she added, knowing Mary would never pay her back.

"I'm good for it," she said as she stuffed the check into her bra cup. "You're a good egg, Belle…no matter what everyone says about you."

"Thanks, Mary. And if by 'everyone' you mean your drama-stirring friends, I won't be losing any sleep over it." She closed the door with a sigh.

Ally joined her in the foyer. "You gave her money?"

"It's easier to give it to her and get her out of my hair. She won't bother me now that she knows I'm seeing someone."

"Look, Belle. I don't know about all this. You made it seem like you guys were over and done with. Next thing I know she turns up on your doorstep, and you're paying her off like a married congressman."

Belle tried to block her from reaching for the doorknob. "No. That's not true—"

"I think you need more time to figure your shit out."

"I know what this looks like, but I swear, it's not even close. My shit is figured out, Ally. I want you, not Mary. Even if I didn't have you in my life, I wouldn't want her."

Ally's arms were tightly crossed, and the rest of her wasn't moving.

"Look, in the last few months my life has really come into focus," Belle said. "I know what I want, and equally as important, I've also learned what I don't want anymore. I look around now, and I see the people who really matter in my life—my college friends, and my family, and you. It's made me realize how different my life was from theirs. I wasted a lot of time with cocktail acquaintances who couldn't figure out what they wanted or were too dysfunctional to keep what they wanted if they'd had it.

"Since I turned forty, I don't want to be around toxic people anymore. And if it costs me two hundred dollars to get the last one out, then that's money well spent."

Belle complemented her plea with big, baby-deer eyes that may have been a bit hyperbolic, but the sentiment was a hundred percent sincere.

Ally resigned herself with a smirk. "What am I supposed to do with you when all my instincts are telling me to run?"

"Don't listen to your instincts. They're just jealous." Belle smiled as she slipped her arms around her waist.

Ally smiled again as she played with the ends of Belle's hair. "They're going to say 'I told you so' when you leave here at the end of summer, and I never hear from you again."

"I hate to disappoint them, but that's not going to happen. I may not even leave at the end of summer."

Ally burst into a luminous smile.

"Not if I haven't found a house at the shore yet. I'm putting my condo on the market next month, so I'll have no choice but to stay."

"Oh." Ally slowly backed away. "You really do have things figured out."

"Ally, what's the matter?"

"Nothing." She padded over to the couch and plopped down. "What time is it?"

Belle landed in her lap. "I decided to sell my condo sooner than later because now that I'm here with you, I have no desire to go back. I'll stay here until I find what I'm looking for on the shore."

Ally wrapped her arms around her but wouldn't give Belle verbal reassurance yet.

Belle lifted her chin and kissed her. "I thought we were going with the flow? Especially since our flow seems more like a tidal wave."

Ally finally turned toward her. "That sounds like a great plan."

"You really think so?"

"Yeah, I do," Ally replied and teased her with a sensual kiss.

Belle began nibbling at her lips and cheeks. "Then what are we doing down here?"

"Wasting time."

Belle got up, took Ally's hand in hers, and led her upstairs.

CHAPTER NINE

Belle sat on a stool at Ethel's lunch counter as she checked her email app. It had been days since she'd emailed Craig's sister about Judy, but she still hadn't responded. Her knees bounced to the Roy Clark song twanging out of Ethel's old-school antenna radio as her Denver omelet sat in the plate getting cold. Maybe it was time to switch to decaf.

"What's the matter with that?" Ethel eyed her and the untouched omelet with a scowl.

"Oh, nothing," Belle said, jolted back to the present. She cut a huge triangle of it and shoved it into her mouth.

"It's those damn things," she said, indicating Belle's phone. "I'd like to toss them all in the river behind the restaurant and let 'em float down to New York City."

"You're absolutely right." Belle placed her phone face down and out of reach. "I've been waiting for an important email."

Ethel scratched at her graying bun. "Hmm. Now how have I ever lived without being able to check my email every five seconds?"

Belle laughed and wondered how long that pencil had been stuck in Ethel's bun. She never wrote down anyone's order. Maybe she'd forgotten it was there.

She also wondered if she should shoot Charlene another email, asking if she'd received the first one, or call Craig to see if he would intervene. After shoving a forkful of home fries into her mouth, she grabbed her phone when Ethel wasn't looking, sent another email politely inquiring of the sister once more, then shoved it into her back pocket.

"Say, Ethel, do you recall any of the boarders that stayed in my aunt's house?"

Ethel bent over the counter, hovering over Belle's breakfast, as she appeared to search her memory.

After a moment, Belle prompted her. "A guy named Phil with three fingers? Or a young schoolteacher?"

Ethel's eyes flashed with familiarity. "Come to think of it, I do remember them, the fella more than the teacher. Marjory was her name, I think. She was only around a month or two."

Hmm. Long enough for Marjory to deliver a secret love child and bury it in the Ashfords' yard.

"Did you know her last name? Or what school she worked at?"

"Afraid not," Ethel said. "I only knew of her because she came in and had dinner by herself once or twice a week."

"What about Phil? Did you know his last name maybe?"

"Nope, don't recall that, but I do remember he was a handsome man, around forty. When the kids were outside here protesting the Vietnam war, he'd get real mad and show everyone his hand and say how he couldn't serve in Korea on account of his accident when he was a boy."

"How long did he live at Marion's?"

Ethel shrugged. "I'd say about a year or two. He worked in the factory over in Putnam and would do all kinds of jobs for Marion around the house. That house looked shipshape when he was there. I always said she should've moved to a smaller place after Wes died. It's really too big for a woman with a young daughter to manage alone. You don't have a husband yet, right?"

"Right, but I'm also not planning to live there after it's finished."

"You're not? I can't imagine an Ashford not owning that place. I remember when my husband was alive, he used to say—"

"So getting back to Phil. Did any of the guys around here hang out with him?"

"I think he may have been kinda friendly with Bob and John Olsen, God rest his soul. John used to run Danville Hardware."

"Bob as in Sheriff Morgan?"

"That's right. He might be able to tell you something about Phil. I'd like to help, but I've never been one to gossip."

"Thanks." Belle smiled and continued eating.

Ethel moved down the line to refill coffee cups, then ended up in front of Belle again. "I will say this though." Her eyes darted left, then right. "After a while people started saying that Phil was helping Mrs. Ashford with more than just the house, if you catch my drift."

"Really?"

"As in having an affair," Ethel added quietly, as if to avoid scandal.

"Yeah, I got that." Belle tried not to smirk. "Do you think the rumors were true?"

"I tend to believe them. You started to see Marion come out of the house on other occasions besides work. She'd smile at ya at the grocery store and come in for breakfast on Sundays with Phil once in a while after church."

"She never told anyone they were dating?"

"Not to my knowledge. We all assumed it, even though they never held hands or kissed in public. Marion wasn't the type to do that."

"What happened to him?"

Ethel shrugged. "He up and disappeared one day as unexpectedly as he arrived."

"Was Judy still alive when he was there?"

"Oh, yeah. Judy was dating that Wheeler boy at the time. That poor kid was always landing in trouble. Nobody knew the back of Bob's cruiser better than him."

"That's what I heard. But wasn't he from a dysfunctional family?"

"Yeah, but he was always polite to me," Ethel said. "They'd come in for cheeseburgers and shakes, and he was always respectful. He and Judy seemed so in love. I was sure they'd get married when he came home from Vietnam." Ethel's gray eyes grew melancholy. "Who woulda believed she'd be the one who didn't survive the war—shame she got so sick."

Belle remembered how Aunt Marion had told everyone Judy had been sick. Apparently, nobody knew she was into drugs.

"Thanks, Ethel. If you can remember anything more about them, please let me know."

"You writing a book about them or something? You're a professor, aren't you?"

"Yes, but I'm not writing a book. Being in the house, fixing it up, changing things around has made me nostalgic."

Ethel seemed to agree, but Belle felt compelled to further explain her probing. "Plus, Judy's my father's cousin, so he's kind of curious about that side of the family."

"I understand. Well, good luck to you. I'll try rattling my old brain to see if I can't shake loose some more memories."

"That'd be great."

She left the café knowing she'd have to confer with Ally on this. Although the sheriff wasn't doing well, it was time to give Ally a gentle reminder to pick his brain.

All day Belle had endured the unnerving ritual of tingling skin and a flip-flopping stomach in anticipation of a date night with Ally. After a dinner of Ally's grilled chicken and a quinoa-and-kale Southwestern salad, they curled up on her sofa under a light quilt for a binge-watch session of *Transparent*.

After they'd settled into the third episode, Belle could no longer keep her focus on the show. She was still simmering over her conversation that morning with Ethel and how easily the right word or two from Sheriff Bob could possibly have solved her Ashford-house mystery.

She drilled Ally with a lingering side glance, hoping to ease her attention away from the TV, but she was too engrossed for subtleties. When Belle resorted to tickling Ally's forearm lightly, Ally turned to her, dotted her lips with a few kisses, and returned her eyes to the TV.

"Ally." She whispered her name like a child attempting to sneak into her parents' bed in the middle of the night.

"What?" she replied, her eyes still trained on the screen.

"Can you pause that for a second?"

Ally complied and faced her with a patient smile.

"I know you said Bob's had a few bad days, but can't we run over there quick, take him a pie, and ask him a few questions about the boarders?"

"Belle, I already told you I'd talk to him as soon as he was over this rough patch. If I start discussing a case with him, he's gonna get all riled up and want to jump out of his pee-jays and into his uniform. Shirley would kill me."

"But he may have some valuable memories that will break the case wide open."

"If he has any info, I'll get it from him. Trust me. The case isn't going anywhere."

"Well, no, but he might be," Belle mumbled.

Ally shot her a scalding look. "You're terrible. He's not on his deathbed ready to kick off at any moment."

"I know, but…"

"Anyway, I haven't heard from the ME's office yet about whether there's enough genetic material to go on. Without that, it's destined to remain cold."

When Ally resumed the episode, Belle fell back against the cushion in a pout. After a moment, she rebounded with, "Unless your friend, Bob, knows something or someone that can lead us directly to the baby daddy."

"Yes, Belle, that's the plan." She put her arm around her and tugged her close. "Now c'mon. Let's finish this episode, and then we'll see if we can find something better to do." She pulled Belle's chin toward her and kissed her sensually on the mouth.

Belle responded with a light moan and some fervent kisses of her own. Soon Ally slowly pushed her down onto the sofa and climbed on top of her.

"Will you go tomorrow?" Belle said, coming up for air.

"What?"

"Will you go talk to Bob tomorrow?"

Ally sprang up. "I can't tomorrow, Belle. I'm driving up to the Berkshires to pick up Chloe. Don't you want to enjoy this last night we'll have alone together before she's home?"

"I do, I do," she said, pulling Ally back down on top of her. "I forgot you weren't working tomorrow."

"You know, I'm starting to think it's not really me you're into."

"What? What do you mean?"

"Maybe you're drawn to the intrigue surrounding this investigation and are attracted to me because I'm investigating it."

"Ally, you can't be serious."

"It's all you want to talk about when we're alone together."

It hurt Belle's heart that Ally might've thought that and hadn't realized how truly into her she was. Hell, it was practically love at first sight, and that was before any of this mess had clawed its way to the surface.

"That's not true," she said as she kissed Ally's neck. "Most times I'd rather be doing other things with you besides talking."

Ally gently pushed her back. "Then can we give the case a rest for the moment and enjoy each other?"

Ally's dreamy eyes seduced her into submission. Those eyes could get Belle to do anything. It was a good thing Ally didn't know that.

"Do you want me to come along for the ride with you tomorrow to get Chloe?"

"That's so sweet of you to offer." She stroked Belle's cheek. "But I think I'd like the time alone in the car to catch up with her, see how her mood is, and tell her about you."

Belle smiled shyly. "Oh? What are you going to tell her?"

"The truth: that I met a really special lady…"

"Yeah…"

"That I've been spending a lot of time with her…"

"And…"

"And what? Some things aren't appropriate to share with a twelve-year-old," Ally said with a naughty giggle.

"Well, I'm honored that you think I'm special enough to share anything about me with her."

"I'm happy that you didn't run for the hills when you heard I'm raising a kid. To some women, that's a deal breaker…not that we've made any kind of deal or anything."

"If those women can't handle you having someone else important in your life, then they don't deserve you…not that I'm saying I'm the one who deserves you or anything."

They broke out in laughter as they wrestled each other, poking and tickling, kissing and groping.

"God, I love you." The words tumbled out before Belle could catch them. She stared at Ally for a moment, frozen in fear of her response.

For her part, Ally seemed struck by the same concern. Then, "I love you, too" floated out like dandelions in the wind.

Belle was never more relieved or more insanely in love. She felt Ally's words fall on her skin like rain, each syllable a single drop that heightened her awareness of everything Ally stirred in her.

She smiled, and then Ally smiled with every feature of her face. Then they kissed, wrapped up in the country quilt and their passion for each other.

So much for keeping her stay in Danville quick and easy.

Almost two weeks had passed since Belle sent out the original and follow-up emails to Craig's sister, and she had run out of patience. With so few people still alive from that era to speak with, she hadn't had much to spare. She mustered up the audacity to call Craig and see if he'd give her his sister's telephone number, but he was willing to do her one better.

"She's here in Connecticut right now," he said. "Our youngest nephew got married on Saturday, so she's here through this weekend."

"You don't suppose she'd have a few minutes to talk about her old friend Judy Ashford over coffee?" Belle's demeanor bordered on groveling. "I'd be happy to meet her anywhere she wants."

He sighed into the phone. "I can ask her. Give me your number, and either I'll call you back or she will."

"Please tell her it won't take long, but it would mean so much to our family."

"I understand. I'll let her know."

She ended the call feeling sleazy for laying it on so thick with Craig, but in the end, if it got her what she wanted, she'd learn to live with herself.

How did politicians do it for a living, she wondered, then tackled the next item on her to-do list.

Belle spent the morning clearing out and sorting the furniture, knickknacks, and various belongings of Aunt Marion's that remained in the house after her death. Some things needed dusting or light cleaning, and they'd be ready for repurposing, while others were ready for a dumpster. She'd called a service that picked up large items to donate for various veterans' programs and was unloading them from the back of her SUV at the curb when Ally rolled up in her squad car.

"This is a nice surprise." Belle ran to the car and poked her head in for a kiss before Ally could unbuckle her seat belt. "Sorry. I'm a sweaty mess."

"It totally works on you," Ally said, bobbing her eyebrows as she got out of the car. "If I wasn't on duty right now…"

"What do you mean? Aren't you sworn to serve the women under your jurisdiction?"

"Not in this context, but for you, I'd definitely make an exception." Ally glanced around and gave her a kiss that left Belle's lips smoldering in the summer heat. "Listen. You're gonna be even more excited when I tell you why I'm here."

"What?"

Ally unlinked Belle's hands from around her neck as she assumed her authoritative stance. "They got DNA out of the blanket."

"No way! That's amazing. Now what?"

"The lab will run it through CODIS to see if they can link it to anyone who's already in the system."

"Is that a database for Connecticut?"

"It's nationwide, so even if the guy or woman took off from Connecticut, theoretically, we could still get a match."

"What do you mean theoretically?"

"One of the parents would've had to have been convicted of a felony sometime after the late nineties, when the database was implemented."

"Oh." Belle frowned as her rush of optimism evaporated in the sun. "So you're telling me this is another one of those 'it's possible but not likely' scenarios."

"Right, but on the plus side, I can ask Craig Wheeler for a DNA sample. Maybe we can at least establish paternity, even if it doesn't lead us to Judy's molester."

"You're going to contact him, right? I think if I call him or show up at his garage one more time, he'll get a restraining order against me."

"Yes. Please let me contact him. It's an official part of the investigation now. Besides, I thought you promised me you'd leave him alone until the case was closed."

"I asked him to help me contact his sister, who was Judy's childhood best friend. She lives in California, so it's not like I could've knocked on her door myself. And then when she didn't answer my emails, I called him again to ask for her phone number."

"Emails with an S?" Ally's sexy-girlfriend demeanor suddenly turned into that of an impatient cop lecturing a group of loitering teenagers. "Belle, I don't blame her for not answering you. Some random woman contacts her out of nowhere to talk about her past? That's not *too* sketchy. In this day of internet scams against old people, she was smart to ignore you."

Duly chastised, Belle mumbled a barely audible response. "She could have vital information that Craig doesn't."

Ally was showing no mercy. "That may be, but unless she agrees to talk to you, you can't keep harassing her or Craig."

"I'm not harassing anyone," Belle said with a coy smile. "I'm a scintillating conversationalist. Who wouldn't want to have a chat with me?"

Ally swirled a hand around her own face. "You see this? I'm not smiling at how adorable you are because I don't want to encourage you."

Belle grinned mischievously.

"Let Detective Gallagher worry about running down leads," Ally said. "If it turns out Craig is the father, then he'll have more leverage in getting the sister to cooperate if need be." She grabbed her hand with a soft smile. "Please, Belle. You need to stay out of this, okay?"

"Okay. But what if his sister calls me back? Can I talk to her then?"

"Yes, but only as a family member of Judy's who'd like to know more about her. You can't grill her about anything relating to this investigation or give her any information I've told you in confidence." Ally's expression grew stern. "Or I won't be able to share anything further with you."

"Okay, babe. I understand. I'm sure she won't even call me anyway. Craig said she's going home this weekend, and I haven't heard from her yet."

"Thank you. Speaking of the weekend, dinner is at six sharp tonight. Are you ready for this?"

"Sure I am. I'm great with twelve-year-olds. I bought her a lip-gloss gift set from Sephora. Nothing too mature or whorish. It's meant for tweenies. I asked the salesgirl."

Ally's sweet smile was what Belle was angling for. "You don't have to bribe her with gifts to get her to like you. Your eccentric charm is enough to win anyone over."

"Thank you…I think."

"It sure worked on me." Ally gave her a soft peck. "You're bringing the sangria?"

"It's macerating as we speak."

"Perfect. See you at six." Ally glanced around again before giving her a longer, sensual kiss and hopping into her car. "Hey, did you call me 'babe'?"

A blush warmed Belle's cheeks. "Too soon?"

"Just right," Ally said with a grin.

Belle waved at her car until it disappeared down the tree-shaded road. She sat on an old parlor end table and exhaled, waiting for the gossamer feeling Ally filled her with to lift so she could resume the rigorous task at hand.

Later, as Belle pulled into Ally's driveway, her confidence in making a winning impression on Chloe wasn't as robust as it had been earlier in the day. She made her way past the girls' mountain bike on its side on the small patch of lawn and hit the doorbell with her elbow as she balanced a pitcher of sangria, a gift bag for Chloe, and a covered dish of homemade chocolate-covered strawberries.

"Look at all this," Ally said as she held the door open for her. "It's like Christmas in July. How did you manage to transport that sangria without spilling it?"

"Don't ask," she said as she headed up the stairs. "I'm sure I committed at least three traffic violations to do it."

"I'm off duty so I'll pretend I didn't hear that." Ally slapped her butt playfully and called out, "Chloe, come here. Isabelle's here."

"Be right there," Chloe said from her room.

"I'm kinda nervous," Belle said. "It feels like I'm a dude meeting my girlfriend's father for the first time."

"You're funny. She's not that tough. However, she hasn't met any women of interest before either, so we'll see."

"What?" Belle's throat constricted. "I'm the first girl you've brought home to meet her?"

"That she'd remember."

Belle's mind suddenly flooded with images of some dysfunctional kid throwing a tantrum because now she'd have to share her mother figure with a stranger. "Well, in the event I don't make it through the vetting process, it was swell knowing you."

Ally laughed. "She's going to approve. I'm completely sure of it. Chloe," she called out again.

"Sorry," Chloe sang as she flounced down the hall toward them. "I wanted to change to look presentable."

Belle and Ally laughed.

"Chloe, this is Isabelle Ashford. Belle, this is Chloe."

Belle held out her hand to shake, and much to her relief, Chloe offered her a pleasant smile as she took it.

"It's nice to meet you, Chloe," Belle said. "I'm not sure if you're into lip glosses, but I thought you might like these."

"I am. These are awesome," Chloe said, studying the package. "Thank you." She surprised Belle with a quick hug and darted off down the hall.

"We're eating now, Chloe," Ally said. "Don't get involved in anything."

"I'm putting these away," she said from her room.

"Good call on the gloss," Ally said as they walked into the kitchen. "I should've known the minute she got her period, the makeup hormones would develop, too."

"Makeup hormones?" Belle held the wineglasses while Ally poured. "Now I know being gay is biological. I've never craved makeup before. I wear it as a public service."

Ally seemed to survey her facial features as though they were brushstrokes on a museum painting. "You're a natural beauty, Belle. The makeup is purely the cherry on the sundae."

"You know just what a lady likes to hear." Belle kissed her, then suddenly pulled back. "Oh, sorry."

"For what?" Ally carried a small charcuterie plate to the table. "Chloe knows I'm gay, and she knows you're my girlfriend."

Belle twirled her wineglass, savoring the sound of that sentence. "I'm your girlfriend, huh?"

"Aren't you?"

"Yeah. I just like hearing you say it."

"You really are a true romantic." Ally kissed her, then instantly switched into harried-mom mode. "Chloe, let's go! And leave the phone in your room."

"I'm coming," she called out. "I was letting Red in."

Chloe and Red scurried down the hall and joined them in the dining room. He ran over to Belle, tail wagging like a windshield wiper on max, and she scratched him behind his ears.

"There you are, you little traitor." She covered his head and whiskers in kisses. "How dare you leave me for a younger woman?"

Chloe laughed. "He can stay over with you. I don't mind."

"Thank you, Chloe," she said. "But if there's one thing you should learn about boys now it's that they're gonna go where their heart is. You can't force them. And this boy's all about you."

"Man advice from a gold-star lesbian," Ally said to Chloe in a deadpan. "You should write this down."

Chloe giggled, half getting it.

"I don't need to have been in a relationship with a man to understand them," Belle said good-naturedly. "I have lots of male friends who've enlightened me over the years."

Ally and Belle shared a laugh and clinked wineglasses.

"Now that I'm a woman," Chloe said, "when am I gonna start being attracted to boys?"

Belle almost spewed out her wine. One thing she'd never expected was to be a dinner guest at a twelve-year-old's coming-out party.

She and Ally exchanged looks.

"What do you mean?" Ally asked. "You have pictures of boy musicians all over your walls."

"I mean like when am I gonna want to date them? I get my period now, so that's puberty, right? But I still find them kind of gross."

Belle snorted into her plate of prosciutto and table cheese.

Ally glared at her but kept her composure as she addressed Chloe's question. "Well, you're only twelve, honey. Getting your period isn't some magic threshold you step through and then suddenly you're ready to start dating."

"And twelve-year-old boys are kind of gross anyway," Belle added.

Chloe shrugged as she picked through the charcuterie plate. "I thought since my friends were getting all crazy over boys that I should be, too."

"Are you going all crazy over girls?" Belle asked at the risk of another searing glare from Ally.

Chloe giggled. "No."

"You know you can tell me if you are," Ally added.

"I know," Chloe said. "Sometimes I just feel weird that I'm not as into boys as Emma and Francesca are. I have more fun playing Minecraft and talking to the kids playing with me online."

"Yeah. Kids who are probably fifty-year-old guys living in their moms' basements," Belle mumbled.

That one warranted a kick under the table from Ally.

"I wouldn't worry, Chloe," Ally said. "You're perfectly normal the way you are. When you're ready, you'll become interested in dating like your friends, who, by the way, are too young to be so fixated on boys. That's high school stuff. Until then, enjoy Minecraft."

Chloe smiled. "Can I have a spritzer?"

Ally returned a smitten smile to her niece. "Sure." She got up and made Chloe a fruit juice and seltzer concoction in a wineglass like theirs.

By the time they were done eating, Chloe had given Belle a thorough education in the rudiments of competitive equestrianism, ranging from when equestrian events first appeared in the Olympics to the difference between English and Western riding.

"Wow," Belle said. "You are amazingly well-versed in your subject matter. You put me to shame as an English professor. I've never even heard of the words 'dressage' and 'equitation.'"

Chloe giggled. "Equitation means judging the rider on form, style, and ability. And dressage is basically how good the horse's training is."

"As you can see, she's quite enthusiastic about her sport." Ally radiated a level of exuberant pride any mother would, and it made her even more attractive. "Her first competition is next month."

"That's so exciting," Belle said.

"Do you want to come?" Chloe asked.

"Uh, I think that would be very cool. I've never been to an equestrian competition before." She winked at Ally. "A bucket-list item for sure."

Chloe beamed. "If I win, maybe I can finally convince my aunt to get me my own horse."

Belle turned to Ally. "Really?"

"I told you I'd consider it, Chloe," Ally said firmly. "Getting a horse isn't like dropping by a shelter and adopting a cat—which by the way, did you clean Bieber's litter?"

Belle stifled a laugh. "Bieber?"

Ally nodded with resignation, then turned back to Chloe. "Did you?"

"Ye-ess," Chloe said with a sibilant hiss. "You said you'd check with animal-rescue groups."

"I have been, honey. But it's a really big expense to board a horse, so I still have some research to do to see if I can manage it."

Chloe scowled into her dish of fresh berries and ice cream. Belle could see how much it hurt Ally to disappoint her.

"So," Belle said, too loudly for dinner conversation. "I think I'm going to really enjoy watching you compete, Chloe. Make sure you let me know when it is."

That returned the smile to her face—Ally's, too.

After they'd finished dessert, Chloe was excused, and Belle insisted on helping Ally clean up while Ally insisted they leave the dishes in the sink.

"I'll take care of them later," Ally said. "Let's sit on the deck with some chilled Moscato."

Belle shrugged. "I really don't mind helping you. We can have it done in no time."

"Why stand around my kitchen cleaning up when there's a breathtaking sunset out there calling our names?"

"Can't argue with that logic," Belle said.

Chloe reappeared in the kitchen carrying a backpack. "I'm going to Emma's now," she announced.

"Text me the minute you get there." Ally walked over to her and hugged her tightly.

"I will."

"The minute you get there," Ally repeated. "Or I'll call her mother."

"I will," Chloe said in a whine as she headed out the door.

"Emma's mother and I always text each other when the girls arrive anyway," Ally said confidentially.

She then led Belle out onto the deck with the Moscato chilling in a bucket. They sat on an outdoor loveseat on the small patio as the setting sun burned orange over distant treetops. After Ally filled their glasses, they kicked back and relaxed on the loveseat shoulder to shoulder.

"She's an awesome kid," Belle said. "I can see why you're so in love."

"I don't know how she's such an awesome kid after all she's been through."

"Ally, after two hours in your company, I see how. You're a great mother to her—loving, supportive, protective, and not overly indulgent. If she doesn't grow up normal, then none of us ever had any hope."

"You think so?"

"Absolutely. You're a testament to the power of a dedicated single parent. And your admiration for each other is enviable. For real."

Ally kissed her. "Thank you."

"For what?"

"For being you. For getting me and understanding what I'm trying to do."

Belle shrugged, earnestly not knowing why Ally was making such a fuss. Maybe she was buzzed. Lord knows she would be if she had to raise someone else's kid.

"It's amazing what you're trying to do," Belle said.

Ally kissed her again, and the warm sweetness of her wine-glazed lips whetted her appetite for more than dessert.

"So…Chloe's sleeping over at her friend's, tonight," Ally said.

"I gathered that. Does this mean we can have a sleepover of our own?"

"Did you bring your peejays?"

"Nope," Belle said with a devilish grin.

"Good."

She gently nibbled Ally's lobe, adding a whisper of warm breath in her ear.

Ally shivered and let out a soft moan. "How about we have our next glass inside? My bathtub seats two."

Belle smiled and drained her glass.

Ally watched, her eyes radiating with urgency.

CHAPTER TEN

The romantic Friday sleepover with Ally followed by an action-packed Saturday with Ally and Chloe horseback riding granted Belle a reprieve from the anxiety of waiting to hear from Craig's sister.

As Sunday morning peeked through her window, she awoke smiling. Spending time with Ally and her niece was wonderfully therapeutic for her mind—for her body not so much. She stretched under the sheets, and the muscles in her back voiced their objections in a chorus of aches. Still, she was already anticipating her next outing with them.

She reached for her phone charging on the nightstand to let Ally know she was on her mind. Lately, she was the first thing to meander into Belle's consciousness the moment she woke each morning. Was it too soon in the relationship to be texting her before she even rolled out of bed? She didn't want to come across as a nudge, but God, she really wanted a text from Ally saying she'd been thinking about her, too.

Before she could decide, her phone chimed with an out-of-state number. She almost hit "decline," assuming it was a solicitor until she remembered Craig's sister. She sprang up in bed and bobbled the phone as she pressed "accept" in her haste.

"Hello, Isabelle? This is Craig Wheeler's sister, Charlene."

"Oh, hi. Thank you so much for calling back."

"I'm sorry for the early hour, but I'm leaving for the airport in a little while."

"No, that's fine. I know how busy you must've been on your visit. I'm glad you found time to call me back."

"My brother said you're Judy Ashford's niece?"

"Cousin. Well, my dad is Judy's first cousin."

"Oh, I see."

"Hey, could we meet up near the airport for a cup of coffee before you go?"

"I don't know," she said. "I have to drop off my rental and get the shuttle to the airport."

"What if I meet you at the rental place? We can grab a cup of coffee on that main road, and then I'll drop you off at your terminal."

"Um, well, I really can't miss my flight. It's at 3:20."

Belle glanced at her clock and was able to convince her that seven hours was a wide-enough window to squeeze in twenty minutes for coffee and still make her flight.

Early that afternoon, as Charlene stirred a Splenda into her black coffee, Belle studied her, noting the often-overlooked nuances of an attractive woman in her early sixties: mauve manicured nails, expensive makeup downplaying slight wrinkles around the eyes and mouth, hands dotted with light-brown spots that betrayed her younger appearance.

That could've been Judy sitting across from her.

"Were you and Judy still friends when she died?"

"Oh, yes. We met in the second grade and remained close until she passed."

"Do you have memories of when it happened?"

The shift in her facial features answered for her. "I'll never forget it. I called the house that day because I hadn't talked to her in a few days, which was odd for us. I phoned a few times in the afternoon, but nobody answered, which was also odd. So I went over there in the early evening. I kept knocking but nobody answered. After about twenty minutes or so, I started back down the driveway. That's when Father McKeenan's station wagon pulled into the driveway. He had driven Mrs. Ashford from the hospital because evidently she was too distraught.

"I can't imagine losing one of my children," Charlene said, "never mind my only one. I don't know how she got through it."

"Did my aunt explain what happened then?"

"No," she said, as if reliving the fear of that moment. "I got out of there and waited for my mother to tell me."

"What did she say?"

"That Judy had a sudden illness. But I knew it wasn't true. I knew what killed her."

"An overdose?"

"I kept telling her to cool it," Charlene said. "She was starting to go overboard with the pills."

"Do you have any idea why?"

She shrugged. "My brother had been away for close to a year, and I think she was trying to cope with him being gone. But looking back now, I think she had some type of depression or maybe was bipolar. Maybe she never properly dealt with the death of her father, being so young when it happened."

"Had she confided in you about anything else that happened to her that might've made her turn to drugs?"

Charlene laughed sardonically. "It was the Woodstock era. We didn't need a reason to do drugs. They were everywhere. My brother knew a guy. We did speed, ludes, and lots of grass. We even went on a couple of LSD trips together."

Belle grinned. "You tripped on acid?"

Charlene smiled demurely. "They were crazy times, but we had fun." Her smile quickly faded. "Only Judy didn't know when to stop. I'd quit everything a couple of months before, after I had a bad trip and ended up handcuffed in the back of a police car. My father beat up my brother and threatened to send me to the girls' home. That's all I needed to hear."

Looking at this classy older woman who probably drove a Lexus and shopped at Talbot's, Belle couldn't envision her freaking out on an acid trip and being tossed into the back of a squad car.

"Her mother had told my family that Judy died from a short illness," Belle said. "That's what we all believed until I came up here."

"I'm not surprised," Charlene said. "Every parent's worst nightmare was catching their kid experimenting with drugs. Only the dirty hippie war protesters did that."

"Did you stay close while she was dating Craig?" Belle heard Ally's voice in the back of her head warning her not to give away any details relating to the investigation.

"Oh, yeah. It was uncomfortable at first." She smiled in recollection. "I felt a little like my brother stole my best friend from me. Judy and I had a few arguments when they started dating exclusively, even stopped talking for a week or two. But that's what girls do. We got over it."

"Was she serious about your brother?"

"He was her first love," Charlene said. "And even though my brother was a couple of years older and had dated other girls, I know she was his first true love, too. Poor Craig was in Vietnam when it happened. I dreaded the idea of having to write and tell him." She frowned, then absently sipped her coffee.

Belle blinked away the tears stinging her eyes and placed her hand on Charlene's. "I'm sorry. I hope I'm not dredging up too many painful memories. It's just that nobody from my family knows much about Judy or my aunt Marion."

Charlene gave her hand a pat in return. "It's okay. In a strange way, it's nice to talk about Judy again. I also have some wonderful memories with her."

Belle smiled. "That's what your brother said. You don't know if Judy ever got pregnant, do you?" She tried to slip that question in smoothly, but all the lube in the world wouldn't have helped.

Charlene's reminiscent smile faded. "Pregnant? Why? Did she have an abortion or something?"

"Not that I know of," Belle said. "She never said anything to you?"

"Well, one time she told me she thought she was. She was so scared. I made it worse by telling her that both her mom and my parents were going to kill her and Craig."

"But she wasn't?"

"No. A few days later, she said she got her period, and we never mentioned it again."

"If she was pregnant, do you think she could've hidden it from you?"

Charlene's brow furrowed. "I doubt it. By the time we started high school she'd got really thin and started wearing outfits that showed off her new figure. That's what caught Craig's eye. She'd been chubby while we were in junior high, and she was afraid of being teased in high school, too, so she went on some crash diet."

Belle scratched her head. She'd been sure Charlene was the missing link in all this. Why didn't she seem to know anything more? If they were that close, wouldn't Judy have told her about the pregnancy even if she'd hidden it from everyone else?

"Now that I'm thinking of it," Charlene said, "if she was pregnant that could've been why she overdosed. But it couldn't have been my brother's. He'd been gone almost a year when it happened."

Well, if that were true, it certainly explained why Judy hadn't confided in her best friend.

"No, no, that's not what I'm suggesting," Belle said nervously. "I'm asking because I found something disturbing at the house when I was cleaning. I'm playing amateur detective to see if I can figure out what happened to her."

"What did you find?"

Uh-oh. Ally's face flashed through her mind again—her beady eyes, pursed lips, finger of reproach waving in her face. She meant business, and Belle had already used up what was left of Ally's good will when she'd called Craig. How would she explain this slip to her?

In a panic, Belle began to babble. "Oh, it's probably nothing. A few scraps of paper with some doodling on it. Something about some guy hurting a girl. Could've been a short story of some kind. For all I know, it wasn't even Judy's. It could've been anyone's."

"Do you have it? I'd recognize her handwriting."

Belle gulped air, knowing it was officially evidence now.

"It's somewhere at home."

"Did the note say what happened to her?"

"No. In fact, it was quite vague. It may have been the imagination of a young storyteller," she said, hoping Charlene would buy that ridiculous excuse.

"I hope so."

The grim look on Charlene's face was familiar. Once she recognized it as the same look her brother had on his weeks earlier, Belle suddenly felt like she should wear a black hood and carry a sickle whenever she conversed with one of the Wheelers.

Charlene glanced at her watch. "Well, I suppose I should head to the airport now."

Belle offered a hand to help her up from the booth and thanked her throughout the five-minute ride to Charlene's airport terminal.

She was supposed to have supplied Belle with the missing piece, some dredged-up memory of her best friend she'd carefully stored away like an heirloom. If anything was there to be taken out and dusted off, it was flying back to California with Charlene.

Belle sighed and drove off in defeat.

When she returned from her recon work, Belle texted Ally to see where she was working, and Ally suggested they meet at the ice cream shop for a frozen yogurt. Belle waited until they ordered and sat on a bench across the street before she broke the news about Craig's sister.

"How did the downstairs bathroom come out?" Ally asked.

"It's not quite done yet. I got a little sidetracked."

"Doing what?" Ally licked her black-raspberry cone.

"Having coffee with Craig Wheeler's sister." She tensed up, waiting for Ally's lecture.

"She agreed to meet you, or am I having frozen yogurt with a kidnapper I'm about to receive a 'Be on the Lookout' for?"

Belle giggled. "She agreed. We met before she caught her flight home. Sadly, though, I don't have any new information that'll lead us to the guilty party."

"That's good, Belle, because you're not an actual investigator, remember?"

"Yes, I remember. Sheesh."

They sat quietly for a moment eating their yogurt in the cool shade of a massive old oak tree, Belle afraid to test Ally's patience any further.

"So?" Ally finally asked. "What did you talk about?"

"Well, since Craig had already told me they had a pregnancy scare once, I asked her if Judy ever told her she was pregnant, figuring maybe she would've confided in her best friend. But Judy told her the same thing, a pregnancy scare." She paused for a spoonful of yogurt. "And she said Judy was thin in high school, so it's not like she could've hidden a full-term pregnancy. Those bones were from a full-term infant, weren't they?"

"Yeah. No doubt." Ally was quiet as she seemed to ruminate over the details. "Skinny girls usually don't hide baby bumps very well. Maybe it wasn't hers after all. I'm thinking Gallagher needs to focus on locating that female boarder."

Belle grew animated. "Didn't I already say that? That woman's plan all along was probably to rent a room at my aunt's so she could have the kid and get rid of it. And it seems to have worked."

"If that's how it happened, then I now have two criminals to find. What else did Wheeler's sister say about Judy?"

"That she knew Judy did drugs—she did them with her—and that she could recognize Judy's handwriting if she saw it."

Ally's head whipped toward her. "Belle, why didn't you lead with that? We can confirm that those writings you found in the crawl space were Judy's."

• 151 •

"I thought we already knew that!"

"Witness corroboration, Belle," she replied, sounding exasperated. "In a murder trial every piece of evidence has to be corroborated."

Belle frowned. "She had a plane to catch."

"I'll talk to Gallagher and see what he wants to do. Craig is supposed to come in tomorrow for the cheek swab. I'm sure he'll be able to recognize her handwriting, too."

"You're going to show him that now? I thought you didn't want to tip him off to anything?"

"I didn't want *you* to tip him off to anything. Gallagher and I are going to have an official conversation with him tomorrow."

"Can I come?"

"No, you cannot."

"Aww, c'mon. Can't you like bestow on me an honorary deputy status for the day? I'm getting good at questioning suspects."

Ally chuckled. "I'm sure you are, but Gallagher and I can handle it. You have a big house that isn't going to renovate itself."

"I'm right on schedule. Your Mom and Pop contractors actually show up on time and finish jobs when they say they will. I wish I'd signed up to teach a summer course to help pay for all of it."

"It's really coming along beautifully. You'll get your asking price for sure."

Belle smiled at the encouragement.

"Then you'll be free to leave this place in your rearview mirror," Ally added with some side-eye.

"Is that what you want?"

Ally turned to face her. "Not at all. But that was your original plan."

"It was the plan before I met you."

Ally gazed directly across the street, perhaps to hide her delight. "So it's changed?"

"It hasn't stayed the same."

Ally's head swiveled back. "What does that mean, Belle? This conversation is starting to make me anxious."

"Why?"

"I don't know. I never expected to fall in love with you, for starters, so now I get like that when we talk about you moving away."

"I didn't expect to either," Belle said excitedly. "Although, if I believed in love at first sight, I should've known from the moment you pulled me over. I don't think my heart had ever fluttered more over anything."

Ally smiled. "Not that I'm confessing to anything, but I've never pulled someone over because I found them attractive."

"Aww, now I'm disappointed." Belle offered her best sexy pout.

"I was very attracted to you from the moment I saw you at the hardware store. I happened to hit the jackpot when I ran your plate and found the expired emissions flag."

"Good thing you don't wear a body cam. You would've caught me drooling over you on tape."

"Lust at first sight is a thing, but love is organic. It has to be nurtured to grow into something."

"Is that what we've been doing for the last several weeks? Nurturing?"

"Beats me," Ally said. "But it's undeniably more than lust." She took Belle's hand and seemed to study her face. "I don't want you to leave next month."

"I don't want to leave you," Belle said and lay her head on Ally's shoulder. "An hour isn't such a bad commute, is it?"

"It's not—for a while anyway. If we want more someday, that's a different story. I'm going to be sheriff here, sooner than later. Bob was planning to finish out the year, but I'm reasonably certain he's gonna make his retirement official by the end of summer. I'm going there for dinner tonight, so I wouldn't be surprised if he tells me then."

Belle sighed. So much to digest. She wanted Ally to question Bob about what he knew about Judy when she was little, but with his illness so grave, she felt like a heel every time she thought to bring it up.

And then there was Ally's less than subtle insinuation that her career was a priority over any relationship. At the moment, she wasn't sure what to do with that new information, but it hadn't left her feeling warm and fuzzy.

"You okay?" Ally gently nudged her with her shoulder.

"Yeah," Belle said, looking straight ahead.

"You got so quiet."

"Why does everything have to be so complicated?"

"I wouldn't recognize my life if it wasn't."

Belle gave a halfhearted giggle. "I love you, Ally."

"I love you, too, Belle."

As Ally was moving in for a kiss, her cell began to ring. "Hey, Shirley," she said with a concerned expression. "Shit," she whispered. "Do you need me to meet you there? Are you sure? Okay. Let me know. I'll be there as soon as I finish up here."

"Bob?" Belle asked.

Ally nodded as she ended the call. "She's taking him to the ER. He's having trouble breathing."

They gathered their trash and started the walk to the station.

"Can I do anything?" Belle asked.

"Thank you, but Chloe's been at her friend's all day. She should be okay there while I run up to the hospital."

"I'll be around later if you need me to stay with her. I can take her for dinner or something."

"That's so nice of you, Belle. But I couldn't ask you to do that."

"Why not? I almost broke my neck flying off a temperamental horse for her. I think we're cool to have pizza together if need be."

"Okay. Thank you." Ally gave her a kiss. "I'll text you later."

Belle drove home hoping Ally would need her. She truly liked Chloe's company, but anything she could do to help Ally was a bonus. She'd been balancing a lot in the short time they'd known each other, and nothing warmed her heart more than seeing Ally happy.

But until she was called upon to don her superhero cape, she needed to get home and don her crummy painting T-shirt and tackle the first-floor bathroom.

Halfway through dinner, Belle could take the awkward silence no longer—well, awkward for her anyway. Chloe seemed content to devour her pizza, picking off the toppings and eating them first, while streaming some TV show on her phone.

She hadn't struck Belle as a rude kid. She must've felt funny having dinner with her aunt's girlfriend alone. Who could fault her? Belle wanted to engage her in a natural conversation as opposed to a Q&A session in which she felt like was trying to shove a watermelon through a garden hose, but how?

And then genius struck.

"So, I had a great time horseback riding yesterday."

"You did?" Not only had Chloe's face blossomed with joy, but she actually put down her phone. "Do you want to go again?"

"Uh, only if you promise to pick me a horse they don't refer to as El Diablo."

"Why?" Chloe squealed. "He was so cool."

"He was very cool but a little high-strung for my level of experience. My hands still ache from my death grip on his reins."

"You're supposed to hold the reins loosely. They're only for steering the horse."

"Well, yeah." Belle said it like she knew exactly what Chloe was talking about.

Chloe narrowed her eyes at her. "Was that your first time?"

"It might as well have been. I was around your age the first and only time I rode."

"You were good for a beginner." Chloe's nod of approval made Belle feel like she'd scored admittance into the most coveted sorority.

"Thank you. Coming from an expert like you, that's high praise." Belle raised her soda glass to toast with Chloe.

"I can teach you."

"I have no doubt. Hey, isn't your competition coming up?"

"It's on the twentieth. I can't wait. I'm going to training camp for five days next week."

Belle smiled at her nearly breathless enthusiasm. "I'm looking forward to it."

Her phone then buzzed with a text from Ally.

"Your aunt wants to know if you're having a good time."

Chloe giggled as she made silly faces into her own phone. "Tell her yes, and she doesn't have to keep checking up on me."

"She says she'll be leaving soon."

"Mmm-hmm," Chloe replied, still captivated by some phone app.

Is she minding her manners? Ally asked in a text.

She's fine, a perfect little lady, Belle wrote back as Chloe let out a belch.

I can't thank you enough for this. You're so sweet.

I'm happy to spend time with her. How's Bob?

OK. A little down though. They're keeping him overnight for observation.

Give Shirley and him my best, Belle wrote.

I'll text when I'm leaving. Love you.

Love you more. Belle added a string of heart emojis.

Poor Bob and Shirley, she thought. They were such a cute pair. For some reason, she projected into the distant future, imagining herself and Ally as an elderly couple. Who would be hooked up to IVs and wires, and who would be keeping the bedside vigil?

Ugh. What a morbid thought.

"Hey, if you want to stop in and visit Bob and Shirley at the hospital for a few minutes, I'll take you."

Chloe looked up from her phone. "Do I have to?"

"No, of course not. Ally told me you're close to them, so I thought…but I understand you not wanting to see him like that."

Chloe crinkled her nose as she wagged her head back and forth.

Belle signed off on the credit-card receipt. "Well, we should get you home and see what Red is up to."

"You can stay and hang out if you want," Chloe said as they got into the car.

She couldn't decipher whether Chloe was afraid to stay home alone or she genuinely liked having her around, but in either case, the offer pleased her. "I think I'll take you up on that."

Later, when Ally got home, Belle was curled up on the couch watching *Modern Family* reruns with Red lounging at her feet.

"Hey, guys. Comfy?" Ally said with a smile.

Belle and Red got up to greet her.

"Did you eat?" Belle asked after kissing her.

Ally shook her head as she stripped off her uniform shirt down to her tank top and tossed her shirt on the recliner.

"Let me warm up some leftover pizza for you."

"Have some wine with me, too?"

"If you insist," Belle said with a grin.

She threw some pizza slices into the oven, opened a bottle of red, and joined Ally on the couch. Ally moaned her approval as Belle grabbed her feet for a foot rub.

"Shit, if this isn't a 'Honey, I'm home' moment…" Belle said.

Ally laughed. "Right? If I was a guy, you'd be single-handedly setting the women's movement back seventy years."

"I can't help it." Belle slid up to Ally's lips. "It's a huge turn-on playing your servant."

Before their kiss could even warm up, Chloe hovered over the couch.

"Can I sleep over at Emma's?"

Belle sprang back to the other side, her cheeks burning with embarrassment.

"Like I've never seen people kiss before," Chloe said, rolling her eyes.

"Uh, why are you going there now?" Ally inquired. "It's a little late to be heading out for the evening."

"Auntie, it's eight thirty," Chloe whined. "C'mon. I already told her I was coming."

"First of all, please don't make plans with people without asking me first. And secondly, I want you to visit Bob and Shirley with me tomorrow."

"Why?"

"What do you mean, why? They've been very good to you, and you haven't seen them in a long time. Bob could really use some cheering up."

"All right," she said with maximum attitude. "Can I go now?"

"Chloe, why are you being like this?"

She sighed in either an attack of conscience or a calculated strategy to gain permission for a sleepover. "I'm sorry, Auntie. I'll visit them with you, but can I stay over at Emma's tonight?"

"Okay, but I'm driving you."

"You don't have to. They're on their way home from dinner, so they're coming by to get me."

"You arranged it with her parents before you even asked me?"

"Love you," she said with a grin and kissed her cheek. "I'll be on the porch waiting for them."

Red followed her out the door to wait with her.

Ally plopped back on the couch and looked at Belle. "What?"

"Nothing," she said with a knowing grin.

"I know. I'm a pushover. I've always been a pushover for her, and now it's coming back to bite me in the ass."

"Don't be so hard on yourself. Most kids have figured out how to manipulate their parents by this age. She's basically a good kid, right?"

Ally agreed. "I'm surprised by her attitude about seeing Bob and Shirley. That's not like her."

"It must bother her that Bob's sick. He looked terrible the last time I saw him. She probably doesn't want to see him like that."

"Good point, but I'll have a talk with her anyway."

Belle took her hand and rested her head against Ally.

"Boy, did I luck out meeting a beautiful college professor who understands kids," Ally said.

"I didn't do so bad either." Belle gazed up from the comfort of Ally's chest and slipped her arm around her torso, squeezing tight.

Ally wrapped both arms around her. "Please say you'll stay over tonight."

"I was planning to even before you asked," Belle said with a kiss.

"That is so not funny."

Belle went to the kitchen to get Ally's warmed-up pizza, absently replaying her chat with Charlene in her mind. She thought about how she said a priest had driven Aunt Marion home the night Judy died. Maybe back in those days it wasn't unusual for a priest to be that involved in his parishioners' lives. But then in those days the archdiocese also traded pedophile priests around parishes like Green Stamps.

She brought Ally a dish of pizza and sat on the couch next to her. "Craig's sister said the night Judy died a priest drove Aunt Marion home. Do you think that's odd?"

"In general, no," Ally said as she chewed. "But in this context, it means I have to put my pizza down and take out my notepad."

Belle laughed. "No. Keep eating. All she said was Father McKeenan drove Marion home that night. She didn't say anything else, and it didn't occur to me to ask."

"It didn't? Well, I guess you're off the list of potential deputies when I'm sworn in."

"I better not be," Belle said as she leaned in for a kiss.

Ally relaxed against the back of the couch and exhaled. "Okay. Tomorrow I'm stopping in at Bob's when he gets home. I'll see what they know about the boarders and the priest. What was his name?"

"McKeenan," Belle said. "I'll text you to remind you tomorrow."

"I'm sure you will."

Belle smiled. "I'm here to serve."

Her head still reclined in exhaustion, Ally pointed to her lazily-puckered lips.

CHAPTER ELEVEN

After admiring the job Angelo had done on the stone fire pit, Belle smiled with approval and offered him a beer, which he accepted. After he'd guzzled a fair amount, Belle revisited the subject of the koi pond—with its new location on the opposite side of the yard.

"Are you out of your mind?" He nearly screeched. "I didn't even wanna come back here to finish the fire pit. This place gives me the creeps."

"Thank you, but Deputy Yates is hard at work finding a logical explanation for whatever went on here all those years ago."

"Logical?" He scoffed before taking another sip.

"Yes," she said, folding her arms across her chest. "This isn't some haunted murder house, so please don't go spreading that around. I'll never sell it."

"Listen, honey, I'd love to forget what my Bearcat dug up— or at least stop dreaming about it."

"How about I add another two hundred on top of your original quote?"

"I'm a mason, not a grave digger. Thanks for the beer." He swigged it until it was nearly gone, then handed her the bottle.

"Angelo, come on. You're not gonna dig up anything else."

"Oh, is that right? Well, the only way I can be sure of that is if I don't dig. Good luck if you ever want to put in a pool." He grabbed his tool bag and headed out of the yard.

Belle sighed and decided maybe one of Ally's flower-garden designs would be best after all. She wouldn't have to dig so deep.

When her stomach rumbled again, she consulted her watch. It was nearly midafternoon. She could go to the grocery store, come home, and make a salad, but by the time she sat down to eat, it would be closer to dinner.

Or she could pedal into town for one of Ethel's garden-salad-of-the day jobs and satisfy her hunger within half an hour.

Ethel flipped the sign on the door to CLOSED and walked back behind the counter as Belle ate lunch. Belle watched her barrel-shaped grandma body move the condiment containers into the fridge and marveled at how agile she was for a woman well into her seventies running a café almost entirely on her own.

"I didn't realize you close at two, Ethel. I'm sorry for holding you up. I'll take this to go."

"Eat. You're almost finished," she said as she waved to the last customer walking out.

Belle glanced around, and upon seeing the place was empty, she went for it. "Do you remember Father McKeenan?"

"Arthur? Oh, yes. What a dear man. You know him?"

"Not me, but he was apparently friendly with my aunt."

Ethel propped herself against the counter and grinned. "He was friendly with a lot of the pretty widows and divorcées."

"Is that right?" Not what Belle expected but okay. She recalled a *Dateline* about a child predator who dated single mothers to get access to their children. "Did these widows and divorcées happen to have young kids?"

"Sure. Some did." Ethel moved closer to Belle even though the café was empty. "Rumors were a couple of kids grew up to look a lot like him." She punctuated her sentence with a wink.

"Nooo," Belle said dramatically, to egg her on.

"Now I'm not suggesting any impropriety on Father McKeenan's part. I'm just telling you what I've heard—because you asked."

"Of course," Belle said with a reassuring nod.

"He was the kind of man you felt comfortable confiding in, telling your troubles to, you know?"

"The kind of man a vulnerable widow or divorcée needed at such times."

"Exactly," Ethel said. "Say, are you asking 'cause you need someone to confide in? I've been known to lend an ear from time to time over this counter."

"I'm sure you have, but, no. I'm fine. I was hoping he was still around is all. Might be nice to chat with him about my aunt."

"Oh, thank goodness. No. He doesn't live here anymore. When he retired, he was fixin' himself up in a little place in Florida."

"I could've bet on that one," Belle grumbled.

"He's one of them snowbirds, you know? If he's still alive. I think he is. Haven't heard otherwise."

"So he didn't move down there permanently?"

Ethel shook her head. "I ran into his sister, oh, about a year or so ago, and asked about him. She said he stays with them up here for a spell during the summer."

"Is she still around?"

"She's not too far from here, down in Coventry. Some ritzy senior-living outfit. If I had brains, I'd be there myself instead of running this place at my age."

By this time Belle had taken out her phone and was typing the info in her notes app while Ethel spoke. "And let someone else run this monument to rustic life?" she said. "Friend, you're a legend in this town."

Ethel's adorable old-lady laugh rolled up from her belly. "Say. Are you sure you're not writing a book?"

"I didn't intend to, but depending on how my stay here goes, I just might. You wouldn't happen to know how I could get ahold of his sister."

"Gorman's her last name, but I don't remember the husband's first name."

"This'll do fine," Belle said as she texted Ally the info. "Ethel, when the book comes out, you'll get the first autographed copy."

She laughed again as she cleared the plate and collected the cash Belle placed on the counter. "Look forward to it."

Belle left the café and walked down the street to the sheriff's station, eager for Ally's take on this new lead.

Belle had relayed the rest of the information to Ally, and the next day they were on a road trip to the Sunset Ridge senior-living community. She'd thought she'd have to go a few rounds with Ally for permission to take the ride with her, but luckily, she was all for it.

"You won't get in trouble for bringing me along on a suspect interview, will you?" Belle weaved her hand through the wind outside the passenger window as she took in the rural scenery and wrinkled her nose at the smell of cow manure.

"Get in trouble with whom?" Ally said.

Belle giggled. "That's right. You practically run the department now."

"I'm not even on duty today. I stopped by the station to file some paperwork with the state. Besides, this isn't an official visit. I'd be going with Gallagher if it was. But since this priest was apparently a friend of your aunt, this is simply a little ole social call."

"You have quite a gift for rationalization."

"I call it 'adjusted perspective.'"

Belle shook her head in amusement. "I taught a course on rhetoric and semantics once. You would've been a star in that class."

Ally offered a cheesy, teacher's-pet-style grin before getting back to business. "Technically, I shouldn't have you tagging along, but your connection to Marion will be an asset in talking with him. If anything seems wonky, I'll bring Gallagher in so we can take an official statement from him."

"Deal," Belle said with a smile.

They pulled into the retirement village nestled in the woods off the main road and found a space in the visitors' parking lot. After speaking with Father McKeenan's sister through her front door, they walked to the pool area and found the retired cleric holding court over a pinochle game with three elderly ladies around an umbrella table.

Ally cautioned her back with an outstretched arm as she appeared to study the scene with Father McKeenan for a moment before approaching. Belle loved watching Ally's mind work, her face as cold as granite, her big eyes locking on her target like a cat before it pounced.

"This guy's got more skeletons in his closet than a haunted house," she finally said with a knowing smirk.

"You got that just by watching him play cards?"

"It's a combination of things. But I wouldn't be a bit surprised if Ethel was right about him—that his genes created a pool of their own in Danville while he was at St. Matthew's."

Belle covered her mouth with her hand as she laughed. "That's so wrong."

"Then why are you laughing?"

"I guess I can't resist a hearty helping of situational irony."

"C'mon. Let's go see what this Catholic Casanova is all about. You remember the plan?"

"Aye-aye, Captain," Belle replied with a salute.

As they approached the table, Belle wondered if they'd even be noticed amid the banter. Father McKeenan was flanked by ladies in floral caftans, beach robes, and big sunglasses, all of whom looked like they were auditioning for an off-Broadway production of *The Golden Girls*. They shrieked with laughter as they faux-slapped or fell dramatically against the good father. He chewed an unlit cigar as he seemed to be regaling them with flirtatious quips.

"Christ. I don't even get that much play with women now," Belle mumbled.

"Seriously," Ally mumbled back. "I almost hate to interrupt him."

"You girls looking for someone," one of the women asked with a smile.

"Uh, yes," Belle said. "Mrs. Gorman said we could find Father McKeenan here."

"You found him," he said, removing the cigar. When he fanned his arms open, the sun caught a gold crucifix nestled in a tuft of white chest hair beneath his hibiscus-print shirt. "What can I do you for?"

"Oh, uh, I'm sorry to interrupt your game," Belle said after Ally nudged her in the back. "I'm Isabelle Ashford. You knew my great-aunt, Marion, and I was wondering if I could ask you a few questions about her."

"Don't apologize," he said. "I could use a break from these chiselers. They're charming me out of my retirement savings here."

"Oh, sure, Artie," one of the ladies bellowed. "We're the ones doing the charming."

All three women cackled as Father McKeenan slowly stood, his posture slightly hunched, and escorted Belle and Ally to a nearby table in the sun.

He groaned as he lowered himself into the chair. "How can I help you gals?"

"Did you know Marion well?" Belle said.

"Oh, yeah, for many years. She started coming to mass fairly regularly after her husband passed. Good woman. Quiet woman but still had a smile for everyone. Always generous when it came to the collection basket, too."

"Did you have a friendship with her outside the church?" Belle asked.

"No. Not for several years. For a long time she'd listen to mass, sometimes take communion, occasionally stay for a monthly coffee-cake social, but never sought individual counsel from me."

"When did your personal friendship begin?" Ally questioned, sounding too official for a casual conversation.

He gave her a guarded glance. "I wouldn't call it a personal friendship. It was more along the lines of spiritual counseling… Why do you ask? Is something wrong?"

Ally looked at Belle.

"Uh, no," she said. "We're curious about my aunt Marion."

"Well, if I remember correctly, she came to me when she started having trouble with her daughter."

"What kind of trouble?" Ally said.

"Typical teenage shenanigans—defiant, stopped doing well in school, talking back. I told Marion the kid was just testing her, spreading her wings a little, but Marion wasn't used to it. She didn't want to loosen her grip on her. They'd been extra close since the husband passed."

"You didn't think it was anything more than typical teenage angst?" Ally asked.

Father McKeenan shrugged. "She was running around with the Wheeler kids. Now that family had their problems. Mrs. Wheeler certainly had her crosses to bear with that husband. Anyways, I figured their attitudes were rubbing off on Judy." He looked at both of them with a combination of concern and confusion. "Are you sure there isn't something wrong?"

"No, no," Belle said. "I'm doing some research—for a novel I'm writing about Danville. I figured I'd base a character on my aunt. I'll be changing the names, naturally."

"Oh, you're a writer?" he asked. "Have you written anything I'd know?"

She and Ally exchanged surreptitious glances.

"This is my first book. I'm a college instructor by profession." Belle pointed at Ally. "She's my writing partner."

"Oh, I see." He smiled, seeming relieved.

Ally seized the opportunity Belle provided. "You mentioned Mr. Wheeler. Some people say he was a nasty guy."

"He was a boozer who liked to smack his wife and kids around—when he'd bother going home, that is. Big ignoramus, you know what I'm saying?"

"Do you think he could've been a child molester?" Belle blurted out.

Ally's eyes sent off a warning shot. "She's asking because she's thinking of addressing that tragic crime in her novel."

"Oh." He glanced between the two of them again. "Well, nothing like that was ever brought to my attention about him."

"So was Marion friendly with any other clergy outside the church besides you?" Ally asked.

"Not to my knowledge. I started there in the early sixties, not long before her husband died. Then I left for a while for Portsmouth. I came back to St. Matt's in the late eighties and stayed until I retired."

"Why did you leave?"

"They caught some son of a bitch in Portsmouth screwing around with a couple of boys and sent him to another parish. I was one of the priests they offered the position to."

Belle shot Ally a look. Either he'd just cleared himself as a potential suspect in Judy's sex assault, or he was throwing some major shade at them.

She decided to go in for the kill. "I'd heard a rumor around Danville that my aunt may or may not have had a fling with a priest. I was curious whether it was true. It would sure help me write some riveting fiction if it were."

Father McKeenan managed an artificial laugh as he put his cigar back between his teeth. "If it were true, I'm sure neither your aunt nor the priest would want that story written about, even if the names were changed."

"Didn't you ever see *The Thorn Birds*?" Belle asked. "Forbidden love, unbridled passion—that's some good shit, I mean stuff. People love reading stories like that."

He smiled. "I saw it. Richard Chamberlain was my hero in the eighties. Darn program almost made me leave the priesthood."

Belle smiled in surprise. "Nooo. Really?"

He affirmed her with a frown. "But I couldn't break the heart of my dear Irish mother."

"So how about that rumor?" Ally said. "Think there's any truth to it?"

He scratched at his balding head under his straw fedora. "Well, if I were to give you my two cents, I certainly wouldn't want to be quoted in a book, but it wouldn't be as outrageous an idea as you might think."

Belle grinned and glanced at Ally, who motioned with her eyes to dial it down. "You wouldn't, by any chance, be speaking from experience, would you?"

Ally's face deflated in defeat.

Father McKeenan leaned forward. "I took my vow seriously, young lady," he said, stern but still kind. "I spent my tenure as a priest in earnest service to God and my community. I never took a penny that wasn't mine and always showed compassion for every one of my parishioners, regardless of lifestyle, but…"

"Nobody's perfect?" Ally said.

He smiled solemnly. "I had my flaws like all men. Suffice it to say, my service to God would've been a lot less complicated had my parents been Protestants."

"It wasn't you, was it?" Belle asked in a confidential tone.

Ally stood and dragged Belle up with her. "Well, thank you for your time and candor, Father. You've been a big help for our story. We have to get going now."

"You're quite welcome, ladies. Sure you don't want to stay for a drink? I make a heck of an old-fashioned."

"Some other time," Ally said, smiling through clenched teeth. "Thanks again."

As they headed to the car, Belle wriggled her arm free from Ally's bear-trap grip. "What's the matter with you? He was about to crack."

"He was about to shut down, thanks to your Spanish-Inquisition-style line of questioning. You can't start accusing him of breaking his vow of celibacy ten minutes after meeting him."

"How long should I have waited?"

"Belle, that's not the point. We had a plan—you'd present yourself as the writer, and I'd ask the sensitive questions."

"I'm sorry. I just got caught up in all the excitement."

"I know you did, babe." Ally offered an understanding smile as she unlocked the car doors. "That's why I had to usher you out of there before he started seeing through our ruse."

"Did I ruin everything?"

"No, honey, you didn't." Ally patted Belle's thigh and started the car. "I have what I need from him for now. We should have the comparison results of Craig Wheeler's sample any day now. If he's the father, then we'll have no need for DNA from anyone else."

"And if he's not?"

"Then we go back and review our list of suspects—Father McKeenan and that fingerless Phil guy. I'm stopping by Bob's tonight to see how he's feeling. I'll have a chat with him about Phil. Maybe I can get some details out of him."

"Finally."

"If you're going to be an honorary deputy, you need to learn some patience."

"Do I get my own badge and Dudley Do-Right hat?"

"No."

"That's okay. The perk of taking spontaneous trips with you is the best one by far." She reached across the console and pulled Ally's face in for a kiss.

Ally nearly swerved off the road when Belle landed one full-on her lips.

"Whoa," Ally said, tasting the gloss Belle left on her lips. "Now that's a job perk I've never enjoyed before."

Belle chuckled. "I would hope not, since the guy you work alongside is almost eighty."

"He was quite a looker back in his day," Ally said, and then her face turned grim. "The poor guy—I wish he was doing better. I talked to Shirley last night. He's been steadily going downhill all summer."

"Cancer's tough on anyone, but he's an old guy. Maybe he's tired of fighting."

"As hard as it is for me to believe, I guess it's possible. I've sure missed him since he's been on leave. He's like an old philosopher, you know? He could talk a dog off a meat wagon, but he's a great listener, too. He loves helping people—which explains why he's been sheriff here for a hundred years."

"Right?" Belle said with a laugh. She squeezed Ally's hand as they drove on, moved by the genuine connection Ally seemed to have with her colleague and friend.

They pulled off the state route and followed the sign around the corner to a country lunch stand near a walking trail. As they munched on grilled-cheese sandwiches and fruit salad at a picnic table, Belle stared at Ally. How elegant and sexy she was even doing something as mundane as eating lunch. Her firm jaw pulsed as she chewed, and then she licked her inviting lips before sipping from a bottle of water.

"I just thought of something," Belle said. "The DNA samples from the guys can establish who the father is, but how are you going to identify the mother?"

"That's the easy part. I'll ask the father." Ally grinned with confidence as she bit into her sandwich.

Belle tapped her index finger against her temple. "Brilliant." She stopped as she was about to bite into hers. "Wait a minute. What if he doesn't want to cooperate?"

"You'd be amazed at how fast telling someone you have enough evidence to charge them with murder motivates them to cooperate."

"Would you have enough to charge someone with murder if their DNA came back a match?"

"No, but they won't know that."

"There's nothing on God's green earth sexier than a powerful woman." Belle leaned over the table and whispered, "What do you say after lunch we run off into the woods for a romp?" She indicated the entrance to the trail across the street with a nod.

"That sounds fantastic, but that's a public walking trail."

"So? It's in the middle of nowhere in the middle of the work week. Nobody's gonna be in there." Belle kicked off her flip-flop and tickled Ally's shin with her toes.

Ally arched an eyebrow at her. "'I'm in line to become the next sheriff, so let's go have sex in a public place' said no intelligent elected official ever."

Belle laughed out loud. "You're right. Most of them wait till after they're in office."

"Touché," Ally said with a grin.

"C'mon." Belle bit her bottom lip. "It's where nature intended for us to do it."

Ally pretended to mull over the suggestion with an innocent face. "Only if you can promise I won't have poison ivy on my ass when I get up."

"Who says you have to lie down?"

"I like the way you think, Professor Ashford. All we need is a sturdy tree."

"Eat faster," Belle said and licked her lips.

"First you want me to eat dairy and then eat it faster? I'll burn the entire forest down if you light a match behind me."

Belle nearly spit out the melon chunk she'd put in her mouth. "Guess s'mores are out of the question," she said, still laughing.

"Thank you. I don't want to be responsible for any wildfires."

"Except for the wildfire burning between us."

Ally patted her heart as though she were swooning. "Isabelle Ashford, you are the sexiest, corniest woman I've ever known." All levity was gone from her voice, and her level of sincerity rivaled that of a marriage proposal when she added, "I love you madly."

Belle dropped the end of her sandwich in its little paper boat and took Ally's hands.

"I love hearing you say that. I love you, too."

"Sometimes it scares me."

"Feeling it or saying it?"

"Both." Ally looked down as she flushed.

"Really? You seem like the bravest woman in the world to me."

"I carry a Glock 9, so yeah, I give off that impression. But full disclosure? I've never felt like this for anyone before, Belle. You worry me, excite me, and care about me the way no one ever has. It's pretty intense."

"Ally," she said as she felt her eyes welling up. "What brought all this on?"

She shrugged. "Just sitting here watching you pick through that container for the perfect cantaloupe square. That's all it takes these days."

"Oh, babe," Belle gushed. "I love that you're such a romantic."

"Follow me."

Ally swept up their trash in her arms, dumped it into the can, then tugged Belle off the bench by the arm. They ran across the street and onto the wooded path, giddy like girls playing doctor for the first time at a sleep-away camp.

Once they found shaded seclusion deep within the woods, Belle pushed Ally against a thick-trunked tree and kissed her passionately, wasting no time as she unbuttoned her Capri pants. Ally was equally efficient, tugging Belle's bra over her breasts.

They tasted each other's lips in the still air fragrant with damp leaves and sweet wildflowers. Belle craved Ally like it was their first time as Ally's physical aggression set her skin on fire with anticipation.

Ally then grabbed her and turned her against the tree, thrusting her thigh into her. Belle's back scraped against the bark, but the pain only heightened her senses. Sweaty against each other in that moment of spontaneous risk and desire, they reached breathless satisfaction together.

CHAPTER TWELVE

Ally's text woke Belle shortly before her alarm, requesting that she come to the station as soon as she could. The imperative compelled her to call Ally immediately with a litany of questions, but she resisted, titillated by the intrigue.

As she showered, her mind bolted off in a myriad of directions. She knew Ally had gone to visit Bob and Shirley and to discuss the case with him. Maybe he'd given her new information. What if Bob had remembered a new suspect? Or Shirley remembered one of the boarders' last names? Or maybe Ally had planned a surprise marriage proposal, knowing how much Belle loved her in her uniform.

She squeezed the excess water from her hair and laughed at where her speculations had drifted. They'd known each other less than three months. And yes, while Ally was the quintessential romantic, she was not the impetuous type. If a marriage proposal was in their future, it was surely in the distant future.

Still, it was fun to allow her imagination to soar with the idea.

Wasting no time, she parked illegally in front of the station and flew inside to find Ally on the phone casually reclined with her feet up on her desk. She ended her call and sprang forward with a smile after Belle crashed into the chair beside her desk.

"Are you ready for this?" Ally's expression created more of a stir than anything Belle's imagination could've conjured.

"Yes, yes, what?" Belle exclaimed.

"Craig isn't the father."

"What? Seriously?"

Ally allowed her a minute for the information to sink in.

"Wow," Belle said. "I did not see that coming. Although, after talking to Charlene, I guess it makes sense."

Ally tossed her pen down on the desk in frustration. "I thought that part was going to be a slam dunk. But, alas, that would've made things way too easy."

"Now what?"

"For starters, I'll be paying the philandering Father McKeenan another visit for a sample of his holiness's DNA. Hopefully, he'll volunteer it."

"I told you we should've gotten it when we were there."

Ally rolled her eyes. "Don't worry. He's not leaving his poolside harem any time soon. Besides, I have another lead."

"From who, Bob? By the way, how's he doing?"

Ally sighed with a thumbs-down. "Not good. Anyway, I was talking to Shirley about the boarders, and she remembered Marjory. She taught for a couple of years at the grammar school."

"She lived at my aunt's for two years?"

"No. She moved in there when she started teaching and stayed until she got her own apartment."

"Or until she had her baby and killed it and buried it in my aunt's yard."

"Whoa, slow your roll there, *Law and Order, SVU*. At this point, a conversation with her would be about what she saw while she was living there."

"Have you found her?"

"I'm checking with my pal over in Vital Statistics to see if we can track her down. That's who I was on the phone with when you came in. I also asked Bob about the other boarder, but he didn't remember the guy's last name. He said he was kind of strange."

"What did he mean? Like child porn on his computer, if computers existed back then, strange or socially awkward-IT-guy strange?"

Ally giggled. "No, like quiet, loner strange—which really isn't so unusual except in the context of this community where people here invite you over for dinner the minute you set foot on Danville soil."

"Yeah. That level of friendliness is a tad unnerving, if you ask me. That's like religious-cult, shackle-your-kids-to-the-bed strange."

"Belle." Ally sung her name admonishingly. "How could you stereotype an entire community like that? I live here. I don't have anyone chained up in my house."

Belle flashed a naughty smile. "Let's keep that one on the table, though."

The phone on Ally's desk rang. "Deputy Yates. How can I help you?" She paused as she listened. "Yes, oh great." She grabbed a pen and began writing. "That's fantastic. Thank you for your help."

"What?" Belle strained to see what Ally was writing.

"Marjory Dixon married a man named George Cambridge in Danville in 1967."

"Google her!"

"What do you think I'm doing?" Ally said as she pecked away at her keyboard.

Belle jumped up and hovered over her shoulder as she searched the computer. She inhaled the scent of Ally's hair, savoring the earthy lavender of her shampoo. As Ally jumped between search screens, Belle tickled the back of her neck.

"Hey. I'm trying to focus here." Ally flicked her hand away. She scrolled down a bit more, then pointed at the screen. "Got her."

"Oh, fuck," Belle said as she read on. "Marjory Dixon Cambridge. That's an obituary." Defeated, she returned to the chair beside the desk. "I skipped my morning coffee for two dead ends?"

Ally threw up her hands and reclined in her chair. "You skipped your morning coffee? I said it was important, not the apocalypse."

"I can't believe this." Belle shrugged. "I'm gonna run over to Ethel's. Want anything?"

"I'll take a refill." Ally handed her an empty paper coffee cup as she scanned her computer screen.

"What are you looking for?"

"Marjory's obituary may not be a dead end after all—pardon the expression."

"Why?" Belle looked at where Ally's finger pointed on the screen.

"Marjory has a daughter, and her last address is in West Hartford."

"So? It looks like she has two sons, too."

"Remember when I explained mitochondrial DNA?"

"Oh. That's the DNA you find through the mother."

"Yup. I can rule Marjory in or out through her daughter."

For some reason, Belle found the thought amusing. "How the hell are you going to explain a DNA sample out of her daughter without suggesting that her dead mother is a baby killer?"

"Well, I'm certainly not going to let you request it."

"No, seriously. I can see asking a guy because there's always the chance he didn't know the girl was pregnant."

"I'll speak to her on the phone first. Then I'll have an idea how to approach it from there."

"Can I come and watch?"

Ally sighed in exasperation. "C'mon, Belle. Aren't you supposed to be having your house painted?"

"I am. I finished the inside, but I've hired people for the outside. Besides, I thought you said that I was an asset in this since I'm a relative. Seeing me with their own eyes helps them develop personal involvement. This makes them more likely to want to help you."

Ally smiled. "You're a good student."

"A good student needs a good teacher to help her realize her potential."

"So you're saying you're free today?"

Belle sat back and pressed the tips of her fingers together. "That's exactly what I'm saying."

"All right. I have a few phone calls to make, so go have some breakfast, and then we'll take a ride."

On the way to visit Father McKeenan at his personal poolside Gomorrah, Belle could hardly contain her excitement. She fidgeted in the passenger seat as she shared her theories on various scenarios they might glean from the retired priest after numerous old-fashions.

"I think I should take Ethel a pie or something," she said out of nowhere.

"A pie? She makes them in her café."

"Maybe she'd like to enjoy a pie she didn't have to toil over in her sweaty kitchen."

"Why do you want to give her a pie?" Ally asked.

"Just as a 'thank you.' If she wasn't such a terrible gossip, we wouldn't have found out about old Father Horndog."

"Good point."

"I wonder if he's gonna let you take the sample," Belle said as she watched the leafy trees whip by her window.

"If he has nothing to hide, he should agree without hesitation."

"What will you do if he doesn't?"

"I have my ways. If I can't charm one out of him, I'll have to get a warrant for it."

"In my experience, you have the power to charm anyone into or out of anything—especially clothes." Belle giggled at her witty repartee.

"With you I don't have to work very hard. You're quite cooperative."

Belle dotted her neck in kisses. "That's because you're so incredibly sexy."

Ally cringed and screeched with ticklish delight.

"If the priest does come back as the father," Belle said, "I hope it was with Marion and not Judy. I like him. I can't picture him as a molester."

"I don't get that vibe from him either. But that doesn't mean he isn't one." Ally then laughed to herself. "I imagine him more like Hugh Hefner entertaining muumuu-clad octogenarians in his silk pajamas."

They laughed together and shared lurid hypothetical accounts of the father's imagined sacrilege until they pulled into the retirement complex.

After locating him calling bingo to residents gathered around the pool, they walked up behind him at the table under the pavilion. When they finally caught his attention, he acknowledged them with a smile and signaled with his arthritis-gnarled finger to wait a minute.

Once someone yelled bingo, he announced they'd be taking a few minutes of intermission.

"To what do I owe this surprise?" he asked as he waved them up on the riser.

"Well, to be perfectly honest, Father, we're working a case," Ally said.

"A case? Are you police?"

"I am." Ally showed him her badge. "Now I can't go into detail with you because it's still an open investigation, but I was wondering, well, hoping you wouldn't mind submitting a DNA sample to the Danville sheriff's office."

Ally smiled so wide and fluttered those insane lashes so endearingly, who could've possibly resisted a request of any kind?

"Me?" His gruff chortle indicated he'd assumed they were putting him on. "What could I possibly have to do with a case you're on? I haven't lived in Danville in almost twenty years."

"It's a cold case," Ally explained, "but recently some new evidence has surfaced."

The father suddenly appeared nervous. Belle tried to catch Ally's eye to see if she noticed his rapid change in demeanor, but Ally was too preoccupied with her eyelash thing.

"Still, I don't know what interest you'd have in my DNA," he said. "I've never committed a crime."

"I'm not saying that you did," Ally said.

"What's the nature of the case?"

"I'm not at liberty to elaborate right now, but I can tell you that we're merely trying to establish paternity. This has nothing to do with you being implicated in a crime."

He tapped his fingertips on the table, seeming only slightly relieved. "Did I mention I was a Catholic priest? We don't marry or have children."

"Priests weren't supposed to seduce pubescent boys either, but we all know how that story ended," Belle said.

Suddenly, his jovial nature evaporated in the heat as he struggled to his feet. "Now just a minute, young lady. If you're suggesting that I in any way hurt a child..."

"No, no, no. She's not at all suggesting that, Father," Ally said. "Look. Between us, a newborn's remains were found, and we're trying to find out who the child belonged to."

"Again, I don't see how that pertains to me. I mean, I can perhaps assist you in your search. My memory's not so bad for my age, but—"

"Father McKeenan." Ally draped her arm around him, her voice soft and reassuring. "I'm gonna level with you—you know, one public servant to another." She waved a finger between them. "The child's remains were found on the Ashford property. We're not looking to arrest anyone. This is about identifying the child. The only way to do that is to collect DNA samples from all the males, still living, who had some sort of connection with the Ashfords."

His noncommittal glance darted between them.

Ally treaded carefully. "You were close with Marion Ashford around the time of her daughter, Judy's death, weren't you?"

He nodded.

"We simply want your DNA so we can eliminate you in the matter of paternity."

Ally's pep talk did little to ease the good father. He was whiter than a baptismal gown. "Did the child belong to Marion?"

Ally shrugged. "See, that's our dilemma. We're not sure since both she and Judy are dead. Our only potential leads are a handful of men."

He tugged at his crucifix sticking to his chest. "I think I should call a lawyer."

"You're perfectly entitled to do that, Father, but it really isn't necessary. An innocent man has nothing to fear when it comes to DNA. It never implicates the wrong person."

"Hey, Artie!" an old woman bellowed from a table across the pool. "Are we playing here or what?"

"I'll be right there, Carmela. Can't you see I'm busy?" he shouted over his shoulder, then turned back to Ally. "So what are my choices here?"

Ally pulled her sunglasses back down over her eyes as she casually glanced out among the vibrant gathering of bingo enthusiasts.

Belle sighed at how powerfully sexy she looked at that moment, so confident, so in control.

"You can call your lawyer if you want," Ally said, "but then I'll have to get a search warrant to swab your cheek, and you'll have to submit the sample anyway. I thought you'd like to get it out of the way so we can stop interfering with your social engagements."

He grunted with resignation. "So…so if my DNA comes back as a match, what then? Can I be arrested?"

"That depends on who the mother was," Ally said.

"If it did come back as my child, it sure as hell wasn't the kid's, I can tell you that right now."

Shocked at his offhanded confession, Belle stared at him. "You weren't joking when you said Richard Chamberlain was your idol."

Father McKeenan glared at her, then addressed Ally. "Look, I'll give you the sample. I'll help you in any way I can, but please, can we keep this out of the papers? The church's reputation has suffered enough bad press with those sons of bitches up in Boston. I swear to you, I did nothing inappropriate with the girl. I'd never even visited the house until she passed away."

"Deal," Ally said with a gentle pat on his shoulder. "Let's go over there under the breezeway. It'll only take a minute."

After they concluded their business, Ally and Belle thanked him for his cooperation and headed back toward the pool and the exit.

"I believe him," Belle said. "Did you see that look of distant yearning in his eyes at the suggestion that he might have been someone's father?"

"Distant yearning? I'd describe it more as scared shitless. But yes, he was very convincing." Ally's face radiated with foreboding.

"You're not buying his claim that he didn't even know Judy?"

"It's not that I'm convinced he's lying about that, but the guy does have a bit of a credibility issue."

Belle shrugged. "As stimulating as this whole saga has been, I'm hoping it is McKeenan's. Then he can explain the circumstances behind the baby's death once and for all. I don't know how families of murder victims do it every single day."

"If it is his, it's highly possible he's the circumstance behind the baby's death. He won't be doing any cooperating then unless he wants to repent before he croaks."

"Isn't it also possible he didn't know that Marion was pregnant?" Belle asked. "She could've done it all on her own after realizing she was knocked up by a priest."

Ally rubbed the bridge of her nose under her sunglasses before backing out of the parking space. "At this point, I wouldn't rule out an alien abduction and impregnation."

"Really?" Belle shuddered at the thought.

Ally contorted her face at her.

"Well, how should I know?" Belle said in a huff. "I thought maybe you knew something about Area 51, being in law enforcement and all."

"Not even close. Anyway, I texted Gallagher earlier. If we come up empty with McKeenan, he wants to send the story to the local news. That might draw out anyone with information. I'm also gonna run it by Bob, if he's feeling up to it. It makes him happy when I ask for his advice."

"Maybe I should call Craig's sister and see if I can pick her brain a little more," Belle said.

"That might not be a bad idea. Maybe she's remembered things since speaking with you. You can tell her about the remains now that her brother's been ruled out as the father."

"You mean I actually have your blessing?"

Ally took her eyes off the road long enough to give her a loving smile. "Yes. Provided you don't give her any other information. Let her talk, and you take down what she tells you. And see if you can get the last name of Phil the boarder out of her."

"What will you give me if I do?" Belle said as she caressed Ally's thigh.

"Hmm." Ally pretended to think. "How about a licentious act to be named at a later date?"

"That's fair."

"Handcuffs and nightstick?"

"Now you're talking." Belle kissed her as she ran her hands through the back of Ally's short hair.

Once Ally dropped her off at the station, Belle wasted no time heading home and calling Charlene. Luckily, she reached her on the first try. After exchanging greetings and verifying Charlene remembered her, Belle jumped right in.

"Do you remember when I asked you if Judy had ever been pregnant?"

"Yes."

"Well, I asked because the remains of an infant were found on my property recently, and the sheriff's department is trying to identify them."

"My God, that's awful," she said. "Do the authorities think my brother's the father?"

"No. He gave the police a DNA sample, but he wasn't a match."

"Have they figured out whose it was?"

"They're still working on it. That's why I'm calling you."

"Me? Well, it wasn't mine. My children were my only pregnancies. And like I said before, if it was Judy's, I never knew anything about it."

"They don't know that it's Judy's for sure either. Your brother told me about the boarders Mrs. Ashford had for a time."

"Yes, I remember. Miss Dixon was my fifth-grade teacher. Such a nice lady. She was new to the school that year, just started teaching."

"Do you think it's possible she could've been pregnant?"

"I don't know. She was a heavyset woman so it wouldn't have been obvious right off. But I don't recall ever hearing any talk of it, not that I necessarily would have, being a child at the time."

"How about the guy, Phil or Philip something?"

"Oh yeah," Charlene said. "The guy with the missing fingers. My brother used to buy pot off him."

"He was a drug dealer?"

"I don't know if he was an actual dealer, but I know he smoked a lot of grass and would sell to my brother once in a while."

"You don't happen to remember his last name, do you?"

"I don't, but I'm almost positive it ended in 'ski' or something like that. My father had referred to him as 'the Polack' after he found my brother's stash once. My dad could drink himself into oblivion half the time, then smack my mother around for sport, but when it came to marijuana use, he suddenly became the moral majority."

Hearing Charlene trash-talk her own father had Belle deliberating over whether she should suggest the possibility that he could've been Judy's molester. But with so many yet unanswered questions about the child's mother, she knew Ally would blow out her O-ring if she shared any new information with Charlene.

"Hmm, so Philip Something-ski," Belle said, thinking out loud.

"I'd suggest you ask Craig, but frankly, I'd be shocked if he remembered anything before he left for the war."

"I'll share this new bit of info about the guy's last name with the investigator. Who knows? Maybe it will be enough to run a search on those high-tech law-enforcement websites."

Charlene sighed loudly into the phone. "I hope the authorities can find out who the child belonged to."

An ominous silence hovered over the line as Belle waited, feeling as though Charlene had more to say.

"Well, good luck," she finally said.

"Yeah, uh, thank you for your help again," Belle said. "If you can think of anything else, please let me know. Sometimes even the smallest detail can be valuable."

Again, Charlene seemed to be stalling before ending the call.

"Would you let me know when the mystery's solved?" Charlene added. "It sounds like a fascinating case."

"Yes, I sure will."

Afterward, Belle went about the business of cleaning and touching up areas with paint around the inside of the house, but her conversation with Charlene kept replaying in her head.

She wasn't sure if she'd realized she had a sixth sense about people or if playing detective alongside Ally had cultivated an unhealthy cynicism in her, but she was certain about one thing: that woman was hiding something.

Whatever it was, Ally would be able to flush it out of her.

CHAPTER THIRTEEN

That night at dinner Belle scanned the wine list at Franco's at the corner table that had become their unofficial spot. As she waited for Ally to return from the ladies' room and for the garlic-bread sticks to arrive, she glanced around the dimly lit restaurant at the décor that was many years past due for an update. In a way, it added to the charm. If she opted to stay here, with Ally, she'd have to get used to such things like a lack of modern style, people who called instead of texted, and having to explain to the bartender what a cosmo was and how it was made.

However, the mere sight of Ally walking back to their table in a plunging black silk, button-down top dispelled those trivial pet peeves. Belle was breathless.

"You look stunning tonight."

Ally smiled and sat down. "You're just now noticing me?" she said in a low, sexy voice. "I picked you up over a half hour ago."

"Some women get noticed every time they walk in a room, no matter how many times." She raised her wineglass to Ally's.

Ally clinked her glass and looked down with a barely perceptible blush. "Some women, yes—Grace Kelly or Sophia Vergara, but not me."

Ally's modesty in the face of a million reasons to brag was one of her most endearing qualities. How could such a radiant woman look into a mirror and not notice what was so tangible to others?

"I didn't mean to embarrass you," Belle said. "It's how I feel." She chomped into a garlic stick that had recently arrived and pointed the bitten-off end at her. "You knock my socks off, kid."

"You don't clean up half bad yourself," Ally said with a giggle as she gently flicked garlic-bread crumbs off Belle's chin.

"Thank you." She dusted her napkin across her chin area for a final sweep. "I've dated attractive women before, Ally, all types, but you're unique. You're a trifecta—gorgeous, empathetic, and super intelligent."

"Gosh. Now you're really embarrassing me," Ally said with a wink.

"By the way, I'm texting you Charlene's telephone number. When do you think you'll give her a call?"

"I said I'd think about calling her. Right now I have—"

"What do you mean, *think about* it? She got really weird on the phone after I told her about the baby. Her whole tone changed. I think it's a sign."

"Of course her tone changed. She went from strolling down memory lane with a distant relative of her childhood friend to learning about a dead infant buried in said friend's backyard."

Belle narrowed her eyes skeptically. "You don't think there's anything to her going all quiet and rushing to get off the phone after that? What if it was hers?"

"It wasn't hers. Her brother's DNA would've indicated some type of relationship if it was."

"What if they were all adopted?" Belle said excitedly. "Then what?"

Ally opened her mouth but hadn't seemed ready for the far-fetched.

Belle grinned. "I'm messing with you. But seriously, what if she knows whose it is and is afraid to speak up?"

"I didn't say I wasn't going to call her," Ally said, clearly trying to suppress her growing frustration. "She's going on the list of leads, and I will most likely call her within a week."

"But what if—"

"Honey, can I interrupt you for a minute to remind you about tomorrow?"

"Yes, I'm sorry." Belle took a breath and spread butter on another garlic stick. "What's tomorrow again?"

"Chloe's equestrian competition." This time she couldn't mask her vexation. "Do you still want to go?"

"Yes, yes. Of course I do. Why would you even ask?"

Ally shrugged. "You're fixating on the investigation again. This is our time tonight, Belle, not a working dinner. We're supposed to be enjoying each other."

"You're right." Belle lowered her head in shame.

"I got to thinking about us this afternoon," Ally said, caressing Belle's forearm. "And I realized that even though we're saying I love you, there are so many little things I don't know about you."

"That's true, but isn't that part of the fun of dating—peeling back each layer of who we are detail by detail?"

"That's the thing—I'm worried we're skipping that part."

"You're right again." Belle put down the bread and grabbed Ally's hand. "What else would you like to know about me, Ms. Yates?"

"Well, uh…I'm not sure. Okay, you're an English professor, but what do you like to read for fun?"

Belle grimaced. "Ugh, really? Favorite authors?"

"Come on," Ally said with a persuasive grin. "Just play along."

"Okay." Belle wiped her mouth and dug into the topic. "Mystery. I'm a nut for Sue Grafton and James Patterson novels. Oh, and I was all about Patricia Cornwell in the nineties."

"I can't say that's a revelation. How about romance?"

"Huge romance fan," Belle said. "But I'll be honest. Over the last few years, my romantic life was such a mess I was finding more pleasure in murder."

"Not that I want to poke a sleeping bear, but that reminds me. Have you heard from Mary lately?"

"Not a word. After I gave her the money for a storage unit, she moved her things out without further incident. Despite her recent miscues, she's not a bad person. We were never right for each other, though. That reminds me. I have to head down there and put my unit on the market."

"You're really going to sell it before you sell this place?"

"What's the worst that can happen? I have to stay up here longer than expected."

Ally's face bloomed into a fragrant smile. "That's the best-case scenario for me. But it would mean a horrific work commute for you."

Belle flicked off her sandals, allowing her toes to roam freely over Ally's bare shins and calves. "When I told my father I'd take on the massive project that is this house, I had only two things in mind—my dream waterfront home and change. Back then I couldn't have defined what kind of change I was looking for, but after falling in love with you, it's Caribbean-water clear. When I'm with you, and even with you and Chloe, I'm the happiest I can remember being in…forever."

"Honey, I'm so glad to hear you say that. As crazy as things have been at times, you've brought my life to a new dimension. And I'm so happy you like Chloe and are including her in your vision. You're the first woman who's truly made me believe a family is possible—not that Chloe and I haven't been a family, but you know what I mean."

Belle luxuriated in the glimpse of Ally's vulnerable side. "I know that both our instincts tell us it's too early to plan for the future, and that's okay, but I want you to know that I can't imagine needing anything else in my life."

As the waitress approached with their entrées, Ally's gaze promised Belle she felt the same way.

Back at Belle's house, she and Ally sat at opposite ends of the antique claw-foot tub with a light covering of scented bubbles. Sipping chilled Prosecco, they gazed at each other in the glow of candlelight.

Belle smiled at the absurdly perfect situation she was soaking in. What was supposed to be a summer of self-reflection, isolation, and drudgery was turning out to be the most thrilling of her life. She was falling deeper in love with Ally each day. From sharing the intrigue of her career as a crime investigator to quiet moments like this, Ally was helping her connect the dots to complete the picture of a future Belle had almost stopped believing in.

"What are you thinking about?" Ally began to massage one of Belle's feet.

Belle smiled shyly. "Nothing."

"There's no way it's nothing. Tell me, or I'll have to use refined interrogation techniques to get it out of you." Ally gave the bottom of her foot a tickle.

Belle shrieked with laughter and accidentally splashed water in Ally's face as she freed her foot.

"You better confess, woman." Ally attempted to grab hold of her leg again as it flailed.

"All right, all right," Belle shouted. "I surrender."

They let the bathwater settle as they gazed at each other again.

"I was thinking about how I could really get used to having you around."

"What a coincidence," Ally said as she gently caressed her leg. "I could get used to being around."

Belle's heart soared.

"Speaking of hanging around," Ally said, "let me know when you want me to do a landscape design for the yard."

"You were serious about that?"

"Sure I was. I've been sketching out some ideas for in front of the porch and in the backyard. All you have to do is pick the spot."

"Why haven't you shown me?"

"I didn't want to seem pushy," Ally said, glancing down as she stroked Belle's calf.

"The painters are almost done with the outside, so any time is good. By the way, nowadays we describe girls as assertive, not pushy. And I happen to find assertive women very appealing."

"Yes, so you've said." Ally added a flirtatious arch of her eyebrow.

"I can be a flirt, too, you know. Just not with that awesome eyebrow thing you do."

"Don't sell yourself short, Ms. Ashford. You have some praise-worthy talents of your own."

Belle reached into the water between Ally's legs and pulled the plug out of the tub. She stood and let the soap suds slide down her body.

Ally licked her lips as her eyes climbed upward.

"I'll be in my bed." Belle wrapped herself in a towel and stepped out of the tub. "Don't keep me waiting."

"Yes, sir," Ally said.

The regional high school's football field had been converted into an equestrian obstacle course for the annual New England Youth Equestrian Challenge. Belle sat in the stands with Ally, Ethel, and Shirley Morgan, already stripping off layers of clothing in the blazing sun until nothing was left to remove but a tank top. Ethel and Shirley had the good sense to bring parasols for shade, while she and Ally had only hats and sunblock for cover.

"I'm so happy you could come with Ethel today," Ally said to Shirley.

"You know Bob and I wouldn't miss Chloe's first competition," Shirley said. "He really wanted to be here, but he's not up to it, so he insisted I go to represent the Morgan delegation."

They all laughed in awe and support of Shirley's strength through her husband's terminal illness.

"Well, Chloe's going to be so excited when she sees all of you here." She clutched Belle's hand in appreciation.

"I'm excited," Belle said. "I've only been to my niece's and nephew's soccer games and dance recitals. I feel like I'm classing up."

"Ally, is that Chloe?" Ethel asked.

She pointed out a girl donned in full regalia: navy riding vest, helmet, beige chaps, and knee-high riding boots. Other than a blond braid hanging from the back of her helmet, Belle couldn't distinguish her from the dozen other girls bobbing along on their horses during warm-ups.

"Yes. That's her," Ally said, clapping and whooping for her.

Belle and the rest joined her in the applause and cheering.

"How can you tell?" Belle asked. "They all look alike out there."

"For one thing, I spent enough money on that competition outfit she's wearing that I see it in my dreams. And the palomino she's riding is Peanut, the horse she's been begging me to adopt."

"You could adopt a competition horse like that?"

"This youth organization uses rescue horses for the kids and also advertises them for adoption. It's an utterly brilliant strategy. What girl isn't going to fall in love with the horse she's teamed up with?"

Belle grinned at Ally's tough façade. "You're going to adopt it for her, aren't you?"

"I really want to, but I'm still trying to sort out the details. Boarding a horse isn't cheap, and it's not like it can live with us in my condo."

Belle thought of her spacious backyard and how it might possibly fit a small barn near the woods to house a horse. She was about to think it out loud, then realized that was tantamount to a marriage proposal in its permanence.

"I'm sure it will work out, whatever you decide," she said with a smile.

The crowd cheered as the opening ceremony began. Belle was mesmerized at the majesty of the girls and their horses in line, standing at attention during the speeches, and then by the precision the young athletes executed in controlling their horses during their individual events.

After the competition, they walked over to greet the athletes, Ally with a dozen long-stem roses from her and Belle.

Chloe ran over to them, red-cheeked and sweaty, smiling like the two ribbons she displayed were bags of buried treasure. She ran into Ally's arms first, then made the rounds hugging the rest.

"You were magnificent," Ethel said. "Ice cream sundaes on me later."

"A ribbon in each of your events," Belle said. "I'm so impressed."

"It's only second and third place, but I had so much fun." Chloe was fidgeting about with adrenaline.

"Only?" Ally asked. "This was your first competition, and you placed. That's awesome."

"I could've used more time to practice." Chloe removed her helmet and loosened her necktie. "I don't think Peanut trusts me one hundred percent yet."

"I don't know much about the sport," Belle said, "but you and Peanut looked like consummate professionals to me."

Ethel and Shirley agreed.

"One hundred percent," Ally said.

Ally couldn't take her eyes off Chloe's smile, and Belle couldn't take hers off of Ally's. Experiencing their bond and being part of this significant event in Chloe's life, she had to agree with Ally's observation—together, they had the makings of a family.

CHAPTER FOURTEEN

As they approached the shrubbery-lined raised ranch of Marjory Dixon's daughter, Olivia, Belle stopped Ally halfway up the sidewalk.

"What's our fictitious reason for being here again?"

"You're not going soft on me now, are you?" Ally asked.

Belle scratched at the hives on her chest. "Having to keep all these lies straight is doing a number on me."

"Belle, what are you nervous about? You're doing some research on Danville and the Ashford family—just like we said when we first talked with McKeenan."

"This is different. We're meeting with her to talk about her dead mother. What if she starts asking me questions I can't answer, and I choke?"

"Follow my lead, and you'll be fine," she said, rubbing Belle's back as she ushered her toward the porch. "I'll do all the talking."

"Just ring the bell and get it over with."

"Hello, ladies." Olivia opened the door with a wide, welcoming smile and held the screen door open for them.

After the introductions, she led them out to the back deck, where shrieks of laughter and splashing coming from the pool grew louder as they approached.

"We're not intruding on anything, are we?" Ally asked.

"No. I'm spending my week off from work watching my grandkids while my son and his wife are on an Alaskan cruise.

What's wrong with that picture?" She laughed, clearly loving her assignment. "Hope you can join us for a little lunch." She indicated a spread of a mammoth fruit salad and platter of finger sandwiches laid out on the umbrella table on the pool deck.

Belle couldn't help staring at the woman, who was somewhere in her fifties. Her life seemed totally average, wholesome, and pleasant. If her late mother was the newborn's mother, it would contradict the picture of Marjory's life after her stint as an Ashford residence boarder to Stephen King level.

"Thank you," Ally said. "But you really didn't have to go to this trouble."

"Honestly, it's no trouble," Olivia said. "After five days with these two, I'm starving for adult conversation. Have a seat."

We'll see how you feel about that after our chat, Belle thought.

They sat around the table on the deck as Olivia poured them glasses of lemon water.

"So tell me, what can I do for you, Deputy?"

"As I said on the phone, it's about your mom."

"Oh, yes. You mentioned someone's writing a history of Danville, Connecticut."

"This is Isabelle Ashford. She's writing the historical piece, a human-interest story for the newspaper there."

"Oh. I'd love to read it when it comes out."

Belle simmered in a mild panic as Olivia's eyes turned expectantly toward her.

"Yes," Ally said. "We understand your mother was a young, single woman who briefly stayed in a rooming house when she took her first teaching job in Danville."

"That's one of my favorite stories of hers," Olivia said with a smile. "That's where she and my father met, in Danville, not the boarding house."

"Well, Belle's great-aunt, Marion Ashford, owned the house where she stayed."

"Oh, how funny is that. My mom would've loved to meet you after all these years," Olivia added with a somber smile.

"I'm so sorry about her loss," Belle said. "It was somewhat recent, wasn't it?"

"Eleven months ago. She and Dad are finally back together." She was quiet for a moment, as if honoring their memory, and then her pep returned. "So what can I help you with?"

Olivia looked at Belle, but Ally intercepted the question.

"Uh, there's actually one other thing you can help with besides your mom," she said delicately. "This may sound weird, but I'm working a cold case related to the house, and I'm hoping you'd be willing to give a DNA sample."

Olivia's face bunched in surprise. "I don't understand. Why would you need that from me for a story?"

Ally took on the air of an old friend, settling into her chair with a smile that suggested she was about to share a juicy bit of gossip. "It's not for the story. Here's where it gets even weirder. The remains of an infant were recently discovered buried on the Ashford property."

"Nooo, that's terrible," Olivia said, reacting exactly how Ally had said she wanted her to. "But what does that have to do with me?"

"It's just routine. We're gathering DNA from the women who were in the home around that time period—to see if we can make an ID on the baby."

"What does that have to do with my mother?"

"She lived at the house for a while," Ally said.

"You're not suggesting she could've been its mother?" Suddenly, Olivia's tone was anything but conversational.

"No, no," Ally said. "It's to rule her out."

Already tense from the awkward downshift in the conversation, Belle stared at Ally, who was casually spooning watermelon into a dish for herself while working over their hostess.

"We have a strong idea who it belonged to," Ally said. "But before we go to the expense of exhuming souls from their final resting place, we'd like to administer a simple test—you know, a formal process of elimination."

"Well, I can eliminate my mother right now by saying there's no way in hell any baby of hers would've ended up buried in someone's yard."

Belle's gaze darted between Olivia and Ally like they were competing in the Wimbledon finals.

"Once again, I didn't mean to imply we think it was your mother's. But now with such amazing advances in forensic science, we can add irrefutable proof to a case, if it ever goes to court, as easily as swabbing a cheek with a Q-tip."

Olivia looked at both of them skeptically, then pointed to Belle. "Did you swab her cheeks yet?"

Belle had to stifle a giggle on that one, prompting a subtle kick from Ally's boot into the side of her foot.

"Unfortunately, she's related to Marion through marriage on her father's side, so it wouldn't provide us the information we need."

"The maternal line carries the mitochondrial DNA necessary for identification," Belle added with a proud smile.

"How come I haven't heard about this case in the news? I live close enough to that part of Connecticut for it to be covered."

"We haven't reported it to the news yet. I'm following up all my leads first before we involve the public. Cold cases like this tend to flush all the nuts out of the woodwork, so that'll be our last resort."

Wow. Olivia's steely-eyed demeanor of a POW against Ally's agile powers of persuasion was impressive. What a showdown. Who was this woman? A retired spy for the CIA?

"I can certainly understand you feeling uncomfortable about this, Olivia, but it's a matter of going through the proper investigative channels. And doing the moral thing. Exhumation." She bowed her head for effect. "It's just so unpleasant."

Deuce! Advantage Ally.

"I'd never forgive myself if I had young Judy Ashford's body dug up and her bones rummaged over without first exercising due diligence in following up every lead, no matter how remote."

Olivia looked at both of them with lingering uncertainty. "Well, I suppose there's no harm in giving my sample, especially if it will help lead to the infant's real mother."

Game, set, match!

Belle's heart swelled with honor as she watched her woman finesse her way through one of the most challenging aspects of her job. She quivered at the outrageous appeal of a capable woman.

After obtaining the sample, Ally cut their luncheon short, much to Belle's relief.

"Will you please let me know when you have the results back," Olivia said as she walked them to the door. "I know in my heart that the child couldn't have been hers, but I'll feel better when you have scientific proof."

As much of an aphrodisiac as it was watching Ally do her thing, Belle felt sorry for Olivia. They'd sowed the seed of impropriety about her late mother into her head, and now who knew what thoughts would haunt her mind as she awaited the results?

In the car on the way back to Connecticut, Belle's mood was noticeably sullen. Ally squeezed her knee tenderly.

"You're so quiet. Anything wrong?"

Belle shrugged. "I feel kind of bad for Olivia. She has her mother so high on a pedestal. What if the DNA comes back a match? Then she'll have to deal with not only her loss but some terrible notion about a sordid past she was never supposed to learn."

Ally sighed. "Look on the bright side—if she does come back a match, the baby will have a sibling and a long-overdue burial."

"Still, not such a bright side for Olivia."

"I doubt it was Marjory's. I'm still banking on it being either Judy's or Marion's."

"Were you serious about exhuming Judy's body for testing?"

"I'm afraid it's probably going to come to that, once we exhaust all the leads. Marion was cremated. But if, as her next of kin, you have an objection, we can call the child Judy's, close the case, and you can bury it as an Ashford."

"Ugh. My father is her next of kin, not me. I'll pass that ball to him. Do we have time to stop for a drink?"

"Sure." Ally grabbed her hand. "You've been a great sport, Belle."

"Yeah, great sport," Belle mumbled as she sifted through her purse for lip balm. She picked up her cell phone and noticed a message from Charlene.

Belle put the phone on speaker and played the message.

"Hi, Isabelle. This is Charlene Highland, Craig Wheeler's sister. I wanted to let you know the other day my brother and I were talking about the Ashfords and the baby, and as we were jogging each other's memory, we sort of remembered that boarder's last name. It was either Rubinski or Ravinski, a B or a V. We weren't sure. I hope this helps. Bye now."

"It sure does help," Ally said, trading smiles with Belle.

"This is awesome," Belle shouted. "This completes the set. Thank you, Charlene!"

"Want to skip the drink and head to the station so I can start running the names?"

"Uh, yeah. I'll start doing it now on my white-pages app."

Ally glanced over at her. "You're so stinking cute."

By the next day, Ally had located a middle-aged man named Philip Rivansky Jr, living in central Connecticut. When she called him, the man informed her that his father was living in a convalescent home suffering from Alzheimer's disease. He was not helpful beyond that.

As had become the custom, Belle rode shotgun monitoring the directions app as they drove down to the nursing facility a few days later.

"This is kind of exciting," Belle said. "We're actually gonna get to meet the legendary Three-fingers-Phil."

"At least we'll know we have the right guy."

"So what kind of information do you think you'll get out of someone with Alzheimer's?"

"You'd be surprised. It works to our advantage that we're looking for info from decades ago. If I needed to know something that happened last month, forget about it."

"Is the son meeting us there?"

"I hope not. He wasn't very cordial on the phone and has no idea I'm making this visit. That's why we're going in the middle of the day. Hopefully he's at work now."

"That's not illegal?"

"I'm going to ask him a few questions, not kidnap him."

"What if he can't answer them? What if he refuses to give you his DNA?"

"Let's not get carried off in *what-ifs*. With McKeenan's sample coming back a negative match, it's crucial that I get one from this guy. He's the last known male connected to the premises."

"If you do get it, and he does come back a match, what good will it do when the guy doesn't even remember his own name?"

"Half the puzzle with be solved," Ally said. "And if we exhume Judy and make a match there, then case closed."

"Then what? Can you even charge him with anything?"

Ally sighed. "You're stressing me out with all these questions, honey. Let's put out positive vibes, okay?"

Despite Ally's air of righteous authority as they checked in at the desk with a bouquet of store-bought flowers, Belle didn't care for the persistent feeling that they were doing something sketchy as they strolled down the hall toward Mr. Rivansky's room.

Ally knocked on the half-open door and entered without waiting for his verbal response.

"Hello? Mr. Rivansky?" She said it loudly enough, but he continued staring out the window from an upright recliner, his left hand shaking on the armrest.

"Mr. Rivansky?" she said again, crouching over him.

He finally turned and looked at her, his eyes vacant portholes.

"Hello, I'm Deputy Ally Yates from the Danville sheriff's department." Her hand was extended to him for a moment before he raised his right one to shake. "This is Isabelle Ashford."

"How do you do?" Belle shook his hand, minus the two fingers, before he retracted it.

He looked at them both with sunken, glassy eyes but didn't say a word.

"Can I ask you a few questions, sir?" Ally said.

His lips twitched, and then he returned his gaze to the gray morning.

"Dinner's on me if you can get one word out of him," Belle muttered.

Ally backhanded Belle's upper arm at her irreverence. "Mr. Rivansky, do you remember living in Danville?" She began a slow, gentle line of questioning. "Danville, Connecticut? About forty or fifty years ago? The Ashford Place...over on Birch Hill Road?"

He coughed a little and patted at his mouth with a balled-up tissue from his lap.

"Do you remember the name Ashford? Marion Ashford?"

He turned to look at her.

"Do you remember Marion Ashford?" she repeated.

"Marion," he said in a weak, raspy voice.

"Yes, Marion," Ally said. "Do you remember her?"

"Marion," he repeated and placed his hand to his heart.

"He remembers her all right," Ally muttered to Belle.

"I'm about to ball my fucking eyes out," Belle replied.

A perky nurse entered pushing her computer on a cart. "Good morning, Mr. Rivansky," she said loudly. "Hello." She acknowledged them with a chin jut. "Sorry to interrupt. I have to take a few vitals."

"No problem," Ally said, and they both stepped back to give her room.

"Who are your visitors?" she asked him as she took his blood pressure. "Your nieces? Granddaughters?"

Belle chuckled. "I wish I was young enough to be his granddaughter."

"Actually, we're friends of the family." Ally pointed to Belle. "Her aunt and Mr. Rivansky were good friends back in the day."

"Oh," the nurse said as she scanned for a temperature. "Well, he doesn't say much, but I'm sure he appreciates your visit."

"Is he able to communicate in full sentences?" Ally asked.

"No," the nurse said. "He'll say individual words occasionally, but he's essentially nonverbal."

"But he hears us, right?" Belle asked.

"He does," the nurse said. "And he understands some simple, direct questions but can't answer them with more than a nod or a word or two. Mostly, he stares out the window or at the television all day."

Belle's heart sank. What if this was her father someday? She couldn't bear the thought. "Does his son visit?"

"I think he has two sons," the nurse said. "They alternate visits once every week or two."

"That's it?" Belle asked.

"When the disease advances to this stage, sometimes children avoid regular visits. It's devastating not to be recognized by your own parent." She suddenly smiled. "I believe deep down inside he knows you're here for him, and it makes him happy."

Belle swallowed her emotions as her eyes stung with tears.

"Let's have a cocktail now, Mr. Rivansky," the nurse said. She poured him a fresh cup of water from his plastic pitcher and held the straw to his mouth. He took several sips, and then she placed the cup on the rolling tray table beside him. "It was nice meeting you, ladies."

After the nurse towed her cart out, Belle and Ally looked at each other. Belle shrugged, wondering what came next.

"So, Mr. Rivansky," Ally said softly into his ear. "Any chance you'll consent to me taking a cotton swab of the inside of your cheek?"

Ally stood straight up, crossed her arms over her chest, and glanced at Belle as the old man maintained his gaze out the window.

"Mr. Rivansky?" Belle said, then turned to Ally. "The only time he even acknowledged our presence is when you said 'Marion.' He can't give you his consent."

With her elbow resting on her forearm, Ally pressed her knuckles against her lips in contemplation. "No. It doesn't appear that he can."

Belle sulked with resignation. "Are we done here?"

"Yes, just about." At that, Ally pulled a small brown evidence bag from her cargo-shorts pocket, plucked out Mr. Rivansky's straw with a tissue, and placed it inside.

Belle was aghast. "What are you doing? What if they have cameras in here?"

Ally sealed the bag and stuffed it into her shorts. "Then we better get going." She turned to the old man and gently squeezed his nearest hand. "Thank you for your help, Mr. Rivansky."

As she followed Ally down the hall, Belle had trouble keeping up with the brisk strides of her long legs.

"Aren't you the least bit concerned about the moral implications of this?" Belle scolded her through clenched teeth.

"Can we talk about this in the car?" Ally replied through a fake smile as they passed the front desk toward the entrance. "Ba-bye now," she said with a wave to the receptionist.

Once in the car, Ally took the bag containing the straw out and placed it in the car's console. She started the car and puckered her lips for a kiss.

"What are you waiting for? They probably have us on tape." Belle turned toward the door, anticipating a small band of SWAT-team members to burst out into the parking lot after them.

Ally snorted in amusement. "They don't have cameras in the rooms. That's an invasion of privacy."

"Sort of like stealing someone's saliva?"

"Yeah. Sort of."

"Ally, I feel like we took advantage of a helpless, sick old man."

"Honey, don't look at it that way. This will probably end up excluding him as a potential biological parent."

"And what if it doesn't?" Belle said, pressing at her heart thrumming against her rib cage.

"Then that helpless child will finally get some justice. Isn't that what all this has been about?"

"Yeah, you're right."

"It's easy to be sympathetic toward him now that he's a frail old man in a convalescent home, but what if he was the one who sexually assaulted Judy? The DNA identification is as much about solving that crime, too."

Belle bowed her head, feeling ashamed for momentarily forgetting about Judy. "Do you think if Chloe isn't sleeping over at her friend's we could hang out with her tonight?"

"Sure," Ally said with a surprised smile. "She'll be home. She has summer reading group tomorrow."

After dinner at an all-you-can-eat Indian buffet, an enthusiastic suggestion by Chloe, Belle's digestion was grateful for the movement afforded by Chloe's other suggestion, miniature golf. She and Ally took their time as Chloe and her best friend were ahead of them by two holes.

Belle enjoyed the cool evening breeze as she ate an ice cream cone and putted her ball around with one hand.

"I don't think this game was meant for multitasking," Ally said. "Want me to hold that cone?"

"This isn't the LPGA." She swirled her tongue around the vanilla ice cream.

"You better be accurately marking your strokes on that card."

"Are you the part-time mini-golf police, too?"

Ally laughed and gently swung her club into Belle's rear end. Her phone then chimed with a call. She put a finger in her ear and answered.

When Ally turned back, the jocularity of the moment had been wiped from her face.

"Everything okay?" Belle said.

"That was Shirley. Bob wants to see me tomorrow morning," she said with a frown. "He's declining faster than expected."

"I'm so sorry, honey. You really are close to him, aren't you?"

"He's the closest thing to a father figure I've had. And like I said, he was a great professional mentor when I first came on."

"You don't see your own father?"

Ally shook her head bitterly. "My parents divorced when I was in sixth grade. My dad moved to Florida for what was supposed to be a temporary job but never came back. There were occasional phone calls and summer visits, but he wasn't real great with follow-through, so my siblings and I basically gave up."

Belle's heart ached for Ally. She treasured her relationship with her father. They were best buds. She couldn't imagine having grown up without that connection to him.

"Ever thought of calling him?"

"Not really."

"Maybe he'd like to have a relationship with you now, but he's afraid you don't."

"Then he'd be right."

Ally's face tightened, and her brown eyes became storm clouds warning Belle to take cover if she planned to pursue the conversation.

"Well, I'm sorry about Bob. My shoulder is available day or night if needed."

Ally melted into a warm smile. "Thanks."

CHAPTER FIFTEEN

A few days later, the moment Ally seemed to have been dreading arrived. At the sheriff's office, surrounded by Ally's colleagues, neighbors, friends, and Chloe, Belle watched as a county judge swore Ally in as Danville's first female sheriff. Sheriff Bob held himself high in his wheelchair, a frail ghost of a figure using all his energy to smile with pride for his protégé. His wife Shirley stood behind him, patting his shoulders, stoic, yet seeming equally proud of the woman they'd treated like a daughter for so many years.

Belle flicked a tear away from her eye as she clapped and cheered fanatically beside Chloe. She'd known this woman barely three months, yet she felt as connected to her as if they'd been family forever. She put her arm around Chloe and smiled when Chloe's arm slipped around her waist, and they fell into a half hug.

The entire scene had Belle feeling part of something much larger than herself.

"I can't thank you all enough for your support," Ally said, her face a tightly wound combination of excitement and sorrow as she glanced over at Bob and Shirley. "Although I've lived in Danville only a dozen or so years, this community has felt more like home than any other place I've been. You welcomed me and, later on, my niece, Chloe, like family right from the start. Ethel, as long as I live I don't think I could ever repay all the home-cooked meals you've sent over to the station for me, and I've worn out the soles of more sneakers than a marathon runner trying to work off your peach cobblers."

Ethel and the rest of the group roared with laughter.

"But most of all, I'd like to thank Sheriff Bob Morgan for teaching me everything there is to know about what it means to be a sheriff in a close-knit community like ours. If I can be even half as dedicated and compassionate as you, Bob…"

Too choked up to complete her thought, she paused for a breath.

"Anyway, thank you all so much for your support, and I look forward to continuing to serve my community to the best of my ability."

"We love you, Ally," a male voice called out.

"I love you all, too," she replied with a chuckle. "Now, Ethel would like to invite everyone to the café for a little lunch and a lot of peach cobbler. Please come and help me eat it."

As the official gathering broke up, people began filing past Ally, offering their congratulations before heading down the street to Ethel's.

Belle whispered in Ally's ear as she received her well-wishers. "I've never experienced anything sexier in my life than you getting pinned with that sheriff's badge."

Ally grinned and muttered back, "I'll have to get a neck chain to hang it from for those occasions when there's nothing to pin it to."

"Hashtag 'winning,'" Belle replied.

Ethel had a buffet of various farm-to-table chicken and vegetable dishes made from raw materials like breads with zucchini from Shirley's garden and grilled chicken and frittatas from Perkins's poultry farm. Belle and Chloe wasted no time digging in as Ally remained hung up in conversations with local muckety-mucks, including the mayor, the selectman, and the ladies' auxiliary, which was much bigger in number than required even for a larger city.

"How's your summer reading club going?" Belle asked as she shoved in a mouthful of spinach and goat cheese frittata.

"Today's the last day, but I finished my reading last week," Chloe replied, picking apart a piece of zucchini bread.

"You're amazing. In my day, I'd leave summer reading till the last week of vacation, and then I'd have to BS my way through the book reports. Kind of incredulous that I became an English professor."

"Not really if you're using words like 'incredulous.'" Chloe grinned like a smart-ass. "And don't remind me that vacation's almost over."

"Why not? You should be excited. It's eighth grade. You're gonna rule the school. Then next year it's on to high school."

"Yeah, that's true. But Auntie and I have already fought over where I'm gonna go. I want a magnet school, but she wants me to go to a private college-prep school."

"Well, you still have time to sort it out. It will all depend on what you want for your future. Have you given it any thought?"

"Yeah. I'm gonna be a veterinarian."

"Then that's easy. A college-prep school's the way to go."

"But the magnet school I want is an agricultural one where we work hands-on with livestock and stuff."

Belle raised her free hand in surrender. "Ooh, okay. I'm out of this one."

Chloe narrowed her eyes in disappointment. "Chicken."

"Don't mind if I do," Belle said and headed over to the buffet of food trays arranged on the counter.

Just then Ally was freed from her conversation with the mayor, a portly man with a shock of black hair, a booming voice, and eyeglasses that dug into his plump cheeks.

"Have you eaten anything yet?" Belle asked, gnawing at a fried chicken leg.

"Not yet," Ally said somberly. "Bob and Shirley are getting ready to leave. Where did Chloe disappear to? This could be the last time she'll see him."

"She probably went out front with the other kids."

"I'm gonna walk them out. Come with me?"

"Sure." Belle caressed her back as they accompanied Bob and Shirley and helped them into their Suburban.

They'd kept the good-byes as short as possible, everyone trying not to tear up again. Ally and Belle returned to the reception inside Ethel's.

"This must be so bittersweet for you," Belle said. "It makes me sad to see you upset when this is such a big moment in your career."

"Thanks. I am proud and excited and all that, but it bothers me so much that their daughter hasn't flown home at a time like this."

"Daughter? Bob and Shirley have a kid?"

"An adopted daughter," Ally said. "They've been estranged for years. As far as I know, she's been back here to visit only once in the twelve years I've lived here."

"I can't imagine not seeing or talking to my parents. What happened? Did they ever tell you?"

"It had to do with her husband. He was undocumented when they first met, and they didn't want her marrying him, so she ended up taking off with him to Florida."

"Are Bob and Shirley racists?"

"No. They're not racists. They just envisioned a more secure future for their only child than to marry an undocumented factory worker who didn't speak very good English. Shirley said Debra was always a stubborn kid, and if you ask me, pretty ungrateful."

"That's a shame. She's going to regret all that wasted time when he's gone."

Ally smiled at her. "You're lucky you don't have family drama. I admire how whenever you talk about your family, it's always positive."

"I guess I'm lucky in that regard. I'm going to have them up for a cookout soon now that the house is almost done. I can't wait for them to meet you and Chloe."

"We're at the 'meet the parents' stage already?" Ally said with a smile.

Belle fluttered her eyelashes. "I think so. But if you think it's too soon…"

"No, no. It's great. I'd love to meet them."

"You've made a wise decision. Every person should have the chance to taste Patricia Ashford's homemade baked macaroni and cheese at least once in their lifetime."

"Then how could I refuse?"

"You can't," Belle said. "Just like I can't refuse anything you offer."

They shared a sweet kiss outside before returning to the celebration.

❖

The next morning Belle made sure she was up and out early. It was Ally's first official day on the job as sheriff, and she wanted her to start it off with a breakfast of one of her favorite guilty pleasures, Ethel's cheese-and-apricot Danish, and coffee.

Bob was also being transferred into the hospice facility, so it was going to require a lot more than pastries to help Ally get through the day.

"Looks like we got ourselves a new sheriff in town," Belle said in her best Sam Elliot cowboy drawl. She placed the tray of coffees and bag of Danishes down and dropped into the seat by her desk.

"And it's gonna be my pleasure to serve." Ally gave her a peck on the lips and tore into the bag. "Camiotti, get out here. If you're gonna be the new second-in-command, you gotta learn how to eat like one."

After a moment, an olive-skinned kid with a five o'clock shadow at eight in the morning came out of the bathroom straightening his belt buckle.

"Sorry. First-day jitters." He grabbed his coffee and Danish, and bit into it with a nod to Belle. "Thanks. I'm gonna take it to go."

"Have at it, Deputy." Ally saluted as he headed out the door.

"So," Belle said with a smile. "How's it going so far?"

Ally looked at the wall clock as she chewed. "It's 8:05."

"I know. I want to make sure you're settling in okay."

"You're adorable." Ally reached across her desk for another peck on Belle's lips.

"What's on your agenda for today?"

"After Shirley gets Bob settled in, she's coming by, and I'm going to help her with his arrangements. He's already told me he wants a wake first, then to be cremated."

Belle grimaced. "Ugh. What a job to have when your loved one's still alive."

"It's not going to be much longer. Bob insisted that we get it all done before he's gone. He doesn't want Shirley worrying about any of that afterward."

"He's a good husband," Belle said with a smile.

"She's a great wife," Ally added. "They got lucky finding each other so young."

"I've come to realize that it doesn't matter when you find the right one, as long as you find her."

"I couldn't agree more."

They exchanged warm smiles.

"How are you doing—you know, about Bob?"

Ally shrugged. "What can I do? It's happening. Right now my main focus is being there for them, whatever that entails."

"Have they heard from their daughter yet?"

"Not that I'm aware of. At one point I'd asked Shirley, but she just shrugged, and then it got really awkward, so I haven't asked again."

"I can't imagine anyone doing a better job at being a daughter right now than you. Danville is in stellar hands with Sheriff Ally Yates at the helm."

Ally smiled with the warmth and attentiveness that were constant reminders she was the one for Belle.

"In the meantime, I have to do some paperwork and sort through this mail, so that will keep my mind occupied until I hear from Shirley." Indicating the mail with a wave of her hand, she knocked over a stack of envelopes, then grabbed one from the pile. "Ooh, it's from the crime lab. This must be Olivia's DNA results," she said, tearing into it.

Belle pressed her palms together. "I hope it's positive. No, wait. I hope it isn't. I don't want it to be Olivia's mother's. It'll devastate her."

"Relax. It's not hers."

"Are you sure?" Belle said.

Ally glared at her. "Zero point zero, zero, one, three is as sure as I'll ever be about anything."

"Then old Phil is the last hope. Did you hear back on his yet?"

"I'll get it by the end of the week, if not sooner."

"If he comes back a negative too, does that mean you'll exhume Judy?"

"We'll have to anyway, but in that case, I'm gonna call the local TV news. Bob had advised me not to because of the negative attention it would draw to the town and especially to your house. He'd said lotsa luck trying to sell it if you have some grisly murder attached to it."

"He has a valid point. Then I'll be known as the Morticia Addams of the Ashford Place. No, thanks."

"Or we could skip the circus and exhume Judy's body. My gut tells me that even if Phil's sample isn't a match, Judy's DNA will be."

Belle glowered. "Then we'll never find out who molested her."

"The chances of that were slim from the start, babe. If nothing else, at least the baby will have an identity…sort of."

Belle was quiet for a moment, her gut telling her Ally was right. "Were they able to determine if it was a boy or a girl?"

Ally gazed at her with eyes sparkling with humanity. "A boy."

Belle managed a wan smile. "Hmm. He'd probably be around your age today."

"Just about."

"I'm gonna take a ride down and see my parents. Talk to them about exhuming Judy."

"Good idea. We could start to get the ball rolling on that."

Belle gave her a kiss, then headed out on the road.

Belle sat on the sofa in her parents' family room watching the Yankees game with her father after dinner while her mother finished cleaning the kitchen.

"Are you sure you don't want to take any leftovers home?" Her mother wiped her hands on a dishtowel in the archway of the family room.

"No. I'm all set. Sit down now and watch the game with us, Mom."

"Who's winning?" She tossed the dish towel at her husband in his recliner and sat next to Belle.

"Nobody. It just started," Belle said.

Her mother picked up her iPad and opened the Candy Crush app. "Are the authorities really going to exhume your father's cousin?"

"They have to if they're ever going to find out whose baby it was. Believe me, I wasn't too keen on it at first—I mean the idea of disturbing someone's final resting place—but Ally's gone through almost every lead."

Her mother looked unnerved.

"Dad, you're okay with it, right?"

"Yeah, I suppose. They gotta do what they gotta do."

Her mother shivered. "I've seen them do it on those crime documentaries. It's so gruesome."

"The whole situation is gruesome," Belle said. "I can't wait till they close the case."

"Have you decided what you're going to do with the house?" her father asked.

"Not yet, but the scale's tipping toward keeping it."

"You're going to live up there?" Her mother sounded alarmed.

"I'm thinking about it."

"Why would you want to move up there when there's so much down here along the shore?"

"There's a lot up there, too. It's just different."

"You mean that deputy sheriff," her mother said, suspiciously.

"Yeah. She's a big part of it."

"Oh, Belle, haven't you learned anything from Mary? It's not wise uprooting your entire life for a woman you met a few weeks ago."

"But Mom, she's not like any…Dad, you wanna jump in here?"

"Nope. I'm good." He waved his hand while his eyes remained glued to the TV.

"She has a child, too. You want all that added responsibility?"

"Mom, it's her child, not mine. Besides, I've hung out with Chloe several times. She's an awesome kid. I've really enjoyed the time we've spent together."

"If it were any other reason…"

"I haven't made any final decisions yet." She faced her mother to plead her position more earnestly. "Look, I know it seems like it's all happening so fast, but you don't understand how I feel about Ally. She's the most amazing woman I've ever met."

"Jim, are you just going to sit there like a boob?"

Her father craned his neck to glance over at them. "Just don't move her in until you've seen her through a winter."

Belle and her mother looked at each other.

"The winter?" Belle said.

"What does that have to do with anything?" her mother asked.

"They get a ton of snow up there," her father said. "See how she is during a bad bout with cabin fever. If you can stand her through a New England winter, you know she's a keeper."

Belle laughed at her father's bad dad aphorisms.

"Is that how you knew you wanted to marry me?" her mother asked.

"Nah…You were working at the restaurant at the time. I didn't want one of those horny Italian waiters getting his mitts on you."

"Oh, Jim." Her mother tried to hold back a smile.

"You snagged yourself a real romantic there, Ma." Belle tapped her mother's knee as she rose from the sofa.

"Would you like some ice cream, hon?"

"I'd like to know I have your support on this if that's the decision I make."

"We'd feel better if we knew you're giving this enough thought, Isabelle," her mother said. "I don't think I have to remind you…"

"But you will anyway…"

Her mother pretended to swat her with her iPad. "I don't have to remind you that your previous hasty decisions have gotten you into more than one fine mess."

"Can't argue with her there, princess," her father said, his eyes still riveted to the game.

Belle sighed. "Okay, fine. You guys win. I'll spend the remainder of my years a cold, hard-hearted woman ruined by bitterness and regret. At least you have one daughter who's made a proper home and life for herself."

Her mother smiled. "Speaking of Carolyn, have you asked her opinion?"

"She said if I was smart, I'd stay single for the rest of my life and enjoy all my disposable income in ways she can only dream of."

Her father laughed. "That's my practical firstborn."

"You know we'll support whatever decision you make, Isabelle," her mother said. "But make sure you give yourself enough time to think it through."

"I will, Mom," Belle said.

She hugged her mother and kissed her dad on the forehead before leaving.

Despite how badly her idealistic heart wanted her parents to be wrong, she knew they'd given her some spot-on perspective.

CHAPTER SIXTEEN

Belle sat on the newly painted steps of the veranda at dusk sipping iced green tea, still reeling from Ally's earlier phone call. Three-finger Phil's DNA had come back a negative match. With no leads left for male DNA, Judy's rapist was all but guaranteed eternal impunity.

She absently raked her fingers through Red's coat, shaking wisps of fur into the air. The tea was supposed to relax her, as was calmly stroking the dog, but she was still stewing.

"I don't get it, Red." She held his face as she vented. "Do you know how many cold-case detective shows I've watched where something as microscopic as a carpet fiber ends up breaking a fifty-year-old case wide open?"

He licked her mouth, then directed his attention toward a couple of blue jays scuffling on the front lawn.

"Anyway, I appreciate you stopping by to check on me."

She draped her arm around him and picked up her cell phone, muttering, "I'm hoping Karma's real, and he's receiving his in some Dante's *Inferno*-type dimension of hell."

She called Craig's sister, Charlene, to give her the courtesy of letting her know how her lead about Phil had panned out.

"Oh, he's alive, and you actually found him?" she asked.

"Yeah. That's something, isn't it? The investigators are top-notch."

"That's wonderful. Was he able to give you the information you were looking for?"

"Unfortunately, no. He's pretty gone with Alzheimer's. They were able to determine he isn't the father of the deceased child, though."

"Oh, I'm sorry. I thought that's what you were hoping to find."

"It was, but it's also essential to rule people out."

"Yes, I suppose," Charlene said.

Belle allowed the silence to linger for a moment as she gathered the nerve to ask Charlene her next and what would possibly amount to her last question.

"Charlene, would you mind if I ask you something personal—about your family?"

"Um, okay…"

"When I'd talked to your brother," she said delicately, "some family issues came up. Craig said your parents had divorced because your dad drank and was abusive."

"Yes, he was. Craig and my mom got the brunt of his violence. He was the oldest and always tried to defend our mom—and us. He'd make my little brother and me hide before Dad staggered into the house. Boy, there were never three kids happier about their parents divorcing than us when Mom was finally able to get away from him."

"Your dad never beat you?"

"I didn't say that. I got it once in a while, too, but I got other abuse, being a girl and all."

Aha! That bastard. Belle was exhilarated at the possibility that she was about to solve the mystery all by herself grilling Charlene. She swallowed her exuberance and steadied her voice.

"Craig said that Judy didn't like to go over to your house."

"She came over a few times. But as a general rule, we never wanted friends over our house. The way we lived was too embarrassing."

"Forgive me for asking this, Charlene, but did your father ever…sexually abuse you?"

"No," she said emphatically. "No. He never did that."

Belle wasn't buying it. Charlene was denying the direct question reflexively out of humiliation, even after all these years.

"But you said he did different things to you, being a girl…"

"Oh, no. That isn't what I meant. He wouldn't punch me either, but he enjoyed doing other abusive things. He'd shove me around or throw his dinner plate full of food all over the kitchen and make me clean it. Or dump the kitchen garbage can on the living-room carpet for me to clean. Charming things like that. He was just a cruel, petty drunk toward me."

Just. As if psychological torture was somehow less devastating.

"Charlene, do you think there's any way the man Judy wrote about hurting her could've been your father?"

"You mean hurt as in molested?"

"Yeah."

After a lengthy pause, she exhaled into the phone. "I honestly don't think so, Isabelle, and it's not that I'm trying to protect the man's reputation. He'd destroyed that and our family name decades ago."

"I'm sorry. I hope I didn't offend you by asking that."

"Don't apologize. I'd never realized how common that was until I finally came to terms with what happened to me, thanks to a wonderful therapist and supportive husband. Only that wasn't one of my father's crimes."

"Wait. Are you saying you were sexually abused, too, but not by your father?"

"Yes," she said firmly. "The bastard has to be dead by now, but my therapist helped me understand that my healing hadn't been about him for a long time."

"Was it another member of your family?"

"No, but he was someone I should've been able to trust."

"They always are. Was it a priest? Was it Father McKeenan?"

"No, it wasn't a priest," she replied but made no offer to name the guilty party.

"Look, I know this must be uncomfortable to talk about, but was it someone Judy also knew?"

"Yes."

"Charlene, who was it? He could've been Judy's rapist and the baby's killer. If he had kids, the cops can question them, get DNA samples from them."

"A guy named Bobby Morgan. His father was a big deal."

"Morgan? That was the sheriff's last name. Was it the sheriff's father?"

"No," Charlene said coldly. "It was him."

"*Him*? Him as in the former sheriff of Danville molested you?"

As she waited for Charlene's reply, she stood as motionless as a mannequin, her mouth parted and her cell phone fixed to her ear.

"He'd only just got on as deputy at the time," Charlene said, "But yeah. I heard he went on to become sheriff."

Charlene had to be mistaken after all these years. She wanted her to be—for Ally's sake. But deep down she knew Charlene wouldn't be mistaken about an incident like that.

Belle inhaled slowly to gather herself before replying.

"That son of a bitch," Charlene spat. "I hope he's rotting in hell."

"He may end up there eventually, but he's not there yet. Not quite."

"What do you mean 'not quite'? You're either dead or you're not."

"He's in hospice now. It's a matter of days, hours even. Who knows?"

"Please forgive my lack of empathy, but I hope his death is slow and painful."

"No need to apologize," Belle said. "From what I've heard, it is."

It suddenly occurred to her that time was no longer their friend in this case. With Bob maybe having literally hours to live, how was she supposed to break this crushing news to Ally and convince her to convince the dying man's wife they needed a sample of his DNA? Especially if it was to corroborate a claim of child sex abuse against him from over fifty years ago?

Sure. No sweat.

"Not that I'm doubting your credibility in any way, Charlene. The problem is I'll have to drop this bomb on his colleague who's investigating Judy's case, a woman who's been extremely close to him…You're absolutely certain Bob Morgan was the man who molested you?"

"I know it was a long time ago, but I'll remember that man and what he did to me—what he took from me—until the day I die."

"Would you be willing to give a statement to the investigators if need be?"

"If I didn't live in California, I'd go with you right now."

Belle smiled at Charlene's moxie. "If you didn't live in California, I'd hug you right now."

Charlene chuckled into the phone.

"Seriously though," Belle said. "Thank you for sharing your story with me. This could make all the difference."

"I hope it does, for Judy's sake. And thank you for letting me. It's even more freeing to talk about it openly and not in the confines of therapy. I guess I really have come to terms with it. Will you keep me posted on what happens?"

"Absolutely. Thank you again."

She ended the call, her hands still shaking from Charlene's stunning disclosure. She needed to tell Ally, but the mere thought of uttering those words to her left her mouth dry and pasty.

She picked up her cell. It was still hot from her conversation with Charlene. Should she call her or text to see where she was? She couldn't tell her something like this over the phone. It would have to be done with sensitivity, in person. But then the look of horror on Ally's face would be permanently seared into her brain. And she'd be the one who put it there.

She went to the freezer and pulled out a bottle of citrus vodka. After a shot that burned her throat like making snowballs with bare hands, she fixed herself a drink and sat at the island counter until she stopped trembling.

❖

After some profound soul-searching and two stiff ones, Belle decided she needed more time to mentally prepare before enlightening Ally. They had dinner plans that evening with Chloe, and she wanted to enjoy them before bringing down the heavens on Ally and the rest of Danville.

Cradling a small arrangement of flowers in one hand, Belle tapped on the half-open door of Sheriff Bob's hospice room before nudging it open. From her chair beside her husband's bed, Shirley looked up from her needlepoint and smiled.

"Belle. How sweet of you to come by. Those are so lovely."

Belle placed the bouquet on the rolling bedside tray. Shirley got up to hug her, then slid another chair beside hers.

Sheriff Bob was asleep. Or drugged. Or both. He looked pitiful—nothing like the uniformed public servant she'd first seen out and about several months earlier when she began working on the house. The disease and the attempts at a cure had ravaged him. His eyes were sunken in his skull beneath blueish, paper-thin lids, his body like a med-school cadaver dressed in plaid pajamas for a fraternity prank. He seemed barely alive as she studied his chest for the movement of breath. This was not at all the figure of a child-abusing monster, yet Charlene's accusation against him pulsed with life.

With a DNA sample, it could be confirmed beyond question.

"Was Ally here?" Belle asked.

"Yes. You just missed her. She left about twenty minutes ago."

Belle sucked at her teeth in feigned disappointment, but she'd known exactly when she'd left and had timed her own visit to ensure Ally wouldn't be there when she arrived.

It was a morose errand on her part. After speaking with Charlene, she'd wanted to see Bob as the predator she'd portrayed him as, not through the filter of the kindly father figure Ally knew, the man who'd hurt one little girl in the most unspeakable way and possibly hurt another—maybe even murdered his own son.

She glanced side-eyed at Shirley as she thought such appalling things about her dying husband. So many more were tumbling into her mind.

They'd had one child, an adopted daughter, who wanted nothing to do with them as an adult. What had Shirley known about her husband's predilections? Had he stopped messing with young girls after he'd married her? Or was his own daughter one of his victims and hanging out at a bar somewhere toasting to his terminal illness?

"Is there anything I can do for you, Shirley? Anything I can get?"

"Thank you, doll. We're all set for now. How's Chloe?"

"She's good, busy getting her summer reading and math work done."

"That's right," she said, finishing a stitch. "School will be starting before we know it. Bob always loved welcoming the kids back on the first day each year."

I'll bet he did, Belle thought, repulsed.

Bob coughed a little in his sleep, and Belle flinched.

"I better get him some more water."

"I can go for you." Belle sprang up from her chair.

"No. That's okay." Shirley laid her needlepoint aside. "I'd like to stretch my legs a bit and hit the ladies' room while I'm up. Would you mind?" She motioned toward Bob as though releasing him into Belle's care.

"Yeah, yeah, take your time," she said, hoping Bob wouldn't pick the precise moment his wife was gone to die.

When Shirley left the room, Belle tightened her stare on him. His lips moved. Was he about to speak? Make a deathbed confession? Should she have taken out her cell phone and started recording?

Nothing. It must've been a muscle spasm or something.

She glanced over her shoulder toward the hall, then pretending to look out the window by his bed, she leaned over him and uttered in a barely audible whisper, "You did it, didn't you? You raped Judy and buried that infant. C'mon. Clear your conscience before it's too late. It's not like you'll go to prison."

If he was at all lucid, that statement would've roused him. Maybe it was too late after all.

Too late for a confession, but not too late for...

She eyed his water cup, then jerked her head toward the door when she heard the squeaks of sneakers on linoleum.

It was only a hospice volunteer passing by.

She exhaled, turned back toward the bedside tray table, and continued slogging her way through the moral quagmire she'd dove into headfirst.

Shirley would be back any minute. If Belle was going to snatch the straw from Bob's cup, she needed to act immediately.

She slid the Ziploc Baggie out of her shorts and deposited the straw, holding it toward the bottom. She pinched the bag closed with her thumb and index finger, and stuffed it back into her pocket.

Whatever came of it from there, at least Belle had made every effort to do right by Judy, baby Ashford, and Charlene Wheeler. And anyone else who'd had the misfortune of being tainted by his evil.

She returned to her chair, her knee bouncing as she pretended to read a magazine, waiting for her opportunity to leave. As soon as Shirley returned, she'd be out of there to stash her plunder until she figured out how to approach Ally.

When she finally came around the corner, Belle leapt up, and the magazine flapped to the floor. "Well, I have to be going now. Are you sure there isn't anything I can help you with?"

"Yes, dear. I'm fine, but it's nice to know the offer is there. Thank you." Still holding the plastic pitcher of water, she gave Belle a peck on the cheek. "Oh, what happened to Bob's straw," she said, more to herself.

Belle panicked for a second as Shirley glanced around the table, then the floor. It gave her an idea.

"Oh, um, I noticed it on the floor, so I threw it out. I'll go get another one." She bolted out without giving Shirley a chance to respond and returned with a new straw.

"Thank you again for taking time to visit with us," Shirley said. "You're a good neighbor, Isabelle."

Belle managed a smile through her mounting guilt. How would she ever be able to look Shirley in the eyes again, especially if she was truly innocent of the knowledge of Bob's secret pastime?

Then again, what if she wasn't?

After dinner and a few games of pool that Belle had lost thanks to the residual angst from going behind Ally's back and stealing Sheriff Bob's DNA, they ended up back at Ally's making s'mores around the fire pit. She'd wanted to broach the subject of Charlene with her since leaving the hospice, but when Chloe and her BFF, Emma, met them at Ally's, Belle resigned herself to having to sit on the secret all night.

In the small yard, she watched the girls through the crackling fire when they toasted marshmallows and giggled as they mashed them between graham crackers. While Ally, sitting beside her, was maintaining a sepulchral vigil at the impending doom of her good friend, Chloe didn't seem terribly fazed about losing the man Ally had once referred to as a grandfatherly influence in her life.

Now Belle recalled the time recently when Ally practically had to shame Chloe into visiting him before he'd gone into hospice.

She shook away the thought that Chloe could've been his last victim. Chloe seemed as normal and well-adjusted as any girl. Yes, she was moody and irritable at times, but what twelve-year-old girl wasn't?

She then silently chastised herself. Not every victim of child sex abuse turned into a raging delinquent. Some suffered quietly living with the trauma. But if Bob had chosen her as his final victim, she would need intervention soon to address any long-term effects.

"Are you okay?" Ally asked. "You haven't been yourself all night."

"Really? Who have I been?" Belle replied with a smirk.

"Well, with your reticent, lost-in-the-wilderness demeanor, I'd say me of late."

Belle turned to her with a concerned smile. "Yeah, that has been you lately."

"I'm sorry. This waiting on the inevitable has me all knotted up inside."

Belle rubbed Ally's knee and smiled reassuringly, feeling like a fraud.

"And not that I have cause for lamentation, given what Bob and Shirley are going through," Ally said, "but when I envisioned becoming sheriff, I'd assumed Bob would be by my side for a while ushering me in with fifty years' worth of sage advice and colorful anecdotes about the job and the residents.

"Now here I am flying by the seat of my pants as everyone's already begun mourning their beloved sheriff."

"Oh, honey." Belle grabbed her hand. "I can appreciate how intimidating it must be to try filling the shoes of the guy who's been sheriff since Moses brought down the commandments, but you got this. You're every bit as intelligent, capable, and dedicated to the job as he was—even more so, especially when it comes to integrity."

Ally's head whipped toward her. "Integrity? Why would you say that?"

Belle gulped. "Did I say integrity? I meant intelligence. I mean you have a degree in criminal justice, after all."

"Back then they didn't need one. Crime investigation was a lot different even twenty years ago."

"But bad guys have always been bad guys. Some just had an advantage."

"That's true now, too."

"And it doesn't matter if they're behind a cassock, a desk in the Oval Office, or a badge."

"Belle, you're being cryptic. If something's on your mind, would you just say it?"

She exhaled and stared into the flames. The veil of heat was drying her lips and eyes. Yes, she had something on her mind, but it wasn't the right time. Unfortunately, if she couldn't switch off the anxiety of keeping that big of a secret from Ally, their night together would disintegrate into one replete with frustration and suspicion.

"I need a drink." She jumped up from her chair. "Want one?"

"We had drinks at dinner, several, I might add. Why do you want more?"

Belle ignored her and went into the kitchen, not to be passive-aggressive, but because she truly was about to collapse under the pressure. Inside, she poured herself a small glass of bourbon over ice, filled the gully under her tongue, then sucked down a burning gulp.

"What's going on with you, Belle?"

"Nothing. I just want a drink."

"Don't tell me 'nothing.' I know exactly what that word and that behavior mixed together mean."

The look on Ally's face devastated her—her eyes brooding and distrustful, her mouth twinging like an aging levee holding back a flood.

Belle grabbed one of Ally's hands dangling helplessly at her side. "I can guarantee you it's not what you think. Maybe we should take this iced tea out to the girls before they come in here for it."

"Belle, if you've met someone or are having second thoughts about where this is going, please show me the respect to say it. I have neither the energy nor the desire for games of any kind."

"What?" Belle cupped Ally's face in her hands to calm her. "Honey, I swear to you that's not at all what's on my mind." She kissed her passionately, a kiss that Ally hungrily returned.

"Are you sure?" Ally kissed her harder. "Do you promise?"

"Yes, yes, I promise." Belle kissed her forehead, down the bridge of her nose, and squarely on the lips, sucking at them as though trying to inhale her essence. "Ally, I'm madly in love with you. I don't want anything more than to be with you. That's why I'm scared to tell you what I need to."

"Honey, if it's not a problem with us or your feelings for me, then you shouldn't be scared to say anything. Just tell me."

"It's not something we should discuss with the kids around. Let's wait till they go to bed. It has to do with the case."

Ally scratched at her chin in apparent frustration. "In the future, you might want to lead with that instead of being all 'cloak and dagger' and practically giving me a fucking heart attack."

"Well, keep your defibrillator handy. When you hear what I have to say, you're gonna need it."

With that, Belle polished off her bourbon and took a new pitcher of iced tea out to the girls on the patio.

Ally trailed closely behind. "Okay, girls. Fill up your glasses and go inside now. It's getting late."

"Late? It's ten thirty," Chloe said. "It's so nice out. We want to stay and hang with you guys."

Ally glanced at Belle. "The other nine hundred and fifty times I didn't want them up in her room on their phones, and the one time I don't mind…"

Belle had nothing to offer except a shrug and a knowing grin.

When the fire finally died out around eleven, the girls had lost interest in outdoor quality time with Chloe's aunt. They said good night and disappeared up to Chloe's bedroom.

Ally gave the sliding-glass door an extra push to make sure it was sealed and soundproof, then hunkered down next to Belle.

"Okay. Spill it."

"All right, but you have to promise me you won't kill the messenger."

"I'm going to kill her if she doesn't give me the goddamn message already."

"I talked to Charlene earlier today. I wanted to thank her for giving us the lead on Phil's last name even though he didn't turn out to be our guy. While I had her on the phone, I figured I'd try to settle the question once and for all about whether her father was Judy's molester. She was emphatic that it wasn't him."

"Of course she's gonna say that. It's her father."

"No. I don't think so. She has no loyalty toward him. She said he was a shit father but insisted he wasn't a sex offender. She and her brother both strike me as sincere."

"What did she say?"

"That she was molested as a kid, too, so I asked her if she remembered who it was."

"And…"

Belle opened her mouth but had to shove the words out. "She said it was Sheriff Bob."

"What?" Ally's contorted face screamed disbelief, but not *how could Bob do that.* It was clearly *that Charlene woman must be out of her fucking mind.* "That can't be. She has to be confusing him with someone else."

"I don't think so. She seemed to remember the incident with stark clarity."

"What exactly did she tell you?"

"After I asked her if her father could've molested Judy, she brought up how she'd been molested, too. I asked if Judy also knew the guy, and she said yes. Then when I asked her who it was, she hesitated. She wasn't comfortable blurting it out, so I basically had to drag it out of her."

"And she said Sheriff Morgan?"

"No, she said Bobby Morgan. He wasn't the sheriff back then."

Ally paused, her mental gears evidently trying to grind out any plausible reason why Charlene could've been mistaken.

"Ally, this is the last news I'd ever want to break to you, but you can't…"

"I can't what, Belle?"

"You can't just dismiss it because you know him."

"I more than know him. I've worked side by side with him for twelve years. He and his wife have been like family to me."

"I know that. Your love and admiration for him have been apparent since I met you. They seem like great people, but—"

"You know, the Wheelers were never model citizens. They had so many run-ins with the law. Hell, her father ended up in prison, partly thanks to Bob. You said Craig still carries a grudge against him for forcing him to get his life together."

"He forced him away from Judy, which, in light of recent developments, seems like the more accurate version of the story."

Ally exhaled and rested her forehead in her hand. Her silence weighed on Belle worse than the burden of betrayal.

"I'm sorry, babe."

She didn't respond to Belle's sentiment or hand on her forearm.

"Ally, please say something."

She turned toward Belle, her face a wall of dejection. "What could I say at this moment? I'm still trying to catch my breath. I need a little time to process this."

Belle hadn't been sure of what reaction to expect, but this one definitely wasn't it. Why did she suddenly feel like they were on different teams? Why hadn't Ally thanked her for the lead and promised she'd follow up on it like all the others?

She was going to—wasn't she?

"Maybe I should leave you alone tonight, let you sleep on it." Belle felt sad even suggesting it.

"That's probably a good idea. Thanks."

What? No, no, no, Belle wanted to shout. She wasn't supposed to agree with her. She was supposed to say she needed her by her side, to make her feel better about doing the right thing.

"Are you going to try to get his DNA?"

She glared at her as though Belle had asked if she could have Bob's car when he croaked. "He's dying. He could've expired as we're having this conversation. Please, just give me some time to digest this."

Ally stood up, a blatant sign Belle was about to be swept out the door. Heartbroken, Belle stood facing her, silently pleading for Ally to change her mind, ask her to stay.

"Will you call me in the morning?" she asked.

Ally agreed but was irritatingly slow following her to the door.

It took all the self-restraint Belle had not to protest Ally's emotional freeze-out. She kissed Ally's lips, warm but unresponsive.

After a plaintive "good night," she barely made it into her car before dissolving into tears.

CHAPTER SEVENTEEN

The next morning Belle's internal alarm clock failed her. She woke late and lay in a daze entwined in the bedding, until dread seized her as she remembered her life collapsing to shit the night before. Still groggy after a bitter battle with insomnia, she reached for her phone. When she saw neither a missed call nor a text from Ally, her broken heart fused together with steely anger.

What the fuck game was she playing?

She flung the covers off and jumped into the shower, refusing to dignify that passive-aggressive nonsense with a follow-up text. Yes, it was a difficult time for Ally, and Belle's announcement had compounded her grief, but still it was no excuse to brush her off like they were only casually dating and she no longer fit into the balance of Ally's world.

By the time she'd concluded her mental rant, she couldn't remember if she'd conditioned her hair or not. Great. Now what? Skip the conditioner and risk the dry fly-aways or use it and have her hair look like she'd shampooed it with olive oil?

After her hair was blown dry and resembled dead cockspur grass, it suddenly occurred to her that maybe Ally hadn't called because Bob had died or was in the process.

Now for her next trick: making a sincere, compassionate inquiry of Ally about his well-being after she'd accused him of being a child predator the night before.

Tearing a page from her freshman-comp students' social handbook, she texted Chloe to ascertain Ally's whereabouts. When she learned she was at work and not hovering at Bob's deathbed, she planned a simple, thoughtful gesture sure to diffuse the tension from last night.

Standing outside the station, she popped a breath mint in her mouth and swiped a lip-gloss applicator across her bottom lip. She had to be ready when Ally kissed her for coming by with a plant to cheer her up.

Ally looked up from her computer with a smile. "Hey."

"Hey, yourself," Belle replied, smoothing down her fly-away hair. "Thought you might like this." She placed it on her desk with an expectant smile.

"A red salvia," Ally said, seeming mildly moved. "How pretty. What made you pick this kind?"

"First of all, kudos for knowing what it is. I'd never even heard of them. And secondly, for a trip to the bonus round, do you know what it represents?"

"Represents?" Ally paused pensively. "Hmm. I'm afraid you got me there."

"Forever mine." Belle blossomed into an ebullient smile.

"That's very sweet, honey. Thank you."

Underwhelmed by Ally's tepid reaction, Belle dropped into the chair beside her desk. "Ally, are we okay?"

"Yeah. Why?"

Was she kidding?

"No reason. I guess I dreamed last night."

Ally sighed and sat back in her chair. "No, you didn't, but I wish I had."

"I didn't mean to cause a problem between us, babe. But it's the lead you've been searching for since Angelo found the baby."

"And the timing couldn't be any worse. Shirley called me this morning. She's been calling everyone to let us know that if we want to say one last good-bye we should come today because they're upping his morphine level to the point where he won't be coming out of it."

"Shit," Belle whispered. "I'm sorry. I'm here if you need me to do anything. I can pick up Chloe and take her by hospice if you want."

"That won't be necessary. She wants to remember him during better days. She's too upset to even talk about it."

"Mmm." Belle uttered her agreement as she wondered if that was a convenient excuse for a girl who'd been creeped out enough by an old perv that she didn't even trust him in a coma.

This time, however, she knew enough to keep her musings to herself.

Ally glanced at the wall clock. "I have a meeting with Gallagher about Judy's exhumation, and then I'm going to head over to hospice. I'd ask if you wanted to join me, but something tells me you're not inclined to pay your respects."

Belle huffed in exasperation. "Ally, you know I'd go anywhere with you if you asked me."

"Under the circumstances, it'll be better if I go alone."

That one stung. "Why are you doing this to me?"

"Doing what?"

"Punishing me like I've wronged you in some way."

Ally's face turned quartz hard. "I'm sorry. I didn't realize my grief was such an affront to you."

"Please. Don't go there. You're angry at what I told you, and you want someone to blame. But you can't just…"

Belle was about to unleash the full power of her fury on Ally when Gallagher walked into the station for their meeting.

"Hey," he said as he pushed his aviators up onto his freshly-shaven head.

"'Morning." Suddenly, Ally was all sugar and spice. "You two have met, right?"

He cocked his head sideways. "Like twice already." He gave Belle a friendly pat on the arm. "Howya doin', Belle?"

Belle twitched a smile, hoping her face wasn't as fiery red as it felt. "Great, great. Good to see you. I'll, uh, let you two get down to business."

Gallagher pulled a crinkly paper from the back pocket of his khakis. "If you want to hang out for a few, you can sign off on this. They can't start digging without your John Hancock."

She searched Ally's eyes for something, the slightest signal that this was only a blip they'd soon glide past. Nothing.

Belle had reluctantly presented her with the difficult task of choosing sides, and it seemed as though Ally was choosing the wrong one.

"I have to run," she said to Gallagher. "Ally knows where to find me."

When Belle had whipped her head back and stormed out of the station pumped full of virtuous indignation, she'd expected a text from Ally by the end of her shift, if not sooner.

Three days later, however, she still hadn't heard from her.

She'd spent the day before with her friends by the shore on an impromptu brewery crawl to take her mind off the debacle that had become her life up in Danville, and also to check in with her realtor regarding her condo sale. She grabbed the laptop she'd left at her parents' house so she could prepare her course syllabi for the fall semester, which was fast approaching.

All morning she fidgeted at the dining-room table that doubled as a temporary home office, typing and answering work-related emails from prospective students and her department chair. The tasks took longer than usual as her fight with Ally had drawn and quartered her mind, and the section containing the ability to focus was the first casualty. After obsessing over her phone to the point of near madness, she finally turned off the sound and stuffed it into a drawer in the kitchen.

Why hadn't Ally contacted her? She understood her needing a day or two to process everything, but she was beginning to feel like she'd become her adversary rather than her confidante. Was Ally not as into her as she'd made her believe, and this was how Belle was going to find out? By being ghosted?

If that was how she wanted to play it…

She shifted in her chair and accidentally kicked Red, who was sprawled on the cool hardwood floor under the table.

"Ooh, sorry, pal." She ran her bare foot over his chest and tummy, then looked under the table at him. "At least I can count on one creature I love to side with me. If I have to blow this taco stand for good, will you hightail it out with me?"

He returned his head to the floor with a lazy groan.

"I'll take that as a yes."

By early afternoon, she could endure no more of her work-related exile. Her eyes ached, and her stomach kept making sounds like she was about to birth an alien, so she hopped on her bike and rode into town for lunch.

After she'd stuffed herself in at Ethel's lunch counter between the wall and some guys from Public Works, she propped the menu up in front of her face and scanned the café from corner to corner for Ally. When the sweep turned up empty, she parked her eyes on the door. If Ally was at the station, she was bound to show up near or around that time to pick up the lunch order.

Unless…now that she was sheriff, she sent Camiotti out on food runs. Crap.

Ethel would know. She lowered her menu enough to attract Ethel's attention through the clamor of the lunch rush. She finally came over to her with silverware rolled in a napkin and a paper placemat covered with ads for every Danville business and a huge congratulatory ad for Sheriff Ally, featuring her mug right smack in the center.

Belle covered it with her water glass and watched the condensation spread over it.

"Hey, stranger," Ethel said with a bright smile. "Thought you'd finished up the house and vamoosed."

"You're half right. The renovations are nearly complete, but I'm still on the fence about vamoosing."

Ethel cupped her ear. "You're putting up a fence?"

Belle giggled and raised her voice. "No. I haven't made any plans to leave yet."

"Oh, oh, I see. How's Ally doing?"

"Fine, I guess," she said with a begrudging jerk of her shoulder. "Did she pick up her lunch order yet?"

"No," Ethel said, obviously perplexed. "She's not working today. Didn't you hear? Bob passed yesterday."

Belle's stomach soured before she even placed her food order. He'd died, and Ally couldn't even trouble herself to call her. It was apparent now how little she'd meant to Ally, how dumb she'd been for allowing herself to fall so hard and so fast for the Baroness of Baggage. The former player had been played.

The warning signs had to have rained down like a meteor shower, but she'd simply refused to see them.

Again.

"Jeez. I'm terribly sorry. I know how everyone here feels about him." Belle realized as she spoke she sounded more bored than bereft. "Can I take my order to go? I want to check in with Ally and see how she's doing," she lied.

"Tell her I was asking for her," Ethel said when she returned a few minutes later with a wrapped sandwich.

Belle nodded, then stood outside the café, frozen in the swelter of mid-August heat like a small girl lost among big strangers.

Bob's straw sat pristine, its Baggie tucked inside her drawstring knapsack. A weightless piece of beach litter to the unknowing eye, it likely contained the answer she and Ally had searched for together all summer. It represented closure—maybe for more than one thing.

Was her love affair with Ally only meant to be fleeting? Summer passion ignited by the mystery of the Ashford place? And now that the mystery was about to be resolved, so would their connection?

When her eyes started pooling, she paced the sidewalk between Ethel's and the sheriff's station, clutching the sandwich in one hand and the knapsack in the other. She loved Ally with all her heart and soul; that she knew for sure. For her, it hadn't been an interlude that spiced up a summer of home renovations and self-imposed exile. She'd thought she was starting the second half of her life on a positive note, with a woman who'd not only ignited passion and desire in her body and soul but also warmed her heart with a stability and contentment always lacking with other women.

She wanted the investigation to be over, but not her relationship with Ally.

Now Bob was dead. He'd never be confronted or held accountable, never tried and never convicted for what he'd done, to Charlene or anyone else—not in this lifetime.

What message would it convey to Ally if she gave her the straw she'd swiped without her knowledge? What if Ally took it from her but, instead of following through with the analysis, destroyed it to protect Shirley and his immaculate public legacy?

The situation was untenable. In either scenario, one of them would end up hopelessly disillusioned.

She exhaled and rested against the bicycle rack outside the sheriff's office, watching a crow pick at the remains of some type of roadkill.

"Isabelle?"

She turned to see Gallagher holding the door open.

"Are you looking for Ally? She's with Shirley now."

"Yeah," she said and looked down at the sandwich. "Actually, I stopped by to bring you lunch."

"Oh. Really? Thanks." He looked puzzled as he held the door for her, and she breezed past him into the office.

"Hope you like chicken cutlets."

"I love 'em. Have a seat."

She sat in the chair next to the desk Ally normally occupied.

"Can I get you a water or something?"

"No, thanks." She looked around Ally's surroundings, absent of her, and felt herself seeping into the fabric of the chair.

"Chicken cutlet, notwithstanding, I'm glad you stopped by." He bit into the sandwich before finishing his thought.

"It's comforting to know someone in law enforcement is happy to see me these days."

He arched an eyebrow, then, "Yeah, uh, we're going ahead with the exhumation Thursday. If they can extract a viable sample, we'll know by the end of next week. The lab's gonna fast-track it for us."

"That's great." She choked back emotion.

"I know this must be tough for you," he said as he chewed, a dollop of mayo lingering in the corner of his mouth.

"It'll be a relief for me and my family." She offered a wan smile of gratitude as she watched him pinch his fingers together to pick up and eat shredded lettuce strands that had fallen onto the paper wrapping.

"Are you okay?" He asked in that *I care about you, but I'm scared you're going to emotionally unload on me* way.

She shrugged. "I wouldn't mind if this summer had a restart button."

"It's probably none of my business, but shouldn't you be with Ally now?"

"Things have gotten a little complicated between us. She hasn't told you anything?"

He shook his head. "You didn't have to be a detective to sense the tension between you two the last time you were here, but she hasn't mentioned anything. She's been really preoccupied with Bob and Shirley the last few days."

"She hasn't said anything to you about Bob regarding the case?"

"Which one? Yours?"

Gallagher's genuine confusion was a full-on gut punch. Ally hadn't even told him what Charlene had said. They were partners on the case. Surely he should've been kept in the loop concerning all the details, not just the ones she thought relevant.

Belle's worst fear about Ally's moral rectitude was being justified, and her rage at the multi-level betrayal it represented impelled her to take matters into her own hands. "I need your help," she said. "But I also need you to make me a promise."

"I'll do my best, but it depends on the promise."

"I knew you'd say that."

"Obviously, I'm not going to promise to do anything illegal or unethical. You know that."

She tightened her lips in indignation. "Detective Gallagher, I'm surprised at you. I'd never ask you to do anything illegal. I'm not stupid." She leaned toward him and lowered her voice. "The ethical part is where it gets a little murky—but only because another member of your team may or may not be dancing on that line herself."

"Ally? You have to be mistaken, Belle. There's no way—"

"Just listen to me for a second. A few days ago I shared some new, pertinent information with her that she should've given you."

"Tell me what it is, and I'll discuss it with her."

"It involves Bob, and I'm concerned that right now, given her grief over his passing, her judgment may be a little off."

He popped the last piece of the first half of the sandwich into his mouth and smiled with reassurance as he chewed. "I can't help you unless you tell me what's going on."

"Will you promise me you'll handle it on your own and won't involve her unless the test comes back positive?"

"What test?"

"Promise me, Gallagher," she shouted, startling them both.

"Okay, okay, I promise." He scratched at his goatee in apparent frustration. "I can do that," he said, as though bargaining with himself. "I can call you a confidential informant. There's nothing unethical about that. It's not like I'll keep Ally in the dark forever. Sooner or later it all comes out in the wash…"

"Bob was a child molester, and I'm positive he's the father of my cousin's baby."

"Holy fuck." Gallagher finally refocused his attention on her. "You gotta be shitting me. How do you know this and nobody else does?"

"I found one of his victims—accidentally. My cousin's childhood best friend."

"Would she make an official statement?"

"She lives in California now, but yes. She said she would."

"Give me her number then. I'll call her right away, get her back here." He picked up the other half of the sandwich and went for it.

"Can't you run his DNA first and confirm it's a match before you make her fly all the way across the country?"

The cutlet slid out the bottom of the bread and landed on the paper. "You have DNA? Why didn't you tell me that first?"

She fished through her knapsack to retrieve the straw. "What did you think I meant when I mentioned a test coming back positive?"

"To be honest, at first I thought you were being dramatic about your spat with Ally. And I was really enjoying the sandwich."

She glared at him and dangled the Baggie in front of him. "This is his straw." When his hand extended toward it, she yanked it out of his reach. "Please send it in without telling Ally. I'm reserving the slightest bit of hope that it won't be a match. Then Ally won't have to know I doubted her."

Gallagher sighed. "Okay. I'll get it off to the lab today."

"Thank you." She squeezed his forearm and got up to leave.

"I still think she deserves the benefit of the doubt," he said.

Belle smiled and crossed her fingers. "I so want to believe that."

She hopped onto her bicycle and pedaled home hard, vigorously, until her quads and shins burned and the loose strands of hair from her ponytail stuck to her sweaty neck. Nearing her house, she savored the woodsy smell of the tree-lined road and the death-metal drumbeat of a woodpecker riveting a tree.

Hopefully, Gallagher wouldn't "lose" the one and only piece of evidence that could tie Bob to such a horrid crime. Without it, Charlene's claim, Judy's scrawled revelation, and the baby's remains would be nothing more than parts of a suburban myth that began and ended with Belle.

She'd done all she could for them. It was out of her hands now.

CHAPTER EIGHTEEN

The morning of Bob's wake Danville was a society observing the same somber holiday. CLOSED signs adorned store windows along Main Street, and light traffic flowed in a steady stream in the same direction. Outside the funeral home, people lined the sidewalk, marveling at the procession of uniformed law enforcement from neighboring towns before filing in to pay their respects to their beloved Sheriff Robert T. Morgan, pillar of all things decent.

Belle sat on the stone wall out front waiting to see if the line would ever go down, apprehensive about facing Ally after her disheartening conversation with Gallagher. She closed her eyes and lifted her face to the early morning sun, finding small comfort in the thought that, after the wake, Bob was going to be cremated.

Give him a little sneak preview of where he was headed in the great beyond.

After a good hour wait, she made her way into the hall outside the room in which he was laid out. She spotted Ally through the crowd standing off to the side, a stoic sentinel ready to assist Shirley in any way. Black was definitely her color.

The thought of kneeling in front of Bob and pretending to say a prayer for him made her sick. But if there was such a being as God, he'd want her to pray for him, as wretched as he was. If anyone ever needed prayer, it was a pig like him.

"Belle." Chloe said her name as she tugged on her shirt sleeve.

She moved out of line to hug her. "Hey, you."

"I miss you," Chloe said, still clinging to her. "Where have you been?"

"I'm around. Your aunt's been wrapped up in all this lately."

"She's been so weird. She really misses you."

Belle smiled, hoping it was true. "I've missed you guys. Are you doing okay? I know he was sort of like a grandfather to you."

She made a face. "Not really."

Impelled by Chloe's cryptic response, Belle escorted her off to the side to settle her suspicions once and for all. "You spent a lot of time with Bob and Shirley, didn't you?"

"Yeah. When I was little. I stopped last summer."

"Really," she said casually. "They seemed like such a sweet old couple."

"I think Bob was starting to lose it."

"Why do you say that? Was he forgetting stuff?"

"He was just...I don't know."

The hair on Belle's neck rose as Chloe looked away. The kid was clearly growing uncomfortable with the topic.

"Did you ever talk to your aunt about him, starting to lose it, I mean?"

Chloe shook her head. Something was buried in there. Should she keep digging? Well, she couldn't just ignore it.

She took Chloe by the arm, cut across the line, and walked her down the hall away from the crowd streaming through the front entrance. "Chloe, I don't know how to ask you this, so I'm just gonna come out and say it. Did he ever hurt you in any way?"

She stared at Belle like an injured bird unsure if the human was about to help or hurt her.

"You can confide in me," Belle added. "I'm a teacher. Nothing bad will happen to you if you tell."

Her lips parted as if her words snagged on something on their way out.

Belle gently clasped Chloe's hand. "It's okay. Just say yes or no."

"No," she said reluctantly. "Not really."

"What does 'not really' mean?" Belle minded her tone, careful not to sound like she was pressing her.

"Well, he never hurt me, but he would try to get me to sit in his lap. I felt like I was too old for that."

Belle gently lifted Chloe's face up by her chin. "You're absolutely right. You are too old for that."

"Then he would try to tickle me, and I started getting these vibes—like I don't know. I didn't feel comfortable being around him anymore."

"Had he made you feel that way when you were little?"

Chloe reflected on the question. "Not really. I think it was when I started getting boobs."

Belle's stomach turned. The son of a bitch certainly had a type.

"I'm really proud of you." She smiled and clapped Chloe's hand between hers.

Chloe grinned in embarrassment. "Why?"

"One, for having the guts to share that with me, and two, for knowing you could stand up for yourself when someone started messing with you."

She frowned. "He did mess with me, didn't he?"

Belle forced a brave face for her. "But he'll never have the chance to do it again. Promise me something, will you?"

Chloe nodded.

"If anyone ever tries to mess with you again, please tell your aunt or me or some other adult you trust."

"Nobody better try," Chloe said with a smile. "I'll donkey-kick 'em in the nuts if they do."

"That'll work, too." Belle wrapped Chloe in a firm hug. "But seriously, don't ever be afraid to speak up."

"Okay," Chloe said, still clinging to her.

"Hey, you two." Ally approached them. "I was looking for you," she said to Chloe.

"Here I am," Chloe said with a flourish of her arms. "I'll go check on Shirley." She gave Belle a knowing grin before leaving.

"I was about to come in when she stopped me," Belle said. "How are you?"

"I'm doing okay. You?"

"Fine...other than missing you like mad."

"I miss you, too," Ally said, looking down. She had to have heard the anguish in Belle's voice. Was she avoiding eye contact because she felt it, too, or was it a requiem for their love affair?

"Do you?" Belle said.

Ally stared into her eyes. "Yeah. A lot. I know I haven't acted like it much lately."

"No, you haven't." Belle pursed her lips and flipped her hair back.

"And I'm sorry for the way I reacted when you told me about Charlene. I was already completely stressed out, and that pushed me right over the edge."

"It was a rather shitty position for you to be in."

"Thanks for understanding that." Ally's smile looked sincere, the first of its kind Belle had seen on her in a while.

"Even if it's true," Belle said, "what does it matter now?"

"Right."

Belle wanted to grab her by her silk shirt and yell, *No, wrong, Ally! It still matters.* Bob might have been dead, but there were people who still deserved their day of reckoning—a baby boy, a lost girl, and a grown woman who'd had to live an entire lifetime with what he'd done to her.

If Ally had known what he'd attempted to pull with Chloe, would it still not matter? As incensed as Belle was with her, she couldn't spring that one on her there.

"I'm gonna go give Shirley my condolences."

"Are you coming to Ethel's after?" Ally asked.

"Uh, I'll try. I have a meeting with a realtor later."

"Oh? For the condo or this house?"

"This one." She lied without compunction, hoping it would get a rise out of her.

And it worked. "Um, okay," Ally said, clearly working at being nonchalant. "If you can't make it to Ethel's, I'll call you tonight."

"Sure." Belle gave her an awkward hug, then turned away before she could gush like a geyser about how much she loved and missed her.

This business of being mature and rational instead of a delirious romantic was no country for old women. No wonder she'd never conducted her personal affairs in that manner until now.

She entered the parlor through the back entrance of the room to avoid the casket. Shirley deserved her respect but not him. She couldn't even fake it anymore.

Shirley was standing in front of the row of family's chairs, lovingly flanked by an assortment of familiar mourners. A middle-aged woman, impeccably dressed, sat behind her, dour-faced and seemingly disconnected as she looked down at her phone.

That had to be the daughter.

Belle gave Shirley a warm embrace and the obligatory, "I'm so sorry for your loss."

"Belle, this is my daughter, Debra," Shirley said as she put her arm around her estranged daughter. "And this is Isabelle Ashford."

Belle offered her condolences as she shook Debra's hand.

The woman smiled appreciatively, but her eyes were vacant. She was there for some purpose other than mourning a beloved parent—a claim to an inheritance perhaps, like a has-been TV star supporting a provocative politician to get his name in print once more.

Oh, what Belle wouldn't give for a private word with her.

She sandwiched Shirley's hand between hers. "You let me know if I can do anything for you."

"I will, dear. Thank you. If you can, please join us at Ethel's later."

When she'd showed up at the wake, she'd had no intention of attending the repast and toasting to that creep's memory, but now that she knew the prodigal daughter had returned...

When Belle arrived at Ethel's for the buffet luncheon, she carried out her usual scan of faces, but this time it wasn't Ally on her radar; it was Debra. Surely, the estranged daughter would have some new insight to share about her father—with the right motivation. She absently glided her hand down and felt for the pint of Jim Beam Honey concealed in her pocket.

She'd schmoozed her way through the crowd, noticing Ally, then swerving in the opposite direction toward the counter. That's where Debra stood cupping an empty wine glass in her hand.

"Hello again," Belle said. "Ready for another?" She indicated her glass.

"I suppose," Debra said. "These bumpkins may know strawberry-rhubarb pie, but they don't know good wine from possum piss."

"I was afraid of that," Belle said with the demeanor of a foreign spy. "That's why I brought my own provisions." She reached into her pocket and brandished the tip of the bourbon bottle.

"Now you're talking." Debra's iceberg face at last melted into what would pass for a smile. She turned around and plucked two Styrofoam cups from the stack near the coffee percolator on the counter.

"To the great Sheriff Bob," Belle said after pouring two shot-size portions.

Debra raised her cup, then looked away as she dumped it down, but not before Belle noticed her roll her eyes.

She immediately refilled the cups.

"If you don't mind me asking, why are you hanging back here like you're a stranger?"

"I basically am," Debra said. "I haven't lived here since I was thirteen."

"Thirteen? What were you, a child bride?" Belle forced a charming laugh as she refilled the cups.

"Boarding school."

Belle immediately sensed a story in there but was treading lightly. "Your mom must be happy you're back—despite the sad occasion."

"It's the only occasion I'd bother coming back for. In case you haven't noticed, I'm not really close with my parents."

"Eh, who is?" Belle poured them another, feeling like a shit for her shameless subterfuge. But in all fairness, Debra seemed like she wanted to get it off her chest, and Belle was providing an attentive ear.

And bourbon.

"Your dad sure was one popular guy." Belle looked around the café. "I think literally the whole town is here."

"Everybody loved old Sheriff Bob," Debra drawled.

"Mmm. Not everybody." At that, Belle hid the mouth that dared utter the suggestion behind her cup.

"I was being facetious."

"I wasn't." Belle looked directly at her.

Debra's eyes met hers and flared with what Belle could only interpret as recognition until she glanced away.

"Look, I'm a stranger here myself," Belle said. "I only ended up in Danville because a distant relative willed me some property. But since I've been here, I've heard some rumors—disturbing ones…"

That won Debra's attention back. "Like what?"

Belle shrugged. "That he roughed up a teenage boy who was dating my dad's cousin years ago. Got him sent off to juvie or some kind of military school. She ended up killing herself."

Debra looked at her, aghast. "Really?"

"Well, I don't know if it was intentional, but she definitely died of an overdose."

"That's rough." Debra drained her cup.

Belle reached for the bottle again. Although her head had started spinning, she couldn't stop now. Debra hadn't waved her off when she splashed more bourbon into their cups.

"My dad's cousin, Judy was her name, had other problems. You know, the ugly kind that sometimes happen to innocent little girls."

"Too often, to too many girls."

"Yeah, especially in Danville it seems. I talked to an older woman who grew up here who was molested as a kid. I wonder if they ever caught the guy." Belle watched for a reaction out of the corner of her eye.

"I'm sure they never did," Debra said. "He probably had connections."

"Probably." Belle sipped her drink for courage and almost tumbled off the stool. "Did you ever hear any stories about it happening to anyone you knew?"

Debra took a drink and paused, staring blankly into the crowd. Finally, she said, "I didn't have to hear them."

A little nauseous now, Belle swallowed the remnants of bourbon on the back of her tongue. "Why is that?" She already knew the answer but put it out there anyway.

With her back against the counter, Debra continued staring straight ahead, the empty cup cradled in both hands. "Why do you think?"

Belle downed the last of her bourbon and allowed a moment to absorb everything before she asked, "Did you know the guy?"

Debra nodded.

"Did getting shipped off to a private school have anything to do with it?"

Another nod.

At that point, Belle passed the rest of the pint to her.

"Did your mother have any idea what was going on?"

"It took me a year after it started to find the courage, but I finally told her." She knocked back her next shot like a cowboy in a saloon.

"What happened?"

She smiled mirthlessly. "I ended up getting the best high school education money can buy at a prestigious prep school seventy miles away."

"She didn't believe you?"

Debra pursed her lips. "I'm certain she did. That's why she got me out of there. She was one of those dutiful wives—the obedient, stand-by-your man type. And after all, I wasn't really theirs. I was adopted." She looked down at her cup, her chin dimpling with emotion. "I never went back either. I went right from Choate to Quinnipiac University. That's where I met my husband."

"You met your husband at college? I'd heard you'd become estranged with your parents after throwing your life away to marry an illegal immigrant."

She laughed derisively. "Illegal immigrant? Miguel was here from Barcelona on a student visa. He obtained his citizenship when he was hired by Dana-Farber as a cancer researcher. We're divorced now, but we have two children and co-parent them with no problems."

"You live up in the Boston area?"

She nodded as she took another swig.

Man, this woman could drink. By then Belle was pretending to sip lest she end up being scooped up off the floor by Danville's fire department that consisted of the two young, burly volunteers drinking Miller Lite by the door.

"I probably shouldn't be mentioning this, but since we're bonding here…" Belle glanced around to see who was within earshot. "There's an investigation going on that'll probably tie him to my father's cousin and the remains of an infant found in my backyard this summer."

Debra's face withered in shock and revulsion. "What? They think he killed the baby?"

"They can't determine how it died. The bones showed no sign of trauma. I've convinced myself he was stillborn."

"Amazing," Debra said. "The fucker got away with everything."

"Maybe not. If the DNA comes back proving Bob was the father, people will find out about it. He sure won't go down in Danville history as a superhero."

Debra shrugged. "Without a guilty verdict, any villain can be remembered as a hero—especially when someone's around to help rewrite history."

Belle assumed Debra was referring to her mother, but she wondered if Ally wasn't a bigger threat to the truth if she intercepted the results of the test.

"Thank you for your candor," Belle said.

On her way to the ladies' room, which seemed a lot farther from the counter than she remembered, Ally sidled up to her.

"You're not putting the moves on Shirley's daughter, are you?"

The attempt at a joke fell flat.

Belle stopped and wheeled around to face her. "Are you saying I'm free to put the moves on someone else?"

"I hope not."

"It's hard to know these days. Am I free or not?"

"Belle, I know this has been hard, but I need a little more time. I want to make sure Shirley is okay and that all her affairs are in order, and I'm still dealing with what you've told me about Bob."

The request irritated her on multiple levels. It was bad enough that Ally was still overplaying her devastation at Belle exposing her daddy figure as a sexual deviant, but Belle's patience was worn too thin for such a lame excuse for why they were apart.

"Don't you mean decide whether Charlene was full of shit or not? Here's an idea. Go talk to Bob's daughter for a few minutes, then tell me whether Charlene was lying."

"I never said Charlene was…"

Belle held up her hand. "Save it."

Overwhelmed with sadness, disappointment, and bourbon, she needed to get away from Ally before this became a two-for-one repast dinner.

❖

A few days later, Belle kicked the shovel down into the soil in the cleared-out area abutting the veranda. She'd picked up a few small azalea bushes at Busby's Farm to add some colorful curbside appeal, still uncertain if it would turn out to be for her own pleasure or luring prospective buyers.

She reached into her pocket to check her phone in case she'd missed the vibrations of a call or text from Ally. She hadn't phoned the night of Bob's funeral like Belle thought she would've—not so surprising after the way she'd stormed out.

It had been three days since the funeral, five since she'd turned over the straw to Gallagher for analysis. She was sure he would eventually rat her out to Ally despite his promise—he'd have to since they were both on the case. By that time, Ally would hopefully have returned to her old, rational self and understood Belle's decision to take it upon herself to, oh, let's call it expedite that critical piece of evidence.

Wasn't Ally missing her? Belle felt like she was dying inside, her petals wilting and falling to the ground one by one till nothing was left of her but a stem.

No notification on the phone's lock screen.

Ally hadn't even fallen into the elaborate trap Belle had set where she'd called her and ended the call before Ally picked up. She was supposed to call her back out of curiosity, and Belle would say she'd accidentally butt-dialed her. Then they'd segue into the reconciliation conversation. The scheme had never failed her before—but then she'd never dated a woman like Ally before.

She sighed and stuffed the phone into her back pocket. She flung the shovel to the ground and crouched down to deposit the second azalea bush into the hole.

That was when the sound of Ally's truck barreling up the driveway, tires spitting gravel chunks everywhere, knocked Belle off balance and onto the damp grass.

She hurried to her feet as the door slammed and Ally marched toward her.

"How fucking dare you? How could you do that to me?" Ally shouted as though she were a trashy crime suspect about to be wrestled to the ground on an episode of *Cops*.

Belle straightened her posture and wiped a forearm across her sweaty forehead. Horrified at this new version of Ally, she licked her dry lips as her heart pounded in her throat. "I'm assuming you're referring to my giving Gallagher the straw with Bob's DNA."

"What right did you think you had to go behind my back to my colleague and insinuate that I can't be trusted to do the right thing? That was totally fucked up, Belle, completely out of line."

"It wasn't just an insinuation," Belle said calmly. "Did you go and get a DNA sample after I told you what Charlene said about him?"

"And if that wasn't bad enough"—Ally's rage was now pulsing in her forehead—"you talked to Chloe about him? Where did you get the balls to betray me like this? I feel like I don't even know you."

"Did you get a sample of Bob's DNA before he died?" she repeated slowly, somehow maintaining her cool.

"Stay out of this case and stay the hell away from my niece, or I'll slap a protective order on you." She turned to walk away.

"I asked you a question, Ally," Belle shouted. "Answer me."

"No, I didn't," she said through clenched teeth. "And that should've been enough for you."

She attempted to storm off again, but this time Belle grabbed her arm.

"You should've done your fucking job."

Ally jerked her arm away. "Who the hell appointed you police commissioner?"

Belle stared her down. "You know it's true about him, don't you? Have the DNA results come back yet?"

Ally glanced up toward the trees, her nostrils flaring like a prize fighter drinking in oxygen between rounds.

"You know your sainted Sheriff Bob is a pedophile." Belle was taunting her. "Maybe even a baby killer, and you did nothing about it."

"What should I have done, Belle? Arrested a man who'd be dead before his fingerprints had time to dry? When I get the results back, do you want to come with me when I destroy his elderly widow with the news? And for what? For Justice? Judy and the baby and the perpetrator will all still be dead."

"That's not the goddamn point. That infant deserves an identity."

"And he's going to get one once Judy's exhumed. At this point, I'm certain she was his mother. And we'll probably know his father, too, once the DNA results come back."

Belle's heart became too heavy to buoy her anger. "He deserves a voice, Ally," she said softly. Her voice quavered as she choked back a deluge of emotion. "Maybe he wasn't murdered. Maybe it was a still birth, but he ended up in a bag in the ground somehow. The circumstances that led to that should be spoken. Even if it won't bring him back and the person or persons responsible can't be punished, it's the right thing to do. You're an officer of the law. I should not be standing here explaining this to you."

By now Ally's face was streaked with tears. "What do you want me to do, Belle?"

"I want them both to finally be able to rest in peace."

"So do I," Ally whispered.

"Then this isn't over—the case, I mean."

"I know." Ally shielded her eyes with her thumb and forefinger against her forehead.

Belle wrapped her arms around her, and they sobbed together on the front lawn. When Ally embraced her tightly, Belle soaked in every drop of her, loving her with every molecule of her being.

Then she stepped back.

"Listen." She wiped her face with the tops of her hands. "You can pretend that Bob wasn't Judy's rapist since they're all dead, but don't pretend Chloe wasn't tainted by his wickedness. Talk to her. Get her professional help if she needs it."

"I will."

They studied each other for another moment, Belle suddenly lost for words.

"What's happened to us?" Ally asked.

"I've been asking myself that ever since you froze me out weeks ago. I don't want a life partner who runs from me rather than toward me in a crisis. That's not what a real relationship is about. That was too hard a lesson for me to learn to ever forget it."

"I get it," Ally said softly. "And I regret the way I reacted to everything initially. But my life partner should trust me and not question my moral convictions."

Belle exhaled deeply. "You know, of all the twists and turns on this wild ride, the fact that you don't find anything questionable about your convictions in this has surprised me most of all. You let me down, Ally."

"It's so easy to judge from your position, isn't it?"

"What do you mean?"

"Why don't you ask yourself what you would've done if your father, your best buddy that he is, was dying in some hospice bed, and someone came along and made that accusation against him?"

"But my father never would—"

"That's not what I asked you. Would you let him die with dignity or do the moral thing and expose him with only days, maybe hours to decide?"

Belle's blood simmered at Ally's flip of the script. "Bob isn't your father. He was a colleague and friend. It's not the same."

"He was the closest thing to a father I've ever had."

Belle stood still as a death's head. Ally must've been as convinced of Bob's virtue as she was of her father's. Could she have answered that question honestly?

"Like I said before, Belle, what do you want me to do? To what ends should I take this to satisfy you? Should I go public with the story and ruin his name so you and your family can file a civil suit?"

Belle shook her head with a weary smile. "I'll be satisfied with ruining his name—before they start renaming schools or libraries or erecting statues in his honor. Leave him on your pedestal if you must, Ally, but keep in mind that somebody loved Charles Manson once, too."

She ran inside and slammed the door, falling against it as she bawled into her cupped hands. How could everything have ended this way? Why had she met the love of her life only to have what they shared decay before it ever had the chance to fully flower?

She took her cell out of her pocket and called her realtor back. She instructed her to reject the offer on her condo, take it off the market, and take a ride up to Danville to get the Ashford place on the market, pronto.

She had to get out of there before the house destroyed her, too.

CHAPTER NINETEEN

The morning of the interment service, Belle, her parents, and sister gathered around Judy Ashford's grave in St. Gertrude's cemetery. The urn containing the remains sat on a green, felt-covered pedestal as the priest droned a series of prayers into the thick, early September air.

Frankie Ashford was finally receiving a proper burial service, his ashes to be interred with his mother in her grave.

Belle stood between her parents holding their hands, silent tears streaming down her face from under her sunglasses. Her mother must've heard her sniffle and produced a tissue for her almost instantly.

A mother's love was instinctual, automatic. Judy must've been inconsolable when her son died, if she hadn't been scared out of her wits considering she was a kid herself.

Belle closed her eyes and let the hope and promise of the prayers lighten her heavy heart. But when the priest recited the part of the Shepherd's psalm that said, "Surely goodness and loving kindness shall follow me all the days of my life," she choked back indignation. What life? What constitutes a life in God's eyes? Sixteen years for a girl traumatized by sexual abuse? An hour or a day for the innocent boy born of it?

She wanted to believe in God at that moment of abject sadness, but the God her grandmother used to speak of was incongruous with an entity that would've allowed all of that to happen—from the moment an adult betrayed a child's innocence to the moment a human being had to die and be stuffed into an old milk crate, unnamed, and in an unmarked grave.

"Are you okay?" Belle's father whispered.

Belle nodded, but she wasn't—far from it. The tragedy of it all was too much, but so was her breakup with Ally. It was all so sad; the worst part was discovering that Ally wasn't who she'd thought she was.

She'd fallen so deeply in love with a woman who was caring, intelligent, and seemingly above reproach. And then one event happened and changed everything she'd understood about her.

It was indeed a time for mourning.

When the service was over, Belle and her family turned to leave. Charlene and Craig were standing several feet behind. Belle wiped the last of her tears and approached them, hugging each one.

"I can't believe you guys came all the way up here for this."

"We wanted to," Craig said. "Judy meant a lot to us."

"I needed this," Charlene said. "I finally feel a sense of closure after what you and I talked about—and knowing my friend and her child are together again."

"I can't thank you both enough for being so open and honest with me. The investigators wouldn't have gotten anywhere in this case without you."

"Do they know who the father is?" Craig said.

"I don't know if the DNA test for the sheriff ever came back, but I'm assuming it's him—given his dubious track record with pubescent girls."

"It's unbelievable," Craig said. "But then it makes sense why he hated that I was dating Judy. If I had known what he was up to, I would've busted his head wide open, deputy sheriff or not."

"I'm glad you didn't," Charlene said. "You would've rotted in prison forever if you had. What would I have done without my big brother?"

Belle smiled, her mood lifted by their love for each other. "Would you guys like to join my family and me back at the house? We're gonna have a little cookout and visit for a while."

Charlene looked at Craig.

"Please," Belle said. "In a way, you're like family."

They agreed and followed Belle's car back to the house.

After a simple cookout of hamburgers and hot dogs, Belle took in the traditional family scene happening on her stone patio. Her parents and Craig and Charlene were chatting like they were old friends, sharing their similar versions of the good old days while her brother-in-law attempted to get Red to chase a tennis ball.

As Belle moved the leftover side dishes into the shade, her sister, Carolyn, approached her with two crimson martinis splashing over the rims of their glasses.

"Try this." She handed one to her as though they were kids again sneaking behind their parents' backs.

"What are you doing to me?" Belle said as she sipped the pomegranate cocktail. "I'm trying to sober up from this insane summer."

"Don't be a wimp. It's the Friday before a three-day weekend."

"I'm trying to detox," Belle said.

They both cracked up laughing as they clicked their glasses together.

"If Eddie thinks he's gonna get Red to chase that ball, he doesn't know who he's dealing with. That dog is so old."

Carolyn laughed. "Let's see how long it takes him to figure it out."

"Is that what twenty-five years together does to couples? Makes them secretly root for each other's downfall?"

"I still adore him, but that doesn't stop me from relishing those moments when his stubbornness backfires on him."

Belle laughed, envying with good nature her sister's enduring marriage.

"Speaking of significant others," Carolyn said. "Where's that deputy sheriff you were so hot and heavy with?"

Belle glared at her. "I told you it's over. Way to bring down the room, Carolyn."

"I know you did, but I thought you guys would've worked it out after the case was over."

"Well, surprise, surprise. We didn't."

"I'm sorry. How are you doing?"

"I'm a mess. I miss her so much, and I'm so conflicted about everything. I have my condo in Guilford and this house, and I don't know which one to sell, but I have to sell one of them so I can pay my bills."

"Don't sell this place." Carolyn glanced around in awe. "You've done an amazing job renovating it. It's just gorgeous."

"I'm so torn. I put all of myself into it, and I love how it turned out, but it's also filled with major negative vibes—my latest relationship disaster, oh, and lest we forget, two kids died here." Belle shivered at the thought.

"We all have to die somewhere."

Belle glared at her again. "Seriously?"

"It's all about perspective, sis. I mean you inherited a free house on a picturesque piece of land, and you fixed it up into a dream house. I know it's in the boonies, but I don't know. If I were you, I'd get a shaman in here to sage the place and call it home sweet home."

"Oh, okay. Some hokey incense ceremony performed by a crunchy granola is gonna solve all my problems." Belle rolled her eyes.

"It would take a hell of lot more than incense to solve *all* your problems. I was only addressing your bad juju issue."

"Making fun of your little sister's heartache? Classy. I think we're done here."

Belle started to walk away, but Carolyn grabbed her arm.

"I'm sorry, Belles. You know I'm teasing you. It's our thing."

"I'm just really bummed. I felt a connection with Ally I'd never felt before, with anyone." She paused to compose herself. "It's been hard moving past this one."

Carolyn put an arm around her and pushed Belle's head onto her shoulder. "Call me more or come visit more. I'm always here for you."

"Thanks. I will."

"Liar. You're gonna keep on pining over your deputy all by your lonesome."

Belle smirked. "Probably. By the way, she's the sheriff now."

"Ugh. Then I guess I can understand your motivation for wanting to sell, even though I'm in love with this house."

"You're not making this any easier."

Carolyn shrugged helplessly as Craig and Charlene approached to say good-bye.

"We have to head back now," Charlene said. "Thank you again for all you've done."

Belle hugged them both. "I wish I could've done more. I wish Bob had to face his victims and account for his actions."

"I'm sure he already has had to account for them at the pearly gates," Charlene said.

Craig agreed. "If there's a hell, that's where he is right now."

Belle wasn't sure about all that, but it was a lovely idea. She needed to believe that justice would be served even if she'd never witness it.

In any event, she found consolation in having seen it through to the only outcome that truly mattered—Judy and her son were finally reunited.

CHAPTER TWENTY

Usually, the week after Labor Day was hectic, and this one did not stray from convention. With the fall semester under way, Belle had been held over on campus with extended office hours to meet with anxious students, both new and returning, and to attend the obligatory staff meeting her department chair insisted was necessary for morale building.

Pretending to take notes, she'd doodled Ally's name and various animals on her notepad, preferring the feel of paper and pen to the laptops her colleagues used. She glanced out the window at the range of trees still lush with the vigor of the late season, but her summer had come to an end.

A pall of disappointment hung over her, rather than the eager anticipation of a new academic year and autumn. She was supposed to feel ready and revitalized, splitting her time between work and house-hunting along the Connecticut shore. Instead, she directed most of her energy into forcing images of Ally from her mind and dreams of their future from her heart.

Her sadness had locked her in a holding pattern. She couldn't sell the condo where she'd lived but couldn't bring herself to let go of the Ashford place either. Her mother had warned her about putting too much of herself into it during renovations.

Really, she'd put too much Ally into it.

She was on autopilot during the hour drive home from work, listening to smooth seventies on satellite radio. Love songs from the seventies seemed more genuine for some reason.

She pulled into the driveway and rolled over the gravel toward the house. Something was different, some detail that hadn't been there when she left that morning. She lowered her window and knew right away by the scent what it was—a small lilac tree planted off to the left side of the veranda encircled by a white protective fence.

She smiled at the housewarming gift, then ran over to it, hoping it was from Ally and that she'd left some sort of note.

Nothing.

Red was waiting for her on the front steps, his wagging tail sweeping the porch behind him. After scratching his ears, she headed inside and toward the fridge, hoping a bottle of something was in there chilling.

She uncorked some white, let it roll over her tongue, and walked to the window to gaze out at the backyard. Noticing something moving in her periphery, she looked to where the koi pond was originally supposed to go. In its place was a magnificent flower garden brimming with vibrant colors, stems, and stalks of all shapes and sizes.

She stepped out onto the patio. That was when Ally stood up and wiped the sweat from her neck with the back of her gardening glove.

"Hi," she said, shielding her eyes from the dipping sun.

Belle smiled and walked slowly toward her. "Hi."

"I hope you don't mind," Ally said. "A promise is a promise."

"It's beyond beautiful." Belle was almost breathless. "But you didn't have to do all this."

"I kinda did. But I also really wanted to."

Ally bent down and picked up an oval garden stone from the center to show Belle. The name ASHFORD and a male cherub with wings holding a flower were carved into it.

"That's amazing," Belle said. "I don't know what to say."

Ally removed her gloves and walked toward her. "Say that you'll accept my deeply heartfelt apology."

"What are you apologizing for?"

"A lot of things, namely for handling everything wrong."

"You can't help the way you grieve."

"No, but there were some things I could've helped. And I chose to bury my head in the sand instead of putting duty before loyalty to a friend."

"It's a slippery slope when that friend is a child molester," Belle said. "Or isn't it? I don't know. I've never been friends with one."

"It's not at all, and if Bob hadn't been days from dying, I would've acted on what you said, without question. I would've taken time to think about it, then acted on it. But during the time I needed to deal with what you told me, he'd already passed. I'm not using that as an excuse. I own what I did. I screwed up on my first big test as sheriff, and I'll have to find a way to make peace with myself for that."

"Did the DNA come back a match?"

Ally nodded.

Belle sighed in relief. She felt vindicated for her part in their breakup, for going behind Ally's back when she'd felt she was wavering. For her, the end certainly justified the means.

"I'm an honest person, Belle. I have integrity, and my ethics may have stalled in this one case that hit too close to home, but they never failed. I would never have let that happen."

"You knew he was about to die, but you didn't take a sample from him."

"I realize that," Ally said. "I knew in my heart Charlene was telling you the truth."

Belle remembered what Ally had asked her. What if someone had made that accusation against her dying father? It was time to stop judging her.

"I made a mistake, Belle, an error in judgment that taught me a valuable lesson." She offered a humble smile. "But I got lucky."

"Lucky? How do you figure that?"

"At the time I had a nosy, mischievous, very slick girlfriend who did my job for me while I wandered lost in a moral wilderness."

Belle pretended not to be swayed. "Are you referring to me?"

"You're the only nosy girlfriend I've had recently. And by recently, I mean in the last five years."

Belle grinned. "You forgot sexy and brilliant."

Ally grinned back. "I couldn't if I tried."

Belle flung her wineglass onto the lawn and lunged at Ally, clamping her arms around her in a grip as sturdy as steel. "I love you, Ally."

"I love you, Isabelle, so much." Ally whispered in her ear. "Can you ever forgive me for the jerk I turned into—temporarily?"

"Yes, my love. Yes," she whispered back, then looked Ally in the eyes. "I hope you can forgive me for doubting you—temporarily."

Ally smiled. "It's been a wild summer. I think we're both entitled to one 'get outta jail free' card."

Belle wrapped her in another embrace, her voice quavering. "I've been so sad thinking it was over."

"God, me, too, honey." This time Ally looked her in the eyes. "I know we can make this work, Belle. Whatever the challenges, if you want to try, I'm all in."

They kissed passionately in the yard as the sun, lowering into the trees, caressed their faces. When they finally came up for air, Belle glanced over Ally's shoulder at the new botanical paradise.

"What's in there," she asked, her arms still looped around Ally's neck.

Ally beamed at the question. "In the center is a red rose bush for love, obviously; some forget-me-nots on the left; and to the right some yellow daffodils, which signify new beginnings—oh, and some jasmine over there because they represent love and sensuality."

"Wow. You must've put a lot of thought into this garden."

"I did." Ally gave her a sly grin.

"Hmm. How am I supposed to sell this place and move away now that you've planted a custom-made Eden of romance for me?"

"Duh. That's the idea—you're not."

"Did you just ask me to go steady?"

"Well, since it would be foolish to propose to someone you've been dating for only three months, yeah. Let's go with that."

Belle laughed. "Good idea. Because it's not like we've ever been fools for love before."

Ally bit her lip in mock shame. As their laughter died down, she stared into Belle's eyes. "It's different this time. I can feel it."

"Me, too."

As clichéd as it sounded, Belle knew in her heart it was true.

After demolishing a pizza and the rest of the wine, Belle and Ally sat together on the outdoor sofa, fingers clasped, shoulders resting against one another's in the waning light of dusk. Belle slid the empty pizza box aside with her foot and extended her legs across the coffee table.

"We had his service over the weekend."

"You did? I wish I had known. I would've come, even if it was just to lurk in the shadows."

"It's okay. My parents and sister were here for it. Craig and Charlene Wheeler even came. He's buried in Judy's plot with her. I'm having a footstone made with his name, Frankie Ashford."

Ally gave her a quizzical look.

"I figured since Judy was such a fan of Frankie Avalon…"

"That's sweet. You'll have to take me to see it one of these days."

Belle agreed with a smile.

"I talked to Shirley the other day," Ally said.

"How's she doing?"

"She's a tough old bird, but after our conversation…" Ally shrugged.

Belle jerked her head toward her. "What did you—did you tell her about Bob?"

"I had to. It was one of the worst experiences of my life, but I owed it to a lot of people, both here and gone."

"What did she say? Did she deny it?"

"No. She just listened with a mixture of shock, guilt, and an emotion I can only explain as relief. She'd believed her daughter when she'd told her about Bob, but I don't think she had the capacity to fathom the full scope of the situation. After I talked with her, she seemed like a woman who'd spent her entire life under the thumb of a controlling man, probably verbal and emotional abuse, too."

"Do you think she facilitated his behavior?"

"Not in an active role," Ally said. "I know it sounds like I'm sticking up for her, but I'm not. She was truly horrified when I told her about the DNA results. She had no idea of the extent of his perversions. She'd somehow dismissed his assault of their daughter as a 'moment of weakness' by an otherwise upright man."

"I guess I should credit her for sending Debra away. Some women in that position would've been too afraid to do anything except turn a blind eye."

"I saw that when I was on patrol in the city," Ally said.

Belle scoffed. "And the evangelicals say gays are unfit parents."

"I'm not perfect by any means, but after six years raising Chloe, I can assure you that nobody would get away with hurting her."

"I'm sorry you had to go through this." She kissed Ally on the cheek. "Does Shirley hate your guts now?"

"Surprisingly, no. She thanked me for everything I'd done for her and Bob. But the best part is that her daughter is speaking to her again. They're going to work on having a relationship."

"I'm glad something good found its way out of this dumpster fire."

"A lot of good did, Belle. Judy and her child are together, Craig and Charlene Wheeler received some long-overdue closure, and best of all..." She waved a finger between them. "Right here."

"This really is the best." She leaned against Ally and sighed.

"You know what else I was thinking?"

Belle's heart fluttered. What was happening? Was she going to throw caution and good sense to the wind, drop down on one knee, and go for it? She swallowed hard and forced her voice to sound casual. "What?"

"I'm thinking of starting a sexual-abuse-survivors' support group."

Belle exhaled the breath she'd been holding and smiled. "That's a great idea."

"You think so?"

"Absolutely. It's exactly what this repressed community needs."

Ally laughed and pulled her closer.

"So, my realtor dumped me," Belle said.

"You were dating your realtor?"

"No," Belle said through a giggle. "After I turned down the second offer on the house for my exact asking price, she said I should stop wasting her time and call her when I'm truly ready to sell."

"Ooh, that feisty little shit."

"I know, right?"

"What did you tell her?"

"Okay."

"You mean it's not listed anymore?"

"She's coming by tomorrow to get the sign," Belle said, casually examining her fingernails.

"Wow. I guess that makes you an official 'Danvillin' now," Ally said with a big smile.

"I guess so." Belle sneaked a coy peek at Ally from the side. "But now I own a house with three huge bedrooms, a family room, and a massive yard."

"Thinking of getting boarders?" Ally asked with a sassy grin.

Belle smiled. "You might say that."

❖

As Ally and Belle guided a blindfolded Chloe through the house and out onto the patio, the three of them cackled as they tried not to trip over each other's feet and Red, who was traipsing along at their heels.

"When can I look? I'm getting dizzy," Chloe said.

Belle and Ally stopped her on the patio, not wanting to get too close to the crate temporarily placed toward the back of the yard.

"Right now," Ally said, then prolonged the torturous suspense a bit more. "Are you sure you're ready?"

"Do you need more time to get your balance back?" Belle added.

"No, I'm ready, I'm ready," Chloe shouted.

They positioned her body toward the crate off to the left and slipped off her blindfold.

"What is it?" she said, then nearly burst with excitement. "Is it a greyhound?"

"Go see," Ally said.

Chloe bolted across the leaf-strewn yard toward the crate, and Ally and Belle trailed closely behind. Belle held up her cell phone to capture the big reveal on video.

"Oh my God," Chloe yelled when she opened the door and saw the brindle rescue greyhound chilling inside on a plush dog bed.

With Red's assistance, she coaxed the dog out of the cage and, after waiting for her to sniff out her approval, hugged and kissed it.

"You like her?" Ally asked.

"I love her," Chloe said. "What's her name?"

"Daisy," Ally said.

"Hi, Daisy." The dog dropped down next to her, rolled on her back, and twisted in the crunchy autumn leaves. Chloe soon joined her on the ground, but Red preferred to sit and watch their shenanigans.

"You want to tell her?" Ally said softly to Belle.

"She'd probably rather hear it from you, don't you think?"

"No," Ally said. "You really won her over. She was furious with me when I told her we'd broken up."

"Really?" Belle said, effusive with pride.

"Don't gloat." She kissed her sweetly.

"Are we keeping Daisy here?" Chloe said.

"It's a good idea, right?" Ally said.

"I guess it's better than the condo. She'll have a huge back yard," Chloe said, sounding disappointed. "But I wish she could live with us."

Belle and Ally exchanged smiles.

"She can't, sweetie," Ally said. "We just don't have the room."

"I know," Chloe said.

"Why don't you come and live here with her then?" Belle asked.

Chloe beamed up at both of them. "Is she serious?"

"Well, since Red spends most of his time here," Ally said, pretending to be nonchalant. "Why not? I'll be coming along, too, if that's okay."

"Yes, yes," Chloe exclaimed with a fist pump. "This is awesome." She ran over to them and pulled them in for a group hug.

Belle kissed Ally while they were still entangled in the embrace. "Thank you."

Ally smiled. "For what?"

"For bringing love and life back to this place."

About the Author

Jean Copeland is an author and English teacher at an alternative high school in Connecticut. Her first novel, *The Revelation of Beatrice Darby*, won the Alice B. Readers Lavender Certificate and the 2016 GCLS Goldie Award for debut author. She's also the author of the Rainbow Awards honorable mention *The Second Wave* and *Summer Fling*. When not writing, Jean enjoys traveling throughout Connecticut discovering its colonial history, and newest wineries and craft breweries. Feminism, organ donation, and shelter animal adoption are causes dear to her heart.

Books Available from Bold Strokes Books

Emily's Art and Soul by Joy Argento. When Emily meets Andi Marino she thinks she's found a new best friend but Emily doesn't know that Andi is fast falling in love with her. Caught up in exploring her sexuality, will Emily see the only woman she needs is right in front of her? (978-1-63555-355-0)

Escape to Pleasure: Lesbian Travel Erotica edited by Sandy Lowe and Victoria Villasenor. Join these award-winning authors as they explore the sensual side of erotic lesbian travel. (978-1-63555-339-0)

Music City Dreamers by Robyn Nyx. Music can bring lovers together. In Music City, it can tear them apart. (978-1-63555-207-2)

Ordinary is Perfect by D. Jackson Leigh. Atlanta marketing superstar Autumn Swan's life derails when she inherits a country home, a child, and a very interesting neighbor. (978-1-63555-280-5)

Royal Court by Jenny Frame. When royal dresser Holly Weaver's passionate personality begins to melt Royal Marine Captain Quincy's icy heart, will Holly be ready for what she exposes beneath? (978-1-63555-290-4)

Strings Attached by Holly Stratimore. Success. Riches. Music. Passion. It's a life most can only dream of, but stardom comes at a cost. (978-1-63555-347-5)

The Ashford Place by Jean Copeland. When Isabelle Ashford inherits an old house in small-town Connecticut, family secrets, a shocking discovery, and an unexpected romance complicate her plan for a fast profit and a temporary stay. (978-1-63555-316-1)

Treason by Gun Brooke. Zoem Malderyn's existence is a deadly threat to everyone on Gemocon and Commander Neenja KahSandra must find a way to save the woman she loves from having to commit the ultimate sacrifice. (978-1-63555-244-7)

A Wish Upon a Star by Jeannie Levig. Erica Cooper has learned to depend on only herself, but when her new neighbor, Leslie Raymond, befriends Erica's special needs daughter, the walls protecting her heart threaten to crumble. (978-1-63555-274-4)

Answering the Call by Ali Vali. Detective Sept Savoie returns to the streets of New Orleans, as do the dead bodies from ritualistic killings, and she does everything in her power to bring them to justice while trying to keep her partner, Keegan Blanchard, safe. (978-1-63555-050-4)

Breaking Down Her Walls by Erin Zak. Could a love worth staying for be the key to breaking down Julia Finch's walls? (978-1-63555-369-7)

Exit Plans for Teenage Freaks by 'Nathan Burgoine. Cole always has a plan—especially for escaping his small-town reputation as "that kid who was kidnapped when he was four"—but when he teleports to a museum, it's time to face facts: it's possible he's a total freak after all. (978-1-63555-098-6)

Friends Without Benefits by Dena Blake. When Dex Putman gets the woman she thought she always wanted, she soon wonders if it's really love after all. (978-1-63555-349-9)

Invalid Evidence by Stevie Mikayne. Private Investigator Jil Kidd is called away to investigate a possible killer whale, just when her partner Jess needs her most. (978-1-63555-307-9)

Pursuit of Happiness by Carsen Taite. When attorney Stevie Palmer's client reveals a scandal that could derail Senator Meredith Mitchell's presidential bid, their chance at love may be collateral damage. (978-1-63555-044-3)

Seascape by Karis Walsh. Marine biologist Tess Hansen returns to Washington's isolated northern coast where she struggles to adjust to small-town living while courting an endowment for her orca research center from Brittany James. (978-1-63555-079-5)

Second in Command by VK Powell. Jazz Perry's life is disrupted and her career jeopardized when she becomes personally involved with the case of an abandoned child and the child's competent but strict social worker, Emory Blake. (978-1-63555-185-3)

Taking Chances by Erin McKenzie. When Valerie Cruz and Paige Wellington clash over what's in the best interest of the children in Valerie's care, the children may be the ones who teach them it's worth taking chances for love. (978-1-63555-209-6)

All of Me by Emily Smith. When chief surgical resident Galen Burgess meets her new intern, Rowan Duncan, she may finally discover that doing what you've always done will only give you what you've always had. (978-1-63555-321-5)

As the Crow Flies by Karen F. Williams. Romance seems to be blooming all around, but problems arise when a restless ghost emerges from the ether to roam the dark corners of this haunting tale. (978-1-63555-285-0)

Both Ways by Ileandra Young. SPEAR agent Danika Karson races to protect the city from a supernatural threat and must rely on the woman she's trained to despise: Rayne, an achingly beautiful vampire. (978-1-63555-298-0)

Calendar Girl by Georgia Beers. Forced to work together, Addison Fairchild and Kate Cooper discover that opposites really do attract. (978-1-63555-333-8)

Lovebirds by Lisa Moreau. Two women from different worlds collide in a small California mountain town, each with a mission that doesn't include falling in love. (978-1-63555-213-3)

Media Darling by Fiona Riley. Can Hollywood bad girl Emerson and reluctant celebrity gossip reporter Hayley work together to make each other's dreams come true? Or will Emerson's secrets ruin not one career, but two? (978-1-63555-278-2)

Stroke of Fate by Renee Roman. Can Sean Moore live up to her reputation and save Jade Rivers from the stalker determined to end Jade's career and, ultimately, her life? (978-1-63555-62-4)

The Rise of the Resistance by Jackie D. The soul of America has been lost for almost a century. A few people may be the difference between a phoenix rising to save the masses or permanent destruction. (978-1-63555-259-1)

The Sex Therapist Next Door by Meghan O'Brien. At the intersection of sex and intimacy, anything is possible. Even love. (978-1-63555-296-6)

Unexpected Lightning by Cass Sellars. Lightning strikes once more when Sydney and Parker fight a dangerous stranger who threatens the peace they both desperately want. (978-1-63555-276-8)

Unforgettable by Elle Spencer. When one night changes a lifetime… Two romance novellas from best-selling author Elle Spencer. (978-1-63555-429-8)

Against All Odds by Kris Bryant, Maggie Cummings, M. Ullrich. Peyton and Tory escaped death once, but will they survive when Bradley's determined to make his kill rate one hundred percent? (978-1-63555-193-8)

Autumn's Light by Aurora Rey. Casual hookups aren't supposed to include romantic dinners and meeting the family. Can Mat Pero see beyond the heartbreak that led her to keep her worlds so separate, and will Graham Connor be waiting if she does? (978-1-63555-272-0)

Breaking the Rules by Larkin Rose. When Virginia and Carmen are thrown together by an embarrassing mistake they find out their stubborn determination isn't so heroic after all. (978-1-63555-261-4)

Broad Awakening by Mickey Brent. In the sequel to *Underwater Vibes*, Hélène and Sylvie find ruts in their road to eternal bliss. (978-1-63555-270-6)

Broken Vows by MJ Williamz. Sister Mary Margaret must reconcile her divided heart or risk losing a love that just might be heaven sent. (978-1-63555-022-1)

Flesh and Gold by Ann Aptaker. Havana, 1952, where art thief and smuggler Cantor Gold dodges gangland bullets and mobsters' schemes while she searches Havana' s steamy Red Light district for her kidnapped love. (978-1-63555-153-2)

Isle of Broken Years by Jane Fletcher. Spanish noblewoman Catalina de Valasco is in peril, even before the pirates holding her for ransom sail into seas destined to become known as the Bermuda Triangle. (978-1-63555-175-4)

Love Like This by Melissa Brayden. Hadley Cooper and Spencer Adair set out to take the fashion world by storm. If only they knew their hearts were about to be taken. (978-1-63555-018-4)

Secrets On the Clock by Nicole Disney. Jenna and Danielle love their jobs helping endangered children, but that might not be enough to stop them from breaking the rules by falling in love. (978-1-63555-292-8)

Unexpected Partners by Michelle Larkin. Dr. Chloe Maddox tries desperately to deny her attraction for Detective Dana Blake as they flee from a serial killer who's hunting them both. (978-1-63555-203-4)

A Fighting Chance by T. L. Hayes. Will Lou be able to come to terms with her past to give love a fighting chance? (978-1-63555-257-7)

Chosen by Brey Willows. When the choice is adapt or die, can love save us all? (978-1-63555-110-5)

Death Checks In by David S. Pederson. Despite Heath's promises to Alan to not get involved, Heath can't resist investigating a shopkeeper's murder in Chicago, which dashes their plans for a romantic weekend getaway. (978-1-63555-329-1)

Gnarled Hollow by Charlotte Greene. After they are invited to study a secluded nineteenth-century estate, a former English professor and a group of historians discover that they will have to fight against the unknown if they have any hope of staying alive. (978-1-63555-235-5)

Jacob's Grace by C.P. Rowlands. Captain Tag Becket wants to keep her head down and her past behind her, but her feelings for AJ's second-in-command, Grace Fields, makes keeping secrets next to impossible. (978-1-63555-187-7)

On the Fly by PJ Trebelhorn. Hockey player Courtney Abbott is content with her solitary life until visiting concert violinist Lana Caruso makes her second-guess everything she always thought she wanted. (978-1-63555-255-3)

Passionate Rivals by Radclyffe. Professional rivalry and long-simmering passions create a combustible combination when Emmett McCabe and Sydney Stevens are forced to work together, especially when past attractions won't stay buried. (978-1-63555-231-7)

Proxima Five by Missouri Vaun. When geologist Leah Warren crash-lands on a preindustrial planet and is claimed by its tyrant, Tiago, will clan warrior Keegan's love for Leah give her the strength to defeat him? (978-1-63555-122-8)

Racing Hearts by Dena Blake. When you cross a hot-tempered race car mechanic with a reckless cop, the result can only be spontaneous combustion. (978-1-63555-251-5)

Shadowboxer by Jessica L. Webb. Jordan McAddie is prepared to keep her street kids safe from a dangerous underground protest group, but she isn't prepared for her first love to walk back into her life. (978-1-63555-267-6)

The Tattered Lands by Barbara Ann Wright. As Vandra and Lilani strive to make peace, they slowly fall in love. With mistrust and murder surrounding them, only their faith in each other can keep their plan to save the world from falling apart. (978-1-63555-108-2)

Lightning Source UK Ltd.
Milton Keynes UK
UKHW041942210119
335961UK00001B/45/P